ROSE & THORNE

Eva Thorne Book 6

Lorel Clayton

LC Books
SYDNEY, AUSTRALIA

Lorel Clayton – Lorel Colgin & Clayton Colgin/LC Books
www.lorelclayton.com

Publisher's Note: This is a work of fiction. Names, characters, places, and incidents are a product of the author's imagination. Locales and public names are sometimes used for atmospheric purposes. Any resemblance to actual people, living or dead, or to businesses, companies, events, institutions, or locales is completely coincidental.

Book Layout ©2013 BookDesignTemplates.com

Ordering Information:
Quantity sales. Special discounts are available on quantity purchases by corporations, associations, and others. For details, contact the "Special Sales Department" at the address above.

Rose & Thorne/ Lorel Clayton. -- 1st ed.
ISBN 978-1-7638008-3-0

"Democracy is beautiful. It's the whole, the collective, coming together to rule—many voices becoming one. Whichever one of you becomes the voice of the people, I hope you will remember: we need that unity."

–Sir Markham (Eva Thorne Book 6)

"Democracy relies on an informed and learned population. Without knowledge of history, of past failures and successes, how can we gauge where our future might lead with the choices made today? Without being aware of the ills besetting our neighbors, the travails they face, how can we find the compassion and will to aid them, and by aiding the whole, improve our own lots as well?"

–General Daniel Moore (Eva Thorne Book 6)

Avian Lands
Highcrowne
Solheim
The Wall
The Three Kingdoms
Gernweld
Fel
Elf Lands
Ihal Favillion
Favillion
Dwarf Lands
Lyss
Goblins
Archon
Fortress of Mages
Metora
Selene
Trist
Lallaloka
Kell
Darrub
Rosh

1 The Cliché

I thought spring and its sneeze-inducing plague of flowers had come early when I saw white and red petals flying toward me. A handful slammed into my face. As I was unsticking them from my tongue, I realized they were bits of paper. Even worse. The muck rakers had a hard enough time keeping this city clean, despite the new sewer system, and clouds of paper flying around didn't help.

Then I heard cheers. It reminded me of the gladiatorial combats in Archon, where bloodthirsty cries of triumph ebbed and swelled with each blow from a fighter's blade.

Highcrowne, thankfully, did not have a coliseum. The elves, humans, and dwarves who dwelled here barely tolerated each other, goblins hating them all, so I had no idea what would gather such a crowd and elicit applause. I hoped it wasn't another war.

I followed the bits of paper blowing down the empty street. Some detective I was, not noticing the quiet in my neighborhood. Even the bazaar was closed, curtains down, 'back in five minutes' signs up for every shop. What was going on?

The mystery was solved when I turned the corner to the Outskirts Temple District and a wall of sound hit me, followed by more confetti. A parade meandered down the cobbled street, hordes of Citizens barely held in check by Guard-manned barricades. Fists were raised, both angry and joyous, and I glimpsed an auto carriage draped in bunting headed up the hill toward the Central City. I fought my way through the crowd and hopped over a wooden barricade, hoping to learn what all the fuss was about.

A needle-toothed grimace from a goblin greeted me. "Back with the others, Citizen."

I waved my Avian badge at the guard. There were no Avians left in the city to enforce my authority, but the magic compulsion on it still worked well enough to give anyone, lawful or criminal, pause. "Official business."

The goblin backed off—a first, as in my experience they usually required sword-rattling threats—and I jogged up the street after the auto carriage. The crowd pressed in behind me now that the excitement had passed. Citizens or no, most would never get access to the Central City to see what happened next, so they returned to business as usual.

How had I missed a tickertape parade?

Because I had been buried in work when not buried in sorrows. The only time I livened up was with Dawn, smiling and playing and feeling happy as I got to be a real mother, not just a bodyguard. She had Mister Gardens for that now. The elf butler often soured my already glum mood. It's saying something when I preferred Nanny's company.

When I went to work (aka drinking whisky at my desk waiting for clients), it really hit me how much I'd given up. I was skilled in magic from all over the world, but it was academic knowledge. The real power I'd once possessed, granted by primal forces, was gone, and even the necromancy I should have been able to command as a Solhan, as a Thorne, had vanished with it. I felt as mundane as Duane.

Was that him in the middle carriage?

Must be seeing things. I rubbed my eyes, which weren't as blurry from drink as they would be at midday, which is when I cut myself off to sober up before supper and Dawn playtime.

Duane had been away for months. No word about how his hunt for Aguragas was going. He could be dead for all I knew. But that niggling moment of recognition wouldn't leave me, and soon I was fighting more crowds and waving my badge to get through, until I was at the base of the Assembly steps where the Crowns were arrayed awaiting the motorcade. Not even I could get past the cordon of EEPs (aka Elven Elite Protectorate) and royal bodyguards protecting the Crowns. The Dwarf King, Harley, the Human King (for now), Moore, and the Elf Queen, Hilja, all looked resplendent in their finest regalia. Hilja was even smiling. Rare for her of late.

I supposed I had a different view of the Elf Queen than most. She often sneaked into my house to visit her half-sister, my daughter. Long story. Suffice it to say that while Hilja and Dawn were getting along well, thanks to shared tea parties with stuffed animals to help act out the political schooling required for a secret heir, Hilja still resented me for 'seducing' her father. Probably also for getting him killed. Essentially. More long stories, which I was not in the mood to rehash in my head as I eagerly awaited the stars of the hour to ascend the dais.

Duane had been with the motorcade. I knew it! I'd recognize his walk anywhere. The fact he was wearing a fancy suit and standing in plain view, rather than skulking alleyways in the Outskirts or hooding his features when slitting throats and performing other Shadow King work, also made it easier to identify him. Since when was the Three Kingdom's spymaster willing to expose himself to such public view?

A shock of white hair against black skin answered that question for me. Gas.

The erstwhile leader of the Upside Down Party, exiled heir to the throne of Darrub, former assassin and current terrorist—otherwise known as Aguragas, or Gas in my mental monologue—was the most hated person in Highcrowne. That explained the angry yet jubilant shouts from the crowd. Gas had blown up the mountain, sent our Avian rulers fleeing for sanctuary in the High Reaches, and killed hundreds of people in the recent uprising he'd started. Now everyone understood why I hated him so much. My reasons went way back and were personal, so I especially loved how he was dragged up to the dais in chains.

By arming disgruntled humans with dangerous rifles from Darrub and recruiting terrorists for his operations throughout the Kingdoms, Gas had also precipitated mass arrests when the uprising was put down. The courts and jails were still full, while miscreants were questioned and ever so slowly processed for release. Working for lawyers trying to win their clients' freedom, with whatever exonerating testimony I could dredge up, was the mainstay of my private investigator work these days.

I hated trying to find little old ladies helped across the street by terrorists so they could have character witnesses. That's why business was slow. I was happy to hand over a stack of exonerating evidence for the guiltless bakers, butchers, and candlestick makers wrongly arrested in the purge—but as soon as I found evidence to support a criminal's guilt, I tended to hand that over to the prosecutors rather than my clients. Unfortunately, word of said betrayals had spread, and I had even less business these days than when I worked as a pet detective.

Poor me. I felt a huge grin spread across my face, though, as an EEP kicked the back of Gas's knees and forced him to bow to the Crowns.

"At last, the notorious Aguragas is brought to justice." Hilja's voice carried over the roar of the mob, amplified by elvish magic.

It was not surprising she assumed preeminent authority among the Crowns. While all were supposed to be equal, some were more equal than others.

Humans had only gained Citizenship a handful of years ago, and the dwarves used to have a ghost as their King until the war, so Harley and Moore were not as well established as Hilja in their power base.

Elves already controlled most aspects of government, from the City Guard to courts and banks and temples, not to mention the ever-growing jackbooted march of EEPs everywhere. They were barely kept in check by the Avians, who now gone, weren't keeping them in check at all. The controversial laws abolishing slavery in Faellion had already been overturned, and there was worry Highcrowne would be next to slide back into old, wretched ways. Ways which elves preferred.

The human and dwarf experiments in democracy were not looked kindly upon by elvish slave masters, and I knew Hilja herself detested anything that eroded royal privilege, so there was a very good chance that most of the people in prison would stay there, and that even King Moore and King Harley could be joining them soon.

Hilja's power was real, and dangerous, and so no one interrupted or dared overshadow her speech.

"With your execution on the morrow, Aguragas," she continued, "we will not only celebrate an end to the ridiculous 'Upside Down Party' but an end to the radical idea than an insignificant Darrubian lordling like yourself can command here, in the Kingdoms, which was forged from the primitive wilderness millennia before your ilk set foot on this world." That was Hilja insulting all humans in case you missed it.

Dwarves helped build the Kingdoms too, but she left out the part that Avians and Solhans were even older, the first nations of this world, and that once upon a time elves had been immigrants as well, brought here from distant worlds through void portals as they escaped the Devourer and the annihilation of 'contaminated' planets and universes.

All that existential, multiverse thinking made me wish I'd brought my bottle of whisky along. The First Soul, the Devourer ... I had more personal experience with the really bad things than I liked. Aguragas and Crown politics were a fun and welcome diversion from my real worries.

"Take this piece of filth to the dungeons." There were huge cheers accompanying this decree, and more fists raised as Aguragas was dragged off to prison.

I knew from his expression that Gas had hoped for a chance to orate, to rile up the few humans in the crowd—and he was good, possibly even able to sway this crowd, all picked by Hilja's, Harley's, and Moore's people no doubt and as loyal as they come—but it looked like he'd have to save his last words for the execution. I hoped it was beheading.

Before you assume I miss the blood of the coliseum, I was only thinking about the certainty that a beheading brings. Poison, hanging, drowning ... lots of things can be messed up, faked even with magic, but not a nice simple separating of head from body. It killed most things, except powerful vampires and Risen.... Okay it wasn't perfect, but I reviled Gas so much, I wanted to make sure I was there. I hate stories where the hero walks away before making sure the bad guy is truly dead. Even worse when the bad guy comes back to life.

I was ready to wheedle my way forward and volunteer to be part of the execution inner circle, but Hilja was not done with her speech.

"More cheers for the Hero of Highcrowne..." That was me. I'd saved everyone, the world really, during the war, only Hilja wasn't looking at me but at Duane. "...Mister Adder Rose, who singlehandedly hunted this terrorist down. I present him with the Crowns Medal of Valor."

She draped something gold and gaudy around his neck. Why didn't I get one of those? "And also, my personal and heartfelt thanks."

The way she looked him in his gorgeous green eyes made a wave of jealousy pass through me I didn't like: Shivers and muscles tightening from my arms to my gut, even my knees. Was I getting the flu? And then she kissed him. On the cheek, but the way his hand was at her waist, her body pressed against his....

Wait a minute. Were Duane and Hilja together?

I turned my back on them and shoved gawking sycophants in the crowd aside, trying to run. I needed my neighborhood, my office, and a dark corner to be sick. I wanted to wretch. The chills were worse than ever, and I really either had the flu, some plague, or ... or I had feelings for Duane and had never told him. I had run away when he told me he loved me, actually, and now he'd forgotten about me. Moved on.

Whisky time.

I couldn't get through the newly reopened bazaar to my office, not with the flood of people on the street after the parade, so I made the mistake of using the front steps to my house. The butler, Mister Gardens, greeted me with a less than welcome look.

"My house, my daughter," I reminded him. Same words I said every time we crossed paths.

Problem was the butler didn't work for me—he worked for Queen Hilja—and he wasn't a butler so much as a tutor and bodyguard for Dawn, heir to the elvish Crown.

Dawn was on the couch, reading and trying not to smile as she watched us from the corner of her eye. She was only part elvish: a golden cast to her skin, sharp points on her ears, delicate features, but otherwise all Solhan from her black hair to her, I suspected, equally black heart.

Mister Gardens, on the other hand, was the epitome of elvish: short, superior, and utterly disdainful. It didn't help that he was the famed Elf Butler Detective, the hero of my favorite dime novels. Although, since I learned he penned them himself, I doubted their veracity. I knew names were changed from his cases, and I knew he was brilliant, observant, and a far better detective than me if we were thrown on a desert island together with no resources but our brains to discover the culprit of the great coconut heist or whatever—where was I going with this? Oh, yes, he was naturally better at all things detective than me, but he lacked my magical talents (admittedly I lacked them too of late) and my Solhan stubbornness, not to mention general willingness to go as far as I needed to go, to cross whatever lines were necessary, to see something through. In this case, it was getting past him and his judgements to reach my liquor stash.

I pushed past him and even snuck in a Dawn hug. She stiffened as all Solhans tended to do—hugs weren't our thing—but she was growing up quick, and I wanted to hold her as often as I could for as long as I could. "See you at six," I said, referring to our mother-daughter appointment time.

Yes, I had to schedule in time with the butler to see her, as her days were packed with studies ranging from history and philosophy to politics and languages, not to mention defense training, including sword practice with Morgan which I had fought tooth and nail for. She needed a proper Solhan education as well as an elvish one. That had meant less 'us' time, but more than fearing her growing up too soon, I feared for her future. Everyone who knew who she was, which was more people than I liked, wanted her as a pawn in their games of power, and I wouldn't be able to protect her from the royal court. She needed to be able to protect herself.

She patted my hand. "I'll be alright mum."

Did she read minds too? And where had this 'mum' come from? Adopting elvish words.

"I believe you were on your way to 'work'?" Mister Gardens reminded me.

I no longer wanted a drink, but I did want to escape the uncomfortable atmosphere, so I snuck in one last kiss on Dawn's forehead and retreated to the kitchen. Nanny was there and glaring out at the butler.

"I've tried poisoning him," she said. "And not with my stew. Good, subtle poison slipped into his tooth polish, laced into his aftershave, sprinkled on the food he prepares himself when he's not looking…. Why won't he die?"

"I suspect he regularly ingests toxins to build up resistance to them. Been doing it for decades, according to Chapter Three of 'The Case of the Ivory Fox'. You're just helping him grow his tolerance."

"Like you've been with alcohol?" She pulled a few bottles from the trash she'd been emptying and gave me the look she once gave me and Viktor when she caught us disrespecting the gods or stealing things with Duane.

Duane. I grabbed a bottle from her and drained the last drops. Can't believe I'd left nearly a thimble full behind in that one.

Then it hit me. I had become the cliché.

"I'm the washed-up detective with suffocating guilt from the people I've lost or gotten killed, full of war stories and reminisces of old glory, shamelessly destroying my reputation by taking on questionable cases, and so full of self-loathing I'm trying to drown in alcohol with ever diminishing success. How did this happen?"

"You tried to be the good guy," Nanny explained. "You should have killed more enemies sooner: Aguragas, Fharen, Ilsa…."

Killing was Nanny's knee jerk answer to everything. "If I'd killed Fharen, I would never have had Dawn," I pointed out.

"Nor that butler." She didn't mean it. Well, she did mean that she wanted Mister Gardens dead, but she loved Dawn. After Little Viktor went to boarding school, she had been at a loss, and Dawn gave her renewed vigor. She'd easily live another century with such restored purpose, and she was loving having a mortal enemy under the same roof as her. Solhans thrived in such situations.

Except me. I got maudlin. Morose. Some other 'M' words if I could think of them.

"I'll be in my office."

She frowned. "Giving up again?"

"Hibernating. Or pickling myself for later. There will come a time when Dawn, Little Viktor, maybe even you, but certainly this city will need me. Until then, I'll make sure I'm numb and have no chance for self-reflection."

That time came sooner than I suspected when I went downstairs to find a mob hammering at my office door.

"Oi, this ain't the bathroom!" I shouted over the banging, not making a move to open it. People often wandered over from the bazaar, but usually not this many. Good thing I kept the door locked anyway.

How am I to get real clients, you ask? I'm not. Gave up that pretense two months ago.

I kicked back in my chair and frowned. Not only had Nanny taken out the trash, she'd cleaned. The piles of papers on my desk were all sorted into neat piles, just like I didn't want, so I scattered them about artfully before reaching into my drawer.

She wouldn't have? My full bottle was gone.

"Nanny! And quit that racket!" I shouted upstairs and at my front door simultaneously.

Nanny's feet pattered down the stairs like repeater rifle fire. She was at least two centuries old already, acted frail when she wanted to, but this burst of energy made me reassess my earlier calculation: she probably had a millennium left. Good old necromancy.

"Have you seen this?" She held out some pamphlet that looked suspiciously like the ones being smashed against the glass of my office door by the boisterous crowd outside.

"I'm not interested in religion or whatever they're selling."

"It's politics."

"My other hated topic. Where's my whisky?"

"Where you can't find it. This is about the election."

"What election? And were you just waiting for me to step outside for two seconds so you could sneak in here and clean?"

"Yes, and you know full well what election—General Moore is keeping his promise of putting the Human Crown up to a vote. He's not even added his own name to the ballot list, but you know whose name is on there?"

"Let me guess. Duane?" The Avians had hand picked him for something, and the way Hilja had feted him today ... didn't want to replay them together on the dais but it kept looping in my mind ... and no one held as much power in the Kingdoms as the spymaster. It was the obvious choice—if he didn't care about his life anymore. "How can a Shadow King function when no longer in the shadows?" I wondered.

"Look here, you idiot girl." She shoved the pamphlet in my face.

Exasperated, I took it and read. It was blurry without the double vision of alcohol poisoning I'd become accustomed to, but I made out quite a few names on the candidate list. Mostly priests and merchants hungry for power—and thieves. There was Duane's name, or I should say 'Mister Rose' as expected. What wasn't expected was the name just above his. The one at the very top, actually (I always read backwards from the end)—Eva Thorne.

"What in the hells?"

"Exactly."

"Who nominated me? Me! Nobody likes me."

Then I spotted a small green goblin with huge spectacles and a smile full of sharp teeth at my door hopping excitedly, fighting back the humans in the mob, biting a few hands here and there, and trying to get my attention through the window.

"Miss Thorne!" he shouted, the sound muffled by my heavily ensorcelled and thick glass.

"Doctor Ghunnan. Of course."

2 IMPOSTER SYNDROME

I signaled to the goblin, indicating he should take the back way. I had no intention of opening my public door. He winked knowingly and disappeared from view.

With a long-suffering sigh, I stood up and went upstairs to the kitchen and out the rear door to the alleyway. I noticed clots in the saucer of cream I kept by the stoop. That wouldn't do. I washed it up and put some fresh cream out, just as the goblin doctor arrived.

"I don't mind if I do." he said, reaching for it.

I smacked his hand away. "This is for Sandy, Viktor's fairy godmother and my sometimes friend. What do you think protects this alley from just anyone wandering around?"

"Perhaps the smell? Nothing impeded my progress."

"That's because I wanted you here. And before you ask, no, you can't come inside. I'm not dropping my good wards for anyone. No one goes into the house except a select few. I prefer the alley for my real work, which is where Sandy's fairy protections come into play. You can enter here if you have a case I'm interested in, but no weapons or double-crosses permitted."

"Fairy magic now? What utter nonsense...." He felt his pockets and suddenly looked worried. "Where did it go?"

"Let me guess, some weapon?"

"A charged lightning pistol."

"Told you the fairy protections work."

"I must have left it at home."

"That's where you'll find it later, I'm sure. So, why did you add me to the election ballot? Are you trying to ruin my day?"

"No. I'm not responsible, but as soon as I saw your name I hurried over to offer whatever help I can. Thus, the lightning pistol. If Highcrowne elections are anything like goblin elections, you will need all the defensive weaponry you can get. Candidates can win simply by eliminating all their rivals so there's no one else left to vote for. That is the goblin way." He winked.

"I though the goblins had an Emperor?"

"Yes, but all the key bureaucratic postings and ministerial offices are appointed by a majority vote. Mayors, sheriffs, even the Postmaster."

"Postmaster?"

"A very influential role—similar to a spymaster."

"I see. Actually, I don't care. That is what I mean. That is why I should not be on the ballot. I am not Crown material. I—do—not—care."

"Come now, Miss Thorne. As your official historian and biographer, I beg to disagree with that statement. Would someone who did not care risk their life to stop the so-called 'Dead God' from conquering the world?"

"Actually, He wasn't my enemy and was really my ally in the end."

"What about advocating for freedom for humans, Citizenship?"

"Just wanted to stick it in the eye of elves everywhere. I hate those annoying jerks."

"And what about defending Highcrowne from invasion?"

"Hello? I live here. A very selfish no brainer."

"I see what you are doing, Miss Thorne. You are very good at protecting your cover, but I was quite the spy myself in my heyday."

What was he talking about?

Oh yes. I had taken to using goblin muckrakers and other invisible workers as informants, and the best way to get them to share information was to claim I was a double agent for the Avians and Solhans and secretly allied with their Emperor. A triple agent. Some tale like that. I tended to weave elaborate yarns that I forgot—which got me into a lot of trouble at times. I thought it wouldn't have hurt for Doctor Ghunnan to think I worked for the same master as him ... unless he'd been responsible for this ridiculous election ballot. In which case, this whole thing was probably my own fault. Typical.

"In any event," the doctor continued his lecture, "I do care. We have been through thick and thin, so to say, you and I, and I do not want to see this election bring about your untimely demise. Regardless of your wishes, you are now a candidate for the Human Crown. You have new enemies."

"Just what I needed."

"But you also have my help to thwart them."

"And mine," a new voice chimed in.

I recognized the dwarf. His suit and fedora were more stylish, but the briefcase was the same one that had once held forged documents used to defend me from imprisonment as an emancipationist. He stood at the end of the alley, not yet bidden to enter.

"Sir Markham? It's been years. What are you doing here?"

"Gypsum sent me." He took a step forward, feeling the barrier drop. I was glad to see him.

"I thought none of Gypsum's husbands were talking to her."

My old friend, turned betrayer turned semi-friend again, was doing time in the highest tower of Northcliff Prison for siding with the enemy during the war. Her many husbands and children had all shunned her for it, understandably, but I'd seen how it had broken Gypsum's heart.

"Gypsum has made a real effort to atone, Miss Thorne. I certainly recognize that. My co-husbands in Gernwold are not as convinced, but I have been in Highcrowne these past months since the terrorist attack working on freeing the dissenters wrongly imprisoned in the purge. Some of their rhetoric has swayed me to be more open minded and forgiving."

"Rhetoric—like democracy and an end to all Crowns?" I said.

I had heard some of the same rhetoric during my investigations for other attorneys. Odd that Sir Markham and I had not crossed paths in the halls of justice. Had he been hiding from me? Was he lying about his real reason for being in Highcrowne? Was I just super suspicious of everyone at all times? Probably.

"An end to Crowns? I wouldn't go that far," Sir Markham said. "Although some dwarves, even King Harley's new wife, do agree with the populist democratic ideal. That is why this election for the Human Crown is so important. All eyes are on what happens next and whether it can serve as a mold for the other races to follow."

"I'm no mold. 'Moldy' some days when I stay in my subterranean office too long without bathing, but I am no example to anyone. And now that you're here, with your legal expertise, you can tell me how to get my name off the hit list."

"That's quite impossible. You have been nominated, and according to King Moore who established the rules of this election, there is no withdrawal. Whomever is called to serve must serve … or be executed for failing their duty to the Three Kingdoms."

"Executed?" This was worse than I thought. Then I relaxed. "This is me we're talking about. No one is going to vote for a Solhan, let alone a known Solhan necromancer and all around bad news femme fatale turned detective. Why am I even worried? They'll take the priest of the Lightbringer temple over me. Even Duane."

"Who?"

"Mister Adder Rose."

"Yes, the Shadow King." Sir Markham went strangely still.

Doctor Ghunnan waved a hand in front of his face. "Excuse me, Sir Markham? Are you alright? …Perhaps it is some sort of epileptic fit?"

"I am quite alright," he said, suddenly blinking again. "What were we discussing?"

"The fact I have nothing to worry about, as no one will vote for me, so the two of you can go home now and leave me to my melancholy. That is the 'M' word I've been looking for!"

"I cannot do that," the goblin said.

"Neither can I. I must impress upon you the seriousness of this election. We have only thirty days, and Gypsum desires that you be triumphant. She told me to tell you that this is the best way to ensure the young one's safety."

She meant Dawn. How could my being a Crown make her safer? It could only make things worse. Nonsense anyway. I hated the Crowns deep down. No way could I be one.

"I'm here!" Another visitor. This one was a tall redhead wearing a white lab coat and lugging a black satchel. Katherine. She ran into the invisible wall protecting my alley and bounced, landing on her backside.

You'd think with such protections in place the alley would be a mess, as no muckrakers were able to enter to collect trash, but it was strangely cleaner, probably because my Bogle friends licked the place clean. One of the leathery skinned creatures dropped its camouflage and started digging through the leather satchel.

"Ick! Get away!" Katherine shooed it off and resealed the bag protectively.

"What in all the worlds are you doing here, Doctor Suttner?" the goblin asked.

"Doctor?" Katherine placed a hand against the barrier, wide-eyed with curiosity. Unlike her mentor, she did believe in magic, so I didn't grant her admittance, giving her a chance to appreciate Sandy's handiwork. She shook herself, finally saying, "Oh yes, still getting used to my new position, Doctor Ghunnan. I've come to offer Miss Thorne my assistance."

"You too?" I asked. Why did so many people want to help? I tried to make people hate me, and obviously I wasn't doing a very good job of it. I needed to try harder.

"What assistance can you possibly provide?" Doctor Ghunnan asked dismissively. "Miss Thorne already has the Kingdoms' preeminent lawyer and the Empire's preeminent scientist ... And why are you standing there petting the air?"

"I'm investigating yet another magical phenomenon you are blind to, and it is precisely the work you shun that will make me invaluable to Eva." She pulled a glass phial out of her lab coat pocket. It was full of green, glowing fluid. "I believe this substance can give her the edge she needs."

"Did you...?" The goblin went wide eyed and hurried over to examine the vial, donning goggles to examine different wavelengths of light. I knew he had fruitlessly been trying to recreate the Avian goo for years. "How did you...?" He reached for it, but she put the vial back in her pocket.

"This is for Eva."

I waved her over. "Okay, I won't say no to that."

I had amassed a vast collection of runes, cords containing concentrated magic, potions, powders—all to offset my missing magic—but Avian goo was impossible to come by anymore, and it was the most powerful magic of all. It could be used to create artifacts with abilities limited only by the craftsman's imagination.

Katherine smiled as the alley's barrier let her through. "Oh, I must understand this invisible force field. How do you control it?"

"With my thoughts." I waved my fingers mysteriously. "Hand the goo over and go. All of you."

Katherine patted her pocket. "In due time. First, we need to make some election posters, prepare for the up-coming debates, craft a victory speech...."

"Whoa, hold on," I said. "I am not campaigning. I am not even technically human, being Solhan, so I cannot be the Human Crown."

"Solhans have the oldest and best claim to these lands now the Avians have abdicated," Sir Markham argued.

"Abdicated? They're just hiding someplace safe." I wasn't sure where, which was the point—they didn't want anyone to know, especially human terrorists, like Gas's compatriots.

"According to the ancient laws, if a Crown representative is absent from Highcrowne for greater than half the length of a year, they abdicate their claim, and the remaining Crowns in residence decide who shall take their place. I am an expert in Crown law."

"So, am I running for the Human or the Avian Crown?" I asked. "Scratch that. I am not running for anything. I'm not qualified to rule anything. I can't even rule my own house!"

Katherine gave me her determined expression. "You are merely expressing the defeatist and repressive cultural training all humans, and Solhans, have been conditioned to feel after years of oppression, slavery, and now second-class, no third-class, Citizenship. Of course you don't believe you're worthy, because every elf and most dwarves have told you that your whole life. Even worse, other humans have told you to be meek and stay quiet."

"You may have noticed I don't do meek and quiet," I said.

"Exactly! We need a woman like you to wear the Human Crown. Did you notice that you were the only woman on the ballot?"

I did. I disliked the idea of being a role model even more than I disliked being nominated.

"If none of you are leaving, then I am." I held up my hands, defeated, and walked out into the main street.

There was so much noise, masses of people pressed together, I thought I'd wandered into another parade. The people were all lined up outside the bazaar, which led to my office, formerly Distant Imports Ltd, which had shut when Kali fled with Bell and Gas's other associates. Another line reached around it all and up to my front door.

This was not happening.

Someone recognized me. "Miss Thorne!" It was the butcher's wife, and she still had a bloody cleaver in her grip, apron smeared with blood.

I backed away and ran into the herbologist, the Widow Kilpatrick, whose husband had mysteriously died shortly after their marriage from what gossips suspected was poisoning. She squinted at me and reached into her satchel for something.

I got clear and pulled my Ashur, the serrated sword hidden in my cane was scary when unsheathed, humming with ghosts of past kills. "Everyone stay back," I warned.

"I have a list of demands for when you are elected." That was the butcher, his bloody fingerprints all over a great sheet of paper with tiny writing he held up and started reading. "The first is lower taxes for small business...."

His wife nodded. "And don't forget a reduction in icehouse fees, or better yet subsidies for switching to warlock power. I'd like our operation to be more environmentally friendly if possible."

"Then I hope your cattle are grass fed," the Widow Kilpatrick cut in. "Wait, that would require you clearing yet more of my forests. Where do you think medicinal herbs come from? Bare rock? We need to protect the old growth trees...."

"What?" I had no idea what anyone was talking about.

Katherine was suddenly beside me, holding some sort of auto recording device. "Go on, Citizen. Your concerns are of the utmost concern to Miss Thorne."

I slunk back into my alley, breathing hard, while Katherine polled the gathered crowd for their top election issues.

"Maybe I'll just stay here," I said, hugging a wall

"Doctor Suttner is right," Sir Markham said, putting a hand on my shoulder, which meant standing on tiptoes for him. "You need to start campaigning. I will work on the more influential members of the human community, those who gather in smoking rooms and the halls of power. Your being a woman is a disadvantage among your kind, so I will ensure we get some leverage. I know where many skeletons are buried. Good day." He tipped his fedora and vanished into the throng on the street.

"How in the worlds did she recreate the green fluid?" The goblin was mumbling to himself. "It's impossible."

"Feeling inadequate? Like a failure?" I guessed. "Welcome to the club."

"We cannot sit still, Miss Thorne. When a challenge presents itself, we must face it head on. Come with me!"

For a goblin one quarter my height, he had an iron grip. Probably because he wore mechanized gloves similar to the mechanical legs hidden under his trousers that whirred as he dragged me back out into the main street.

"Important person coming through," he said, using his enhanced strength to push people aside. Katherine came behind us, being conciliatory and adding more information to her poll.

"Where are we going?" I asked. Pulling free would require me cutting his hand off, so I tried the diplomatic approach first. Not killing or maiming as a first reaction? Maybe I could be a politician?

"To assess the competition," the goblin said.

Soon we were out of my neighborhood and nearing the air docks. We couldn't reach them, because there was a crowd three times larger than the one outside my house blocking the way. A dirigible hovered a little off the ground, and its lowest level of windows were open. I saw Duane there waving and smiling, tossing out gifts which were fought over by the jubilant crowd.

"We love you!" One young girl called out starry-eyed. She wasn't even voting age.

I thought I had a lot of female supporters, but Duane had more, as well as plenty of men waving placards which said things like "Humans Out of the Shadows", "Real Power for Real People", and my favorite, "Will You Marry Me?".

"He was voted Highcrowne's most eligible bachelor in the last issue of the Times," Doctor Ghunnan noted. "It was on page three after the announcement of the parade to celebrate capture of the terrorist."

That's how everyone knew what was happening. I made it my business to never read the news, figuring I was unhappy enough as it was, and if something important happened I'd find out about it by word of mouth. That hadn't worked out so well.

"Duane!" I shouted. He couldn't hear me above the cheers and whistles. "This is not you!"

This wasn't me either. I couldn't get the image of Hilja and Duane out of my head, and it made me mad. Seeing him surrounded by an adoring crowd that didn't know the first thing about who he really was made me mad. He was a thief, an assassin, a killer ... a survivor.

So was I.

Damn him. I couldn't huddle in the dark anymore, being pathetic when he got back up again, over and over. I would not go down without a fight.

I was going to win this stupid election if it killed me.

By the time Doctor Ghunnan and I finished the rounds, scoping out the other human candidates and listening to their speeches in temples and on soapboxes at street corners, I was certain Duane was my only real rival. The rest were idiots.

Katherine, unable to get into my house or office, had taken over the vegetable shop in the bazaar, transforming it into my election headquarters. The greengrocer was her assistant campaign manager, and in between fetching her ink and parchment, poster paints and signage, he was trying to sell lettuce and the flavorless tomatoes grown in Highcrowne greenhouses. I really missed ripe Keshian fruit and vegetables grown on the vine.

"Based on the polls," Katherine was saying as she scribbled, "I think our platform should be about small business, supporting the average hardworking human to succeed and build a future for their family. A better world for their children."

"Not the woman issue?"

"No, and if any of the others bring it up, we attack them on their backward thinking. How can a Human Crown afraid of a female rival ever hope to stand up to the Elf Queen?"

"I like it." I wanted to more than stand up to Hilja, I wanted to smack her smug face.

How many times had she been over visiting Dawn and never once mentioned Duane? Were they sending letters to one another? Had she been out to Faellion to see him? He'd kissed me not six months ago, and we were kind of working on things. Admittedly, six months to a human was a long time, but for Solhans and elves it was an eyeblink. She knew she had crossed a line.

"Mister Rose's criminal past is not forgotten among our constituents," Katherine added. "They resent shakedowns and gang law, and now they are Citizens, they want full access to all the privileges elves and dwarves enjoy."

I squirmed. "You do know that it was my uncle who ran all those gangs and shakedowns? Duane was just working for him. The Thorne name is not as beloved amongst our 'constituents' as you might think."

"You saved the world, defeated the Dead God. Fought for their Citizenship. That's what people remember," she said, waving away my worries. "The data backs me up. Now, we just need a slogan."

Doctor Ghunnan's face lit up with an idea. "How about 'No choice? Vote Thorne!' I fully intend to make sure her political rivals are all dead before the election. Poison is crude, and difficult to place in their food now that their guard is up, so I was thinking of setting up a device on their doorstep which will electrocute them as soon as they step outside for the morning paper. There may be collateral damage, but we can always blame freak weather phenomenon."

"I know it's the goblin way—and I know how un-Solhan this sounds—but we should try not to kill anyone. Especially Duane," I said.

"Whatever for? I know he has been our ally and travelling companion on numerous occasions, but a politician should never place morals above winning."

"I admit I'm no expert on morals, hypocrisy yes, and Katherine's platform of middle-class family values is as boring as a cardboard sandwich ... where am I going with all this? Oh, yes, I think our slogan should be a bit more radical, truthful: 'Thorne was borne to piss them all off' or 'She doesn't care who she angers' or 'She'll fight for your rights because she just likes to fight'...."

"Needs some work," Katherine said, musing. "You are on to something, though. They don't need you claiming to be a mother and small business owner like them, because you are, from all accounts, terrible at those things. They need someone scrappy, someone willing to do what they're too afraid to do."

"'Beware, she's too dumb to care'." Doctor Ghunnan was starting to have too much fun with this.

"No slogans," I said finally. "We all suck at them." I grabbed poster paint and roughly scrawled 'Vote' and drew a tick box with my name next to it. "I'm at the top of the ballot: that is the key factor in my favor. People will not scroll down."

"Very shrewd, Miss Thorne." Doctor Ghunnan pulled out his own copy of the ballot which was already covered in his scribbled notes. He rubbed a wetted thumb across it and frowned. "This was printed using human technology; I'd recognize the imperfections of a handset typeface anywhere, yet the ink and paper are indestructible. Clearly more sophisticated materials, such as those used by elves and goblins. I wonder who produced it?"

I wanted to know who had put my name on it. And strangle them. "I think I have a private investigation case—mine. See you both later."

"We need to campaign!" Katherine protested.

"Doctor Ghunnan can help, right?"

"I will gather my miniature printing press," he said. "It will enable mass production of high-quality campaign flyers. I'll also retrieve a few electrical devices ... just in case you change your mind and want to eliminate Mister Rose and the others."

I still had the image of him and Hilja burnt on my retinas. "Ok. Just in case."

I left Katherine and her ever growing horde of volunteers (the greengrocer had roped in the rope seller and the urn painter) to designing the signs and pamphlets, while I headed for the Central City.

The one benefit of having the Avian sanctuary and half the mountain blown up by Aguragas was the opportunity to redesign. Goblins had built an embassy, and humans were using all that felled stone to build a proper palace for their Crown. I knew I'd find the current person wearing that title, if not a real crown because he preferred his military uniform, overseeing the operation: General Moore was the hands-on sort of ruler.

"Daniel," I said when I found him. I usually called him 'General', never 'King' so the use of his first name made him frown at me.

"Miss Thorne."

"You have some explaining to do," I said.

"Do I?"

"The election. Bad idea. You know I think you should just stay in charge. It' so much simpler, and you're so much better at this than Duane or I could ever be."

"I made a promise to the people of the Kingdoms, and I intend to keep it. My home is the river lands, the Fortress of Mages, what remains of it, and I intend to go back there and reclaim what belongs to me and my people. I will not be staying in Highcrowne, and so you need someone else to rule."

"You're leaving? With all your people? Do they know this?" That would take a significant chunk out of the human population in the city.

"Not all of them, not yet. I need to make things safe for their return, and then they will come."

"Is that the reason for all the strange voting rules? Surprise nominations, thirty-day campaign, serve or die? Let me guess, you want to retake the Fortress of Mages from the risen in late spring."

"Yes, after the water recedes but while the soil is damp enough to impede the movement of the undead."

"If you remained our Crown, you could have all of Highcrowne's forces at your command if you wanted."

"The others will not fight. Harley is concerned for dwarves, Hilja for elves. As they should be. Someone needs to be concerned for the humans."

"And the Solhans?"

"Is there any chance of saving your people from themselves?"

"True. Okay, so why did you put me at the top of the ballot?"

"It was randomized. As much as I feel you would be an adequate candidate, I do not want to interfere with the process. All nominees had equal chance."

"Adequate? Thanks, I guess. But that listing does not look random. Me then Duane? Who nominated me any-way?"

"It was anonymous. Not me, in case you were wondering. I need to remain impartial if I am to oversee a fair and peaceful transition."

As much as I respected General Moore, I couldn't believe how naïve he was.

"While I appreciate that you told everyone to make it random and impartial—not everyone obeys orders. People have agendas, other allegiances, and you can be certain some of those people may be responsible for making or printing ballots, or at the mercy of those with money or power who understand how much this election can influence the future of the Kingdoms."

"Who would go to the effort of rigging the ballot just to put you first on the list, Miss Thorne?"

"That is what I want to know. Who tallied the nominations? I want to question them."

"My personal aide, Laric, who should be working in my office now."

"I'll start there. Thank you, General."

"And Miss Thorne..."

"Yes?"

"Good luck."

"That doesn't sound very impartial of you."

"Then I should say I wish both you and Mister Rose luck—and the rest of the candidates of course."

So, the general did have some favorites. I smiled as I made my way to the barracks where Moore's office was located. The smiling must have made people think I was campaigning, because random Citizens waved or stopped to shake my hand or tell me about their problems. By the time I reached my destination, I wasn't smiling anymore and was in fact darting from the concealment of one shrub or statue to the next. I rushed into the general's office unannounced, to find the aide standing and staring at nothing.

"Hello?" I waved a hand in front of his face. "Laric?"

He blinked. "Yes? What can I do for you?"

"Is the general overworking you? Maybe you should get more sleep? And not while standing up."

"The general is not here, Miss Thorne."

"You know me?"

"Of course. I was responsible for screening all nominations to ensure they were eligible—Citizens and human being the only requirement."

"How was I nominated?"

"Same as everyone else. Following our call for nominations in The Times, names were placed in the collection box outside the barracks here."

"Not everyone reads The Times," I said, annoyed there was more news I'd missed by never reading the news. Some investigator I was. But I shunned being spoon-fed other people's facts. I preferred to discover them for myself.

"Town criers were used, that big sky sign hung from a dirigible, a letter drop...."

"Fine, I get it. So, you must have got thousands of nominations as everyone wants to be king."

"Fewer than you think, but the rules were that every nomination had to be seconded."

"So at least two people nominated me?"

"Hundreds. You are the Savior of Highcrowne."

"I think Mister Rose holds the title now." Still, it was good to know I wasn't forgotten. "Just hundreds? Never mind. Since the nomination is apparently legit, my question then becomes—how did I make it to the top of the list?"

"I'm not sure. I sent all the validated nominees to the ballot designer and told her to make sure it was random, not alphabetical."

"You left it up to a designer? An artist?"

"How is that any less valid than leaving it up to me? I presume you want to pounce on her next? She has a delicate constitution, and I ask you not to disturb her."

"Wait? Is she your girlfriend or something?"

"What? No. I simply admire her work. While I am used to having generals and other soldiers bark orders at me, she seeks the quiet of nature, the chorus of song-birds, as she paints watercolors when not forced to design hideously utilitarian ballots and other government documents."

"So, you're mooning over her. Where can I find this delicate vision of artistic genius?" Who happens to be privy to many government documents, and potentially secrets. Interesting.

"In the Central Gardens, and if you must interrupt her serenity, then let me take you to her." He suddenly seemed eager for the excuse to interrupt her himself. Nothing turned my stomach more than noxious gardens or blind love ... at least when I was feeling unloved of late. Election nominations and enthusiastic scientist friends aside, I felt terribly alone. Quiet contemplation was the last thing I needed, but the gardens wouldn't stay quiet for long. Not with me there.

"Show me to her."

The artist was a goblin. And not pretty. Maybe Laric did only love her art? No, he was looking at her more than at what she was painting. Love is blind. Which explained why he thought her watercolors were any good. They were muddy and dripping and looked more like a marsh than the manicured elvish gardens around them. She stood poised before her easel, but her eyes seemed to be on the Assembly building visible just beyond. If that was what she was painting; her art was even worse than I thought.

"Nina," General Moore's aide said ever so gently. "Do you mind?"

She hadn't heard.

"Hey!" I shouted. "I have questions."

She dropped her brush, and Laric rushed over to pick it up. He stared dreamily into her eyes as he handed it back on one knee.

"Thank you." Her voice was soft as butterfly wings and a contrast to her dry, scaly, and toothy appearance. She wore a lacey dress with puffy sleeves, another contrast and so unlike every other goblin I'd met who wore leather. Admittedly, most I'd met were mercenaries, muck rakers or commandos in their Emperor's service, other than the professor, so my expectations were probably skewed.

No other words were spoken, and she made no move to take back the paint brush. They just stared into each other's eyes. I hated young love. Did I say that already? It was just so melodramatic, every glance and unsaid word charged with subtext. Enough already.

"Okay, Nina," I said. "I have things to do. This can't be your office, so where do you design things like official government ballots?" Not that I had ever imagined ballots needed an artist's touch before. They were just words. I guessed someone had to put them in a coherent order and add the symbol of the Crowns etcetera.

With a blush to her greenish skin, she finally tore her gaze from Laric and said, "At the printshop my father owns. I'll show you, Miss Thorne."

"You know who I am?"

"I'm familiar with all the human candidates. I had hoped to add sketches to the ballot to aid the poor illiterates of our fair city, but King Moore was in such a hurry there was no time to complete them all."

"How tragic," Laric said. "Not only were you unable to help those poor wretches, but we were all robbed of seeing the beauty of your work."

"Please..." I began in my less than politic voice but quickly added in a more chipper tone "...show me the way."

I was supposed to be campaigning for office. As we walked and people waved, I practiced my smile. That hurt. Not doing that anymore. I'd be the one unsmiling candidate.

The print shop was in the goblin district of the Central City, near the new embassy. Goblins screamed spies to me. Every single one was in the service of their Emperor. Mercenaries were too feral to do anything other than kill, but I suspected every servant, cleaner, scientist, or craftsman with green skin to be a secret agent in disguise. I bet that's why Nina had been watching the Assembly building earlier.

What I couldn't figure out is why a goblin-owned printing business, with access to top quality paper, inks, and magical processes was using human equipment?

The answer was clear when I met Nina's father. He was human.

"Miss Thorne!" He shook my hand so enthusiastically I thought my arm would fly off at the shoulder. "It is an honor. A real pleasure. I was one of those who nominated you, you know?"

Why I was at the top of the ballot was becoming clearer.

Only, I noticed a line of glossy posters that had just emerged from his presses hung up on clotheslines to dry behind him. They all featured Duane's handsome face, green eyes so alive they snatched my breath away. He wore a beautifully embroidered cream suit with top hat to match, fingers set to tip it in greeting. His slogan was something brilliant, of course—"Your most eligible King"—and sure to set many female hearts aflutter. Not mine. Nope. Wasn't working.

"What was I saying?" I asked, dazed.

"Nothing." The printer noticed my reaction. "Yes, my wife Bettina is a fan of your rival. We can't play favorites when it comes to our work, but never fear, my vote is the only one in this household that counts, and I'll be casting it for you."

"Thank you," I said, absently. "That must be Bettina."

An older goblin woman, uglier than Nina in my estimation, hauled a cart full of paper out from the storeroom, humming as she worked. She kissed two fingers and placed them against an image of Duane's lips, and I shuddered for him.

Nina and Laric were frozen, staring into one another's eyes. They didn't move even as Bettina shoved the cart between them and ran over their toes. They were like statues.

"When did you settle in Highcrowne?" I asked the goblin matron when she drew near.

She blinked, surprised to see me. "Miss Thorne. I understand you have met Mister Rose in the flesh?"

"That is such a weird term 'in the flesh'. We have stood fully clothed next to one another many times." And we'd kissed. I didn't say that out loud for fear she'd want the skin from my lips as a souvenir. "Back to my original question. When did you arrive in Highcrowne? And what work did you do for the Emperor? Perhaps I should say, still do?"

"What Emperor?" She kept working, showing no surprise. A consummate spy that one.

"I suppose you've been teaching Nina the trade?" I said. And by 'trade' I meant spy craft. She must know I knew, but she kept whistling and working, ignoring my questions.

"Apologies," the father said. "We are a quite busy with the election announcement, and my wife is a bit absentminded on her best days. It was lovely of you to pay our humble shop a visit. I am most grateful."

I knew when I was being asked to leave in the politest way possible.

"I may be back," I said loud enough for Bettina and Nina to hear. They were listening, whether they pretended to or not.

I came out to find Doctor Ghunnan hanging a poster of me, proud of the work of his miniature printing press. It wasn't in color like Duane's. I felt a bit disappointed.

The doctor caught sight of Nina's father standing behind me, and his eyes slitted with fury.

"You."

"You!"

"What's going on?" I asked. "Doctor, put down the lightning pistol."

"We were once rivals for the fair Bettina's hand," Doctor Ghunnan explained.

The printer hung Duane's glossier poster next to mine. I was entranced all over again, but the doctor tore it apart before my eyes. "No," I said involuntarily.

Then my poster was torn down.

"Hilja?" She was in the hooded disguise she used whenever visiting Dawn. Strange to see her without a swarm of EEPs around, although there were a few looking conspicuous in big hats and sunglasses, leaning in nearby doorways. and glancing at us over copies of The Times.

"Eva," she said, venom in her voice.

"Why are you angry with me?"

"I never thought you would stoop so low as to try and steal Mister Rose's victory. He deserves the Crown."

"I didn't want it, didn't even know I'd been nominated until this morning."

"Then why the posters?"

"My friends have their own ideas. And well, let's be truthful as that's part of my campaign platform—I do want to beat Duane just so I can stand next to you wearing a Crown and jab you in the eye without fear of EEP reprisals. How dare you."

"How dare I what? What are you talking about?" Hilja asked.

"You know." I glanced at the poster Doctor Ghunnan had torn, precipitating Hilja's reprisal.

"Our relationship is purely professional."

"He wasn't good enough for you before, but if he's a Crown, he would be. Keep your grubby elvish fingers off him."

"And what right do you have to claim him? Does he have a slave mark I missed? A wedding ring?"

"Don't play dumb. You have me watched, and him watched, so you know how he feels about me."

"Feels about you?" she scoffed. "I think you are the adoring fan, just as pathetic as those who gather for his trinkets at rallies—yours is the unrequited feeling."

"Just keep your paws off my posters."

"Then keep your goblin hound's hands off of Mister Rose's posters."

"Fine."

"Fine."

Hilja and her cloud of poorly concealed bodyguards hurried off, and I stood arms crossed, watching them go. I'd won this territorial match.

I turned around to see the printer and Doctor Ghunnan had both set aside their enmity to watch me and mine.

"I did not understand a word of that conversation," the doctor said.

"Come on. Let's go. No one here is admitting anything—unless you want to brew me some more truth serum?" I asked.

"I am all out of ingredients, I fear."

"How about whisky? You have any of that in the history wing of the palace?"

"Certainly. And stronger stuff. Have you heard of Absinthe?"

"Let's go."

Three hours later, I stared down at the green, wormwood extract in my glass. Untouched.

It wasn't whisky, so that could be the reason I resisted. Or maybe it was because I had renewed purpose? A reason to fight, to show Hilja and Duane both, to show everyone who had ever doubted me ... Or maybe it was just because the green alcohol looked gross and a little scary.

The goblin had given me a tour of all his latest inventions—things like automatic orange peelers and pogo sticks, a prototype which I refused to test as I didn't want Dawn breaking her neck—when Katherine had found us to complain about our lack of campaign enthusiasm and to rub in how much more progressed her own research was. She was showing off her magic-infused, long distance communication device, powered by her own green goo, when Doctor Ghunnan had started on the absinthe.

"Magic." He kept mumbling while swatting at invisible things floating in front of his face. Maybe it was the hallucinations that had kept me from downing my own glass. I had whisky tolerance, but this stuff?

"Here, take one," Katherine said, handing me one of her paired speaking devices. It was rectangular and black, a slim glass box with two holes and only one button on the side.

"Why glass?" I asked. "Won't it break? And have you ever heard of ergonomics?" It didn't fit well in my hand, and the button was in the most annoying location and hard to press.

"With this we can talk, even when on opposite sides of the city. We can coordinate rallies, debates...."

She should be the one on the ballot. I had lost most of my enthusiasm right after Hilja accused me of stealing the election from Duane.

I hadn't asked for this. Someone had placed me first on the list because they had wanted me to win or at least make sure Duane didn't, it was hard to say. Nothing would have come of it if I hadn't let

Katherine take over, a dynamo of action, obviously fulfilling her dreams vicariously. She wanted me to be something I wasn't: a positive example, a leader. I didn't think Duane was those things either, but it wasn't my place to tell him what to do. If he wanted this....

"I'm withdrawing from the race," I said.

"No, you can't," Katherine argued.

"I do what I want."

"Have you even read the election rules?"

"No one gave me a copy ... wait. Let me guess. They were published in The Times?"

"Yes, and those on the ballot cannot withdraw. Not participating is tantamount to being a traitor, punishable by loss of Citizenship and exile. And as you know, if you win and deny yourself the Crown, you can expect execution. Serve or die."

I'd lived the life of an exile, and I remembered how it was before I was a Citizen, not even allowed into the Central City without a babysitter. It had been tough, but I could endure it—if not for Dawn. I had come back to Highcrowne for her. I would stay and do this for her.

"Fine. But we don't have to campaign. If I don't win, there's nothing to say no to, and so I can't be executed. That means no more posters."

Katherine started to argue when Doctor Ghunnan swayed and fell straight back onto the floor. He reached up towards the ceiling and smiled. "I see magic."

"He may have a concussion. You should check on him," I told Katherine. She was already grabbing her medical kit.

I used the distraction to escape all the election talk. I grabbed the absinthe bottle and ran. Best to keep the stuff away from the professor.

When I got home, I stashed it in my office where I hoped Nanny wouldn't find it, under the floorboards alongside a few dark magic relics, and then climbed the stairs to the house.

Dawn and I colored pictures while sharing our day. I loved her giggles as she deliberately made a few strokes outside the lines and glanced around nervously as if Mister Gardens was watching. I always activated privacy wards to make sure he wasn't, and that Nanny wasn't eavesdropping either. This was our time.

She told me she had snuck out the back to pet a stray cat, before Nanny dragged her inside by an ear. I didn't scold her because I knew the alley was safe. I wished she could explore the streets as I'd done as a kid, going everywhere, but it wasn't possible. Being a hated Solhan refugee had given me far more freedom than the child of the Elf King would ever know. I kept smiling for her, but inside those maudlin, morse, melancholy feelings were bubbling up again, if they had ever gone away.

After supper—Mister Gardens and Nanny split meal preparation duties, and Nanny's dishes always had leftovers—I tucked Dawn into bed and kissed her forehead, before gathering all her favorite stuffed toys and tucking them in beside her.

"Are you going to be a queen like my sister, Hilja?" she asked.

"Not if I can help it," I said.

I read her to sleep, nothing that could be labelled learning, just a fable with funny animals doing silly things that made her smile as she drifted off.

Early risers all, everyone else was asleep except me. I was alone in the silence of the night. I looked out the window at moonlight on cobbles, its bluish cast distinct from the orange glow of streetlamps farther away.

It was this quiet time that was hardest. The world slipped away, and I had only my memories. I recalled Thane holding me as we danced, holding me as we looked out on our last sunrise together. His words in a dozen voices, the voices of all those people he had possessed, mostly Fharen's, but even Duane's, how he had said my name. How I had sent him away one last time without a proper goodbye. Was he dead, consumed by the Devourer? I no longer had a connection, no way of knowing. He was just gone.

I missed him, but over the last six months I'd missed someone else too. Now he was back, I'd learned he had spoken to Hilja and crowds of admirers ... but not to me. Why hadn't Duane come to find me?

I couldn't sleep, and there was no whisky in the house, so I dug out the absinthe and took a careful swig.

Nasty.

I hoped it would show me magic like it had the goblin doctor. I missed my magic. Not the wards and runes and enchanted objects anyone could draw on—I missed real power.

Like the soul sense that had allowed me to know what anyone thought or felt, to know what they knew, effortlessly. Even the ability to pull souls from their bodies, to consume and transform them. It had terrified me before, but now it was gone, I couldn't remember why I'd been so frightened. It had all been Thane's power, not mine, and with him gone, it was too. I felt like I'd been given wings only to have them torn off. I knew what it felt like to soar, but I was stuck on the ground forever.

That power, Thane's love, all of it had made me believe I was special. For once in my life, I had not floundered— I'd saved the city, the world!—and I had believed in myself.

Now, I was just a failed detective. Again. Nothing.

Who could want me to be a queen?

 # STORMCOMING

The rainstorm and a dark foreboding provided the atmosphere for my absinthe-fueled dream. It began in the Void between worlds, the pathways you could walk to reach other places, even other universes, if you knew the way. If you strayed from the path, you would die, lost, swallowed by nothingness until you felt the pull of the Dead God drawing your soul to Him and His eternal embrace.

Thane, I thought, but it was not Him in the dark. I slipped on limestone. Icy rain jolted me, and I was no longer in the Void but in the karst plains outside Solheim. The silhouette of the ruined city was like skeletal fingers rising from the ground. The great tower shone with turquoise light, a beacon for Death, an emanation of His power, and once again His power was mine.

All my necromancy awoke, like it had merely been asleep, never lost, and my soul sense surged outward searching for life. I felt Conrad, the Risen monster I had created after I killed the man who had loved me. I'd killed so many, but he deserved it the least. He deserved nothing but love and forgiveness, and my arms around him—nothing I could ever give. My warm embrace was reserved for another.

Thane. I searched for Him, emptiness everywhere, until suddenly He stood before me, the light from Solheim's tower reflected in the luminous blue of His eyes. He wore Fharen's form. *Are you alive?* I asked. *Have you come back to me?*

Yes.

I awoke when lightning flashed so bright and so close that thunder immediately shook the house, rattling my windowpane, where torrents of rain clawed to get in. I gasped, reaching out for Thane, for Conrad with my soul sense, but it was gone. It was only a dream. A nightmare. I was still powerless. Weak.

Wind tore the window open, howling through the room and tossing the curtains into knots. I rushed to close it, worrying it would wake Dawn. Then I remembered she had Viktor's room now, with him away at school. I was alone.

Water plastered me as I fought to close the shutters, and in a flash of lightning I noticed a figure below on the street. A face inside a dark hood looked up at me, more lightning dancing through the clouds beyond him. Green eyes.

I felt the electricity in the air, lightning drawing closer.

I went downstairs and opened the front door. Rain hammered the roof so loudly I couldn't hear anything else; it splashed up from cobbles, getting even under eaves to soak my nightgown. I was already wet, so I stepped out into the storm and took his arm. "Duane? Are you insane?"

He was soaked through, black hair plastered to his cheeks, rivulets like tears streaming down his face. "She's dead, Eva."

"Who?"

"Hilja."

I was stunned, wondering if I was still dreaming. I swore I would never drink absinthe again. "Come inside. Now."

Duane moved like an automaton, pausing unexpectedly, needing me to steer him into the salon. I barred the door and fetched towels from the cupboard. We were both shivering as I wrapped him up and set him on the couch. The towel barely helped my chattering teeth, so I wrapped blankets around us both. Soon heat built. Duane emanated warmth like the baked sands of his homeland. I'd passed through there once and thought of him. Soon, I was uncomfortably hot and pulled away, tossing my soaked towel on the parquet flooring.

"Tell me everything."

"Not here."

"My home is the most warded place in Highcrowne. No one can get in."

He pointed up the stairs, and then I noticed Mister Gardens in the shadows, watching. He knew he was discovered, so he strode boldly down, saying, "You've drenched the cushions. What were you doing out in the storm?"

"My house, my prerogative," I said, annoyed. "Go back to bed."

He ignored me and set about cleaning and mopping up. Being powerless in my own home, as well as when it came to magic, had helped drive me to the bottle of late. But every time I became determined to kick him out, to put a sword against his throat, or even to scream in his face, I stopped myself. Mister Gardens could teach Dawn things I couldn't, things she needed to survive. Even more so now that Hilja was dead—Dawn was Queen.

Mister Gardens couldn't know, not yet. I wasn't ready for this.

"Let's go," I told Duane, directing him down the stairs to my office.

I had a privacy rune set into my desk which I activated. We wouldn't be overheard here, but the icy blanket of silence that descended made me hurry to the metal stove where I built a fire. I rubbed my hands before it, my back to Duane.

"I'm sorry, Eva."

"For what?"

Being angry at Duane for ignoring me while he was busy with parades and speeches seemed foolish now. My life was changed forever. I was mother to a queen.

Unless Dawn and I ran.

But there was Mister Gardens and EEPs who would follow. They'd found us before, and they would never stop until they found us again. No, we couldn't run. This was why I'd been training Dawn, but six months was not long enough. She needed sixteen years.

"I went to see her," Duane said, dazed. "She kissed me. I don't know what happened. I woke up and she was dead in my arms. Blood everywhere and a black rose in her hand."

"You slept with her?" Some fury resurfaced.

"No. I don't know. I don't remember. The rose...."

"What's so important about the rose?"

"It was my signature mark as an assassin. I always left one with my victims, my calling card."

"I didn't know that's where your name came from." I'd known he was once an assassin but not who he'd killed. The black rose was found in the hands of dead powerbrokers, mercenary leaders, and mages. Everyone who had ruled Highcrowne a decade ago had fallen, making way for new powers to rule. "Wait. Did Hilja hire you to kill for her back then?"

"I helped her rise, eliminated those Fharen relied on, and yes, I did it for money and for her."

"So, when I saw you together on The Malthésis, you hadn't just met. You'd been together...."

"Since I was sixteen, after you went to Gernwold."

I was stunned to silence, but he didn't move, didn't look at me or reach out. He waited, as if I held the executioner's blade and was only biding my time before I dealt his punishment.

"Did you kill her?" I hated that I had to ask, but I didn't know Duane as well as I thought. I thought I'd known the worst, but those were only sketchy outlines, never the details.

"I would never .... Perhaps? If someone made me? Drugged or compelled me? Never willingly."

I supposed that was what mattered. If I believed him. If I knew him at all. I had no truth serum to be sure, but as he stood before me lost and afraid—as I'd never seen him before—I knew I wanted to believe him. I had to try.

I let my detective instincts kick in, pushing away my doubts and feelings of betrayal. Who would want Hilja dead? The list was too long: political rivals, anyone not an elf, me .... Why did I think that? I did hate her a bit, was jealous of her certainty and for being with Duane, disliked her elvish disdain for the rest of us, but not enough to kill her. An assassin had wounded her once, which had been their only aim, else she'd be dead. I thought I'd stopped the ultimate person responsible,

Ilsa, but now it was clear that case had never been closed.

"Who else knew you were the Black Rose?" If too many people had motive, then I needed to discover who had opportunity. Who could get into her private chambers and frame Duane.

"Aguragas."

"Did he escape?" His execution was scheduled for today, and that was a great motive.

"I don't know. There's so much more going on, Eva. My people are acting strangely. My networks, my information ... it's all wrong. I didn't feel I could trust anyone—except you."

The Shadow King powerless, framed for murder. Maybe this was more about Duane than Hilja? Aguragas remained at the top of my list for that reason. He loved to destabilize the monarchy—killing one Crown and disrupting the election of another would be just like him. Getting vengeance on an old rival at the same time would be the cherry on top for him.

Had he wanted to be captured? "Tell me how you tracked Gas down in Faellion. Every detail."

Duane spoke for an hour, his thoughts clearing, his memory sharp. It seemed he had been drugged before, groggy, but he was coming back into focus, and he told me all about his hunt for Aguragas.

"...I knew he'd gone to speak to House Uanal before the explosion, so I started there. It was information from Kali, so I trusted it more than chasing after all the supposed sightings of him and his followers in Gernwold or at the Wall. I had some of my people go and look into everything, of course, but me and my best people went to Faellion."

"Who are your best people?" I probed. "Why do you trust them?"

"I don't trust anyone, remember?"

"Allies and future enemies you said. Except me?"

He was silent.

"You say you trust me now, but you still worry I could one day be your enemy?"

"Mister Gardens certainly is, once he learns what happened, and you will protect Dawn above all else. What if he threatens her to get to me?"

"She is his Queen now. He wouldn't."

"If he does? Always think the unthinkable can happen. That's what it means to be spymaster. I thought I had everything covered: people who didn't know my best people watching them, people watching those people.... And before you ask, they are not all street thugs like the Tinker Twins. Those I grew up with I know better, I know all their secrets, but I've gathered a lot of secrets on merchants, guards, soldiers, Matriarchs, bureaucrats, royal family members ...."

Secrets I use as leverage to get them to spy for me, and because you can't trust people who fear you, I've also recruited a lot of patriots who want to protect Highcrowne or the Kingdoms. I've even recruited just civic minded citizens looking out for their neighbors. Bogles, goblin muck rakers ... I tell you I had everything covered."

"How could all of that be disrupted then? What did you mean when you said earlier 'it's all wrong'?"

"I can't explain. It's like this sense that something is off. Like when you're getting an ear infection and things feel strangely tilted. Not everyone has betrayed me, not yet, as that would be impossible. But it feels like many of them are lying to me, making it so information from two different places does not add up. I don't know which is the lie or why. It's like someone has tossed gum into the gears, and the machine I've built is malfunctioning."

"You've spent too much time with Bell to come up with an analogy like that. You also spend far more time thinking than I ever imagined. I feel inadequate now."

"No. By being outside of it all, you can provide clarity, a new perspective."

"That's trying to find a silver lining to my myopic selfishness and all the wallowing I've been doing lately. Thanks. So, how did Gas slip up?"

"You're making me worry he didn't. He was clever in Faellion, staying out of cities, away from roads. He had anti-magic protections, so there was no tracking him that way. I got lucky in that one of my eyes spotted him on horseback in a valley and tracked him, sending me a message when they could, so I made sure fury descended on him in a heap and there was no escape."

"I worry about luck," I said.

"Me too."

"So, what next?" I asked. News would be out that Hilja was dead. Maybe no town criers yet, as the palace kept things under wraps, but people knew, and one of those people might well be Mister Gardens—and soon. "Did anyone see you covered in blood?"

He looked down, frightened, but the blood wasn't visible to anyone but him. He wore a black cloak over everything. "I got out using secret ways, but there's no guarantee someone didn't see me. I shouldn't stay in Highcrowne, but how else am I to find out who did this?"

"You don't. Hire me."

"Will you work for free, for old time's sake?" He held out his empty pockets. I knew he had plenty of money stashed for emergencies like this. Probably some in his shoes too, but never in his pockets where thieves like him would find his coin.

"No way. You will owe me big for this. Very big."

"I thought you told me you'd 'never ever' work for me?"

"I do a lot of things I think I'll never ever do. It's like a jinx. I really need to stop saying that.".

4 UNDERNEATH EVERYTHING

Duane might no longer be drugged, but he was still stunned. He looked glassy eyed when I held a hand to his chest as he tried to follow me up the stairs. "Stay," I told him.

I thought he had seen everything, but there was something about Hilja's death that had gotten to him. Something he wasn't telling me.

Clients always lie. So, what was Duane's? Now wasn't the time to investigate, however. I'd figure it out as more pieces fell into place. In the meantime, I needed to clean house.

A cigarette glowed red in the darkened living room. A shadow lounged on one of the moth-eaten chairs.

"Mister Gardens," I said.

"Miss Thorne." His tone made me guess someone in the palace had sent him a message—probably via enchanted mirror or some other top secret elvish method—and he knew about Duane.

I had my Ashur. I'd grabbed it as soon as the nightmare woke me, and I closed my shutters against the rain. It was my binky, my baby blanket in times of stress, and it hadn't left my grip since. I drew it now, serrated steel glinting in the light from the streetlamps outside.

He didn't draw anything, which meant he already had a weapon readied.

"We only want Mister Rose for questioning," he said reasonably.

"I've seen how elves ask questions—lots of chains, pincers, and pokey things of torture. A waste of time with a disciplined spymaster. Time better spent finding the real killer. You know he was drugged?"

"Or says he was. A disciplined spymaster could feign anything, make you—especially you—believe anything."

"What's that supposed to mean?"

"You are less than objective when it comes to him."

"I choose my clients—and I choose him. My reasons don't concern you. Now, you can either play nice and leave now or...."

"Or what?"

"I can't think of an alternative either of us will enjoy. Actually, I might."

I took a step closer to his silhouette, worried about a knife, wanting to test him, to see how far he would go. I didn't see anything, and with my reduced magic sense I feared a glamour was hiding whatever he was really up to. I hated being blind, and I chickened out.

"Goodbye," I said, as I silently invoked the wards I'd placed on the house back when I had real power.

Mister Gardens vanished with a surprised and somewhat annoyed grunt. The dagger he'd been holding fell to the floor not more than a step away from me. My magic was gone but not my instincts. I was glad I'd played it safe.

I hurried up to the third floor to check on Dawn. She was Queen now, if only a few knew it, and I didn't think Mister Gardens would have hurt her—but he could have told her what was happening, which would not be good either.

"What's wrong?" Dawn asked first thing. She was awake, sitting on her bed with hands folded serenely. The door was ajar, so I knew she'd been listening.

"Just a bad storm outside. And I have a new case. I need to work all hours on this one, so Nanny is in charge."

"What happened to Mister Gardens?"

"Nothing. He's just been called away to the palace. Elf business."

"You know that Nanny's cooking is awful?"

"Yes, it is."

"I'm likely to starve."

"It will grow hair on your chest."

"Ew. I don't want hair there."

"It's a saying. I've no idea what it really means. If it's Solhan, it probably translates to 'makes you tough enough to survive real poison when you need to, so it's a good thing'."

Especially if she was Queen.

No, I would not accept that reality. Not yet. Better if the rival elvish faction responsible for Hilja's assassination took over the city—until they found out about Dawn. Then they'd need to eliminate her too.

The shifting clouds of worry roiling through my insides must have shown on my outsides, because, alarmed, she said, "Mommy?"

She never called me that anymore. I hugged her tight. I grew as uncomfortable as she was, and it was a relief when she pulled free and said, "Uncle Duane?"

"He can't help...." I began, but he could. He was there in the doorway.

"Dawn." The sadness was in his voice, the way he stood, and I watched him struggle with it, his expression as changeable as mine, pushing it down deep inside like some enemy he was trying to wrestle into submission. When calm settled on his features, it was even more disturbing. A mask. "Everything is alright. Just stay inside and don't go out."

"She never goes out," I said. It was the tragedy of her birthright. She was meant to rule, but all her life she'd been imprisoned.

"That's not true, is it Dawn?" Duane said.

She looked sheepish.

"To the alley but no farther. There's no way past my wards," I argued. Then I remembered I hadn't sealed the drains. Stray hairs from Dawn's head, flecks of skin, all had to be allowed to pass, but there shouldn't be a drain large enough for even a mouse.

"Okay," she admitted. "I dug a hole in the cellar. Looking for treasure, mind you. I happened to find something awfully stinky and ran the other way. Until I realized what it was."

"What?" I asked, clueless.

"The sewers," Duane explained. "I own the company in charge of construction and made sure they dug under your house. I thought you could use an escape tunnel in future."

"Or a secret way in, just in case I didn't invite you?" I had to say it, and this time he looked sheepish.

My wards penetrated to the bedrock, so I didn't need to worry about incursion. The protective spell on Dawn, however, was newer and not as all encompassing. I did want her to leave one day, and so I'd made it weak, breakable, and apparently circumnavigable.

"We're sealing up the basement," I said.

"No," Duane argued. I gave him good glare and he hastily added, "I mean, Eva, we can use the sewers. No one will know where we are in Highcrowne. The tunnels go everywhere, under everything important. I saw to that."

"You mean every place you might want to rob some-day?"

"Yes. Or escape from. We can find out what's happening and never step in daylight." It was obviously a dream for him. I was pale as snow and used to eternal winter, but I did crave sun. It wasn't meant literally, I knew. A Shadow King needed the shadows, and if I was to figure out what was happening, I'd need to be his shadow. Walk in his shoes.

"Alright. We go, but I get Nanny to seal the wards behind us, so this too curious little one can't follow." I wanted to scold Dawn, but I was a little proud of her curiosity and resourcefulness. I ended up smiling instead.

I woke Nanny, told her to place a repelling hex over the sewer hole once we'd gone, and told her to watch out for Dawn: "My little hellion. Go back to sleep".

Then Duane and I descended into stinky, damp darkness.

"The smell is enough to make me vomit," I complained.

"Every full proof secret highway has its drawbacks," Duane pointed out. "Keeps everyone else away."

"So, what happens to all this crap without the muckrakers hauling it away?"

"Oh, the muckrakers still take care of it. I didn't want to put them out of a job—that would be a huge blow to my voter base."

"They're always goblins. They can't vote in human elections."

"There are rules, and then there are rules, or more flexible policies. The point is, I am all for the working man, woman, thing, whatever. The sewers collect waste, so it doesn't run down the streets and into the river. The muckrakers screen the central pool for any valuables, then shunt it along to...."

"Let me guess. The river?"

"Yes, but way downstream. Out of sight, out of mind."

"And I bet you made a fortune from the Crowns too, who paid you to install it all?"

"Yes. Plus, a maintenance fee from the merchants and landowners served."

"Wait. Am I paying for this with my taxes?"

"No. Friend's discount."

"Are we friends?"

"If not, then what?"

I didn't want to answer that. Didn't even want to think about it now that I'd learned he and Hilja had been working together for so long. More than working— they had been 'together' for so long. Right after my first teenage crush kiss with Duane, she had swooped in and stolen him away. Did I mention how much I was not sad she was dead?

He knew me too well, well enough to stay silent as we climbed down into the muck. The newly cut stone had green things growing and creeping over it already. Some of it glowed. The professor should have been doing goo studies down here. It was warmer than above in the snow, and so I wasn't surprised when I saw a snoring goblin curled in an alcove. There would be nests of them soon.

Duane finally broke down and spoke first about everything we weren't saying.

"You know, it was never like with you and me when I was with Hilja. I couldn't stop thinking about you. Then you changed. When you came back from school, it seemed you didn't feel the same about me."

"Not the best ambiance for this talk." I pinched my nose as a cloud of some noxious gas drifted by. "And yes, I changed. My soul had been in a jar all my life until Uncle gave it back to me at my Coming of Age ceremony. You fell in love with a different Eva."

"I never stop falling in love, whichever Eva I see, and she changes every day."

It was the most beautiful thing anyone had ever said to me. I was still mad at him about Hilja. But ... something softened inside me, and I changed the subject.

"It must have been hard digging all these tunnels in frozen soil."

"Everything's hard on the streets, especially in Highcrowne. The workers were grateful for the job."

"More people should settle in Kell. It's nice there. Of course, I had no trouble with risen, but others might…. I'm sorry, by the way. I didn't like Hilja, but you did, so I'm sorry."

He nodded, unable to speak or tell me how much he was hurting. I felt it, though, even without my soul sense. I knew him that well.

"Look at us, saying nice things to one another. Maybe the end of the world is nigh again?" I laughed.

"It's always nigh. My networks send me word of every threat, every war, every death 'of import' or shift in political power across the Kingdoms from Faellion to the Wall, and what Ulric and Calka used to tell me was worse. I feel cut off from everything tonight, and in a way—I've never felt more at peace."

"Ignorance is bliss. Before it gets you killed. We need information. Once we surface, I'll send Bitten Belly and my other bogles out to learn what they can, but you must have someone in the elven palace, some servant or guard, who can tell you who else was there tonight? Who else could have killed her?"

"Yes. I'll send word to them, ask for a report. I just need to guess which messenger I can trust."

"Send several, pigeons too. Hedge your bets."

He nodded, and I could see his confidence returning. I hadn't said anything he didn't already know, but he'd been doubting himself, doubting everything, and he needed someone to reassure him that his instincts weren't all wrong.

"This way." He led me through a side tunnel where the path alongside the sewage canal became so narrow it was like walking on a tightrope. I slipped and got my boot wet, cursing and limping with disgust all the way to the ladder he indicated we climb.

We emerged in an alley that was somehow filthier than the sewer below. The snow drifted in the corners was yellow and speckled with dirt and garbage. Rusted scrap metal left red stains against the tenement walls on either side, and despite the cold, the sickly-sweet stench of something dead wafted from one corner.

I pinched my nose shut. I should invest in a clothespin or some of those perfumed posy bouquets the ladies used to protect their nostrils from the stench of this city. That would be weakness, though, and something no Solhan liked to admit. I forced myself to unclench my nose.

"I hope your messenger isn't whoever is dead and stinking up this place," I said.

"No. That's a cat. He always leaves some carcass rotting to deter visitors."

Duane whistled, and a window opened on the floor above us. I noticed most of the windows on either side were blocked up with wood or bricks except for that one.

A balding man with a greasy shirt leaned out. His already huge eyes bulged even more. "Boss. What you need?"

Duane waved him down, and a moment later the lackey had lowered a ladder and joined them. He'd been too startled at seeing Mister Rose himself that he'd forgotten a jacket and stood shivering and rubbing his hands like some frightened rodent.

"Tell Alfonse in the kitchens I need a full report. He'll know what about. Have him use the wax recorder and leave the spool for me in the usual place."

"Sure thing, Boss. Can I grab something warm before I head out?"

Duane nodded. "First, I'm curious about the fish market. Any big orders, like for a banquet?"

"Strange you should ask. There was an order for today, Jollups too. You know what the occasion is?"

"Do elves need a reason to feast when we starve? Get goin' now before your bols freeze." Duane adopted the speech mannerisms of whoever he was speaking with. It was automatic for him and disturbing how easily he shifted personas.

The flunky nodded gratefully and climbed back up, wincing at the icy wooden rungs before sealing his window shut against the cold. Duane watched his blurred figure for a moment and then led me back to the sewer. I'd hoped we were done with that means of travel, but apparently not.

"Do you think that was odd?" he asked me when we were back underground in relative warmth.

"I don't know. A coded and seemingly senseless conversation with a pudgy human fish hawker in a stinking alley? For you, I suppose it's normal?"

"I have people who talk to people like that these days. He seemed a bit surprised to have 'Boss' there in person, but the strange thing was that your picture and name is as famous as mine, especially since our supporters have been plastering posters all over town. He never asked what you were doing there, my supposed political rival."

"Maybe he was just too scared to question. I do have that effect on people."

"Ego much?"

"Look who's talking. At least I don't invent imposing titles for myself, 'Shadow King'. And why were you asking about a banquet? I assume at the elven palace?"

"Someone will want to celebrate Hilja's death, or someone knew to plan for a funeral. Alfonse is a chef and may know who our eager party planner is. I still need more information on members of each house and clan staying at the palace, just in case. More servants' gossip is required."

We visited several dodgy streets and rundown basements, sending messengers off to collect intelligence, and I set my own bogles doing the same. Reports should be rolling in soon, so Duane and I cooled our heels in one of the mausoleums in the above ground cemetery. It was a favored place for clandestine meetings, made all the better with the new sewer entrance and egress routes.

"Your workers have been busy. No one questioned the need to put tunnels under graves?" I asked. Bodies were never buried anymore, because of risen, only urns full of ashes, but still it must have been a bit of work to dig beneath the old catacombs.

Duane shrugged. "Government is corrupt."

"Do you hear that?" I asked. It sounded like shouts.

Duane pressed his ear to the mausoleum wall, unperturbed by a skeletal hand that hung from a nearby shelf of bones. These were ancient dead, no ghosts about and no souls to yoke and turn them into risen, so I wasn't disturbed either. It's when a loud thud made Duane jump and back up from the wall that I worried. I drew my Ashur.

The ancient stones of the wall shook, and a section broke free, throwing up choking dust. After I coughed and cleared my teary eyes, I saw slashes in the stone, thin grooves which I recognized. Werewolf claws.

Werewolves were highborn dwarves cursed, or blessed, depending on your perspective, with the ability to transform into vicious killing machines. Ancient Solhan magic made them the ultimate warriors for the ultimate empire which had once spread across the world like a malignant fungus of evil. Not the nicest way to think about my people, but I knew Solhans, and I knew they were not nice.

My sister, before her recent incarceration by the frightening league of Unmentionables, had been set on reviving the Solhan Empire, especially when she learned the august family Thorne had once ruled it from time immemorial. My sister was an undead vampire, so she knew that had meant Dawn would carry on the inheritance—Ilsa had something against the male line inheriting, so she always forgot about Little Viktor—but I wanted my daughter to have a normal life. With Hilja dead the likelihood of that happening grew slimmer every minute.

In any event, the main point of my internal monologue was that werewolves were dangerous and deadly, and so it was not good if one was trying to break through the mausoleum wall.

"I'll see what's happening." Duane headed over to investigate. I thought exiting, rather than being trapped in this small chamber with a rampaging werewolf, was a good idea, so I followed.

It was dark outside, the streetlamps too far away to illuminate the gravestones and tombs in the cemetery. Solhan vision allowed me to see clearly enough, and Duane's history of skulking in shadows made it navigable to him too, so we had no trouble slinking up to the neighboring mausoleum entrance and peeking through the crack in the door, which was slightly ajar.

"Elves be damned! This is not their decision."

"What about our own traditions? What disrespect to our mothers and grandmothers? Democracy is an affront to our elders, no respect for their wisdom. Do you dare presume to be wiser than the wisest of us?"

"If they are wise, then they shall win the election."

"If they deign to run. Why should our mothers solicit the respect they naturally deserve? And you, please, turn dwarf again. Give up your rage. No one will vote for a wolf."

"Why not? We are the truest of the lineage, the chosen of old. We should rule—not the Matriarchs."

I looked at Duane. "Democracy, yeck," I mouthed. Seemed we were listening to a heated political debate between two dwarves. Based on the name above the mausoleum, I guessed it to be a family plot of a high-ranking dwarfish clan. That's why at least one was a werewolf, the other clearly a conservative supporting the Matriarchy and traditional values. How mundane.

"Not so private after all," I said silently. I knew Duane read lips. I didn't speak for fear the werewolves would hear, so I gestured we should get going, as this was no longer as private a meeting place as we'd hoped. Like I said, the cemetery was notorious for clandestine rendezvouses.

We found ourselves on deserted, frozen streets, kicking empty tin cans to score points whenever they made it into gutters or crates on the side of the road.

I couldn't help remembering so many days spent doing exactly this, nothing, with Duane and my brother when we were kids. I felt young again, not jaded and regretful. I felt like anything was possible. I felt like me again. When had I lost myself?

"Is that a smile?" Duane asked.

"Maybe."

"Your high score is going down. Next crate is mine." He kicked hard, and the tin can hit the sweet spot. He raised his arms, triumphant.

I shoved him, and he nearly careened into a street-lamp.

"Hey. Sore loser." He was smiling too.

I didn't want the moment, the memory of another life, to end, ever. An impossible dream.

Inevitably, one of Duane's messengers signaled to us from a side street. I noted a campaign poster tacked to the building behind him. It had my face next to a checkmark. I had wanted the checkmark, but I had not approved the painting in my likeness, and this one was particularly bad as it had me smiling. Few had seen me smile, so the artist—probably that goblin girl—had taken liberties and made me look so honey sweet fake it made me want to vomit. That was not me.

I was distracted and hadn't been listening to the messenger's report, until there was mention of "a visitor from the Wall."

"What's this?" I asked, hoping for a rewind.

"All I heard was that the banquet was organized by the Seneschal, on behalf of the Royal Privilege Party, in honor of 'an esteemed guest newly arrived via the castle at the Wall,'" the informant repeated.

The castle at the Wall meant they had crossed from Solheim. "Who is this guest?"

He shrugged. The informant was a greasy human, likely a delivery boy or cleaner who passed for a slave among the eleven elite in the palace.

"Royal Privilege," Duane emphasized. They-were a key rival party, with many members hungry for Hilja's for power. And they opposed democratic ideals such as those the dwarves had been so energetically discussing.

I couldn't stop wondering about this special guest. I had travelled via the Wall with Dawn on an airship. It was the quickest route from Archon and Kell, even Lyss, not that anyone came through there but me. So, the newcomer didn't have to be from Solheim. Still, the Wall was heavily garrisoned, and travelers were usually turned away unless they were particularly convincing or rich enough to bribe the commanding officer. I had been both.

The messenger didn't know any more details, so I filed the information away for later and asked, "What's the word about Hilja?"

"The Queen has taken poorly and is confined to her rooms at present. She is unlikely to attend the feast," the messenger said.

"That's all?" Duane asked, hesitant to mention he knew she was dead and had been covered in her blood until recently. I'd seen him wash up, repeatedly, every chance he got, but I suspected he desperately wanted to change his clothing as soon as he had time.

"No. What should I be on the lookout for, Boss?"

"Just tell me who is keeping people away from her room," Duane said.

"The Seneschal."

"Ernest?" I asked.

"Yes."

I knew him. A notorious democrat. Actually, more a socialist.

Duane waved the informant away and activated his privacy bracelet again, so we could theorize as we walked. The can kicking game was over, but murder investigation was high on my list of fun too, if only it hadn't been Hilja.

"Do you think democrats are behind this?" I asked. "You know where Hilja's true convictions lay, and after last year and the truth serum I gave her, the other Crowns knew too. Ernest lurked in elvish inner circles, always listening in, so maybe he learned she has no love for his cause after all, and that angered him enough to kill her?"

"The Seneschal is a quivering pile of sycophantic goo who would never take unilateral action on his own," Duane said.

"All signs point to a high-ranking elf," I mused. "Murder in the palace, covered up, able to order a banquet ... Hilja always spoke as though she trusted no one. Whether she sided with democracy or not, all her rivals were out to get her. Who has the best claim to the throne now that she's gone? Assuming they know nothing about Dawn?"

"A few. Prince Gallan's Clan, Teiran, although they are mostly ancient, with little ambition now that their prince is dead. Although, if they guessed Hilja was responsible for his death, they would want vengeance. I don't think they know, however. I made sure of it.... There's Clan Lellyn."

"Hilja mentioned them before," I recalled. They made her very nervous.

"Powerful landowners who control most of Faellion's slaves, and accomplished soldiers. Many EEPs come from their clan, Guard commanders too, like House Uanal."

"Sounds like Clan Lellyn is a winner to me. Let me guess, Seneschal Ernest is from there?"

"Yes."

"I think we question Ernest next."

"He never leaves the palace."

"Your sewers can't take us there?"

"No, but maybe we can lure him out. Snatch and grab something he cares about."

"What would that be?" I had allied with Ernest once, briefly, but I had not paid much attention to his prattle. I knew he liked sandwiches was all.

"His hound."

"Pooch snatching?" I'd been on the other end in my pet detective days, so I knew full well how much ransom petnappers could get from the insanely rich.

I didn't even smell the sewer anymore, as we climbed back down. I was trying to remember where I'd stored my pet catching gear, the basement I think, and wondering if Kali had left it or tossed it when building up the business.

Because I was distracted, I touched some of the green stuff on the wall, a glowing vine surrounded by moss that was attracting cockroaches and other nibbling insects. I felt a presence. A soul. I jerked my hand away.

I had not sensed souls in months. I hesitantly reached out to touch it again.

"Really, Eva? That stuff is foul. Wear gloves." Duane wiggled his fingers clad in silk. The light gray fabric was stained from all the climbing in and out of the sewer.

"I had no idea you'd grown so soft," I teased. He used to live in the Central City sewers when I first met him. Eating sewer mushrooms. "Now shut up a minute."

I shooed insects away and touched the glowing vine. The soul was vast. Alive. No mere ghost. And familiar. This time I backed away, nearly running into more vines along the walls. My hairs stood on end.

"We have to get out of here." I wanted to run but for some reason my body wouldn't obey.

"What is it?" Duane knew better than to dismiss my worry. Few things made Solhans fear.

"You remember that valley near the Wall, where you and my uncle allowed your 'war ally' to dwell? I thought there was a bargain struck where it promised to stay put."

"Yes."

"It broke its bargain."

Duane took hold of my shoulders and shoved me toward the ladder. I climbed back out as fast as I could, him right behind. I wiped my hand in the icy snow, shaking, trying to get whatever chemicals it used for communication off me. I didn't think it was its soul I had been sensing so much as its mind.

"We need to see Ulric." Duane said.

"He's in the Central City, and we can't use the sewers. Besides, he may be compromised too."

"Why do you think that?"

"This explains your hunch, Duane. People not acting right, deceiving you—it's that plant creature. It's loose, somehow, and if Ulric was the one keeping it to its bargain and that bargain is now broken, we can assume my uncle is too. It's got to him."

"That's a scary thought. You go to worst case scenario even faster than I do, Eva."

"Oh, that's not worse case, not by a long shot," I said. Things could get really dreadful. "We need to discover what's happened to Ulric, but I'm not going anywhere near him. I'll dream walk."

For that I needed a safe place to sleep.

Getting back home without travelling the plant-infested sewers meant exposing ourselves to the zig zag of frozen streets in the Outskirts where shadows lurked, and eyes watched us. The plant creature had touched my mind for a moment, so it knew I suspected something. Like ... there was no telling how many people it had sunk its hooks into.

Another chilling thought sent shivers down my mind.

"What if it's been controlling people all along?" I asked. "All those people it protected in its pods during the war? What if it never let go of them?"

"Worst case scenario yet?" Duane asked, a tremble in his voice.

"Still going deeper."

Doctor Ghunnan had been in one of those pods, if briefly. I didn't know who else in my inner circle. This could be really, really bad, if I was right.

This is what paranoia felt like. Walls closing in, itching under my skin, fear shooting fire through my muscles at random and unpredictable intervals, making me want to run, but there was nowhere to go.

Shadows came towards us.

5 Worst Case Scenario

The shadows stepped boldly into the street, illuminated by warlock crystal-fueled lamps. They were no longer amorphous shapes but people, short, tall, thin or wide, brightly or plainly dressed, and from social classes who would normally never associate with one another and generally behaving ... wrong.

A goblin in mercenary leathers came forward first, calm, emotionless. That was odd. They were usually all teeth and bluster and crazy eager to fight. A dwarf stepped up beside him, a soldier, but not one with werewolf blood, I didn't think. I'd learned the dwarven lineages and who was able to turn—a bit of midnight study as I was working on tracking down information to indict or acquit prisoners of the state—and this one didn't have any of the distinctive eyes the wolf lineages possessed.

Three humans were with them: an old man in a rich robe, like he'd been woken up to join this unlikely crew; a leatherworker, distinguished by the tannin stains on his skin and clothes; and a boy. A little boy who looked so much like Vikky used too, a fringe of straight black hair, baby blue eyes, and wearing pajamas too. His gaze was so grown up, dispassionate. I felt a chill.

"What do you want?" I asked.

Duane was readying knives. I glimpsed steel slide from sleeve to palm out of the corner of my eye, and I waved him back. These were just people. Whatever had been done to them.

"We want you, Eva. We want Dawn." They spoke as one, and for a moment I wondered if it was Thane controlling them. He'd been able to speak through others, but He was gone. I'd sent Him away—twice. Besides, they didn't say my name in the same way.

"Why?" I asked. "I can't be the only reason you've come to Highcrowne. What do you want?"

I remembered when I had read the plant's soul during the war. It was vast, an alien, not of this world. Just as elves and dwarves and humans had come here long ago, taking over from Solhans and Avians, the plant alien was a portal traveler. It had arrived by chance, but it was a conqueror by nature. Its last world had belonged only to it. So, I knew the answer—it wanted to control us all—but I was hoping for specifics, some evil plan-sharing that I could use to defeat it.

"You. Come, now." It wasn't going to make things easy.

"Do you have anything non-lethal?" I asked Duane.

"Not my style, but yes, sometimes 'capture and interrogate before killing' is a useful approach." In a blur, he unwrapped a pair of bolas from around his waist and swung them in both hands, letting fly at different targets. He went for the goblin and the dwarf, smart, and they gazed down wonderingly at their suddenly bound legs.

The boy reached for me, and I knew the plant knew (for it had been connected to me before too) that the child was my weakness. Fortunately, I did carry nonlethal goodies in my belt pouch.

I felt for the braided string that indicated a powder pellet tied in cloth. I was low on magical sundries, as it had been a long time since I'd gone shopping and nothing in Highcrowne was as good as Kell. The yellow stuff in the pellet was derived from mustard seeds, mundane and not magical, but still highly effective. I tossed it down and ran, pulling Duane along with me. We did not want to get that stuff in our eyes.

I glanced back to make sure it was working, and sure enough, a yellow cloud had obscured the plant's minions. Hands reached blindly for us, but there were none of the cries of pain or curses usually elicited from using such blinding bombs. It was unnerving, the silence.

I could tell Duane was torn between running and fighting, but he got his shot as we rounded a corner of a building and saw more people under the alien's control. A flying dagger took out a burly, human mercenary who had a giant club in hand. The blade nicked his throat, so he dropped the hammer and went to one knee, trying to stem the flow of blood.

"I knew that guy," Duane explained. "Definitely on the 'to kill' pile."

"I'm glad to see they have some self-preservation instinct." I'd begun to worry they were like risen, mindlessly throwing themselves at castle walls or into barrages of arrows without fearing death. There were still people in there, underneath the plant's control, and that meant there was hope.

There were thugs and ordinary looking citizens in this new group, and I thought about tossing another mustard pellet, but I only had two more and chose to save them. This group was far enough away and small enough, so we were able to dodge past them and into an alley that connected with mine.

I was almost to the invisible line of protection produced by my wards, when Doctor Ghunnan stepped out in front of us.

"Oh, there you are Miss Thorne. Miss Student, I mean Doctor Suttner, whatever Katherine calls herself these days, sent me to ask you if you are prepared to give a speech in the town square tomorrow before the debate?"

"Debate?" I felt like I was in some dream that had just shifted from creeping horror of one kind to creeping horror of another.

Duane knew what he was talking about. "All the candidates on the ballot get three minutes to state their platform and then are randomly chosen to debate a key issue against an opponent."

"I don't believe the pairings are random at all," Doctor Ghunnan said, holding up a document barely visible in the dim light. "I was able to retrieve this—don't ask how—but it shows that you and Mister Rose will be going head-to-head."

"Of course we are." Maybe all this was a nightmare? I pinched myself, really hoping I'd wake up.

"I think we should go prepare in private, Miss Thorne, without your rival here listening to our stratagems." The goblin doctor reached for my arm, and I jerked back.

"You were taken by that plant in the valley by the Wall," I said.

"What? Oh yes, the entity. That was some time ago."

"You said you wanted to study it more. Did you go back to that valley?"

He went still, calculating. I used the pause to roll past him and into the alley where my protections kept everyone out except those I chose. "Duane," I beckoned.

The goblin's hesitation was gone, and he took Duane's arm, saying, "Reason with her."

Duane shoved him away with a powerful blow to the sternum, mechanical legs and servos whirring to compensate, and then Duane was inside the protections too.

"Did the plant touch you?" I asked, Duane's arms were covered, no bare skin, but still I worried.

Duane shook his head. "I don't think so. What does it feel like?"

"Like losing yourself."

"Then how would I know? I feel like that all the time." His green eyes gazed into mine, and I awkwardly looked away.

"Let's get inside, where my protections are even stronger." I held open the back door to the kitchen for him and felt my skin tingle as he passed close enough to touch.

I glanced back and saw Professor Ghunnan standing there calmly, like he had the patience to wait forever.

Nanny and Dawn were asleep, and we didn't wake them. Duane moved even more quietly than me as we crept into my room. It was small, a single bed, and no chairs. He crouched in one corner, back against the wall.

"I'm not sure I can sleep with you watching me like that," I said.

"You told me you were going to dream walk."

"Which requires sleep, or a good trance at least."

"I can be quiet."

I knew he could slow his heartbeat so it was barely perceptible, his breathing gentle and silent, and that he could crouch for hours without shifting his weight. To everyone but me, he could be invisible.

I didn't exactly have my old soul sense, but I was a necromancer, and I felt his life. That was something he couldn't hide. Even if I wasn't Solhan, I would have found it hard to ignore Duane's presence. His scent was warm, not quite cinnamon but something more like ginger and cloves. He didn't wear any elvish perfumes; it was all him—and I found it very distracting.

"Please, just wait in the hall. I'm safe. If I say anything out loud, you can hear it as easily through the door."

"Alright. If that's what you want."

It wasn't what I wanted at all, but I wasn't going to say what I wanted. Now was not the time. Besides, I was still angry at him for being in Hilja's room, not that I believed he killed her, but he'd been there with her. I was still angry, wasn't I?

"Thanks," was all I said as he slipped out and shut the door behind.

I lay on my bedcovers, stiff and not feeling relaxed at all. Duane's scent still lingered.

"Get a grip, Eva." I exhaled. It wasn't all romantic discombobulation: it had been years since I'd dream walked, and that had been when I had all my powers. When the Dead God went away, he took my confidence and everything that was easy about necromancy. What remained was the hard work, the craft of it, the discipline, and I had never been a very disciplined student.

"Ulric," I whispered. My uncle was good enough to compensate for my rusty skill set—if he were listening. If he wasn't dead or consumed by the plant already. He had been the guardian, keeping it to its bargain. "How did you let it escape?"

I closed my eyes.

I felt old magic, like that which had seeped into the ruins of Archon, into the bones of Lyss. I sensed Solheim, like gravity, always a weight on my awareness that pulled me, even without the Dead God there calling my name.

There was someone else in Solheim, calling for me. I saw Conrad in his white armor: lacquer paint flaked off, leaving blotches of caked-in grime and rust. His face was still the same, alive somehow, although his hands were skeletal, a bony finger pointing somewhere behind me. His mouth moved soundlessly. It seemed like a warning. I turned to look where he pointed, and suddenly the ground flew beneath me, like when I'd rode on the back of a dragon, crossing the continent in a day and a night. This was faster, nausea-inducing. Gray limestone plains of karst gave way to mountains, forests, golden fields, desert ... and then the tropical shores of Faellion.

I jerked to a sudden stop and fell, screaming as soundlessly as Conrad had. I reached out for something to hold as I plummeted from the sky and down, down, down.... I hit painfully, unable to wake up like in normal falling dreams. I felt soil swallow me, the flesh still on my bones, life still struggling inside me. I was not dead, but I was slowly buried. Dirt choked me, and I closed my eyes, expecting the end.

I was suddenly in darkness deeper than what existed behind my eyelids, like a prison, the walls thick stone, absorbing my words, absorbing any light, and I only knew they were stone because I reached out and felt the rough, granular surface. Not Highcrowne granite, Faellion sandstone. The scent of salt air carried, as did the sound of distant ocean waves.

"Uncle?"

"Eva." Ulric's voice was faint, like wispy clouds. He sounded old.

"What are you doing in Faellion?"

"I don't know. I woke here. In darkness. I am chained, my power bound with magic."

"Then how did you help me dream walk?"

"I did not. You came here of your own accord."

That was a surprise. Maybe I had learned something after all.

"Elves must have captured you. Was it Hilja?"

"I told you. I don't know. I was asleep and then I woke like this. Whoever was responsible would have to be very powerful."

That was an understatement. Ulric was one of the Solhan Nine, the cabal that had summoned a god.

As if sensing my thoughts, he added, "In the Dead God's absence, my power is weakened. I rely on the devotion of His few remaining worshippers. It was the perfect time to strike against me."

I'd sent the god away. So, this was my fault. As usual. I chose to ignore the barb.

"How do we get you out of here? The plant alien is running amok in Highcrowne without you around to control it."

"In this dream walk, you have given substance to your projected soul, but you can fade, grow incorporeal, and rise up through the ceiling. Look and see where I am and then come to me. Find me and free me."

He tended to give orders when he spoke, and my rebellious instinct made me stiffen, ready to argue, but why? It was exactly what I should do. Sure, there was Hilja's murder and an election to deal with too, but getting Ulric back and stopping that plant was top priority. It would be a relief to get away from the election anyway. Couldn't win in absentia could I? I might have read that on some scrap of paper Katherine shoved in my face.

I decided to do what he said.

I tried to forget the sensations of my body, be present only in thought. A dream without touch or smell, only vision. I became awareness. I felt light, rising effortlessly. I stuck on the roof of the chamber a moment, but then I held my breath, trying to shrink to nothing, and I kept rising like one of those dirigibles emerging through layers of cloud cover.

I was high above the ruin. It was an elvish castle, its ancient, sandstone walls shattered by some long ago siege. It perched on a small, defensible hill above the jungle, the steep slopes covered in scrub and twisted trees, a sandy, crescent-shaped beach at its base.

I blinked and realized the scrub brush had moved. A tumbleweed? No. They were all moving. Hundreds of them dotted the hillside and even more were visible among patches of rainforest beyond the outcropping.

They were like giant bean pods, brown with black spots and long, tangled, reaching vines spread every-where, wriggling and dragging them around, shifting them like they were some kind of animal or insect. One pod opened along a seam, and a vine retracted, dragging a squealing, red-tailed deer into it. The pod sealed shut over it, and soon the squirming stopped. More pods were opening, dragging in animals ... an elvish worker....

The plant wasn't just in Highcrowne. It was in Faellion too. It was spreading, growing. I didn't know how fast or how much land it had covered. But as I wondered, I accidentally made a connection with its mind. The same mind that had been in the sewers, the same mind from the valley years before—vast and alien.

It reached out a tendril towards my incorporeal form, and I worried it could trap me even without a body. With a yelp of terror I retreated, not saying another word to Ulric.

I woke, gasping, feeling like I might never sleep soundly again.

It took me a long time to stop trembling enough to tell Duane what I'd seen. I didn't tell him I had made note of the mountains and other landmarks, the position of the sun relative to them, the bright moons too. I could find my way to Ulric and rescue him. I just needed to think first. Make a plan that wouldn't end up with me being swallowed into one of those pods. I didn't want Duane to know, because he would go without me, and I couldn't lose him too.

"That bad, huh?" he asked.

"You can't imagine."

"Is he dead?"

"No. But we have no way to get to him. I think we should find another solution. Tell me how you discovered the plant to begin with? You were always by my uncle's side. Do you know how he gained control over it?"

"Magic, you mean? I've no idea how all that worked. I discovered the plant at the same time Fharen's army did. It was just after the Dead God took Archon. Refugees fled from there, and my best guess is that one carried a pod. A seed. There are lots of strange things in the Archon jungles."

"That's an understatement." I'd nearly died there three times. Knowing this alien plant had come from Archon made me even more terrified. Yet ... the Archonese jungles had not been overrun with animal-eating pods. If it came from there, maybe it had only been a seed? Something dormant and ancient? I had dug up many relics in those ruins, searching for a way to expunge the First Soul.

"How did Fharen yoke it then?"

"He set his mages to studying it, learning to speak with and bargain with it. My spies observed the whole time. I relayed everything to Ulric."

"The bargain was people, I remember. People it turned into hybrid monsters for Fharen's army. Part plant, part... whatever they had been before. But I remember those things—they had burning sap for blood, tendrils and flowers growing out of their misshapen bodies. They weren't like the people who came after us tonight. Those pod creatures had been mindless mon-sters."

"Because that's what Fharen wanted. Deadly, unquestioning soldiers. It doesn't mean that's the only thing the plant can make. Ulric bargained for protection, for our people to be hidden from the Risen hordes and the soul sight of necromancers, like Lili of Solheim."

"So, you think it's like a queen ant or bee—able to transform people as much or little as needed to perform a function?"

"Yes."

I shuddered again. Doctor Ghunnan was one of the new pod people. How many more of my friends?

"I need time to think." I made kaffe, and we drank in silence, steaming mugs in hand, and neither of us looked to be warmed by it. Duane's gaze had grown thoughtful, his body stiff, chilled with fear, like mine.

We waited at the window in the salon, watching the street as the sky glowed with sunrise and lamps went out. There were a few pod people lurking, until crowds of merchants and ordinary people going to work filled the streets. If any lingered in shadowed recesses and doorways, they were impossible to distinguish from the beggars and peddlers. I noticed a few dwarfish guards patrolling, checking for papers and moving the beggars and loiterers on, so the shadows were empty.

"What's that about?" I asked Duane.

"New policy. Beggars are restricted to Beggar's Block, not just to sleep but for their 'livelihood'."

"How's that supposed to work then? No one will go there for fear of being asked for a handout."

"Exactly. It's an elvish solution to a human problem—make the poor starve until they'd prefer to be slaves again."

"And you liked Hilja?"

"Wasn't her doing. Exactly. And you're right ... she's past tense."

Too soon. She wasn't really past tense to him, while to me she was just the murder victim in the case I was working. I could be cold and Solhan when I needed to be.

"At least we can go outside again." I said it, but I didn't make a move. The plants could be controlling anyone.

A bang on the door made me jump. It sounded like a troll knocking. I peeked through the spy hole and saw it was the next best thing—a grall: a ten foot tall slab of gray muscle, wisps of gray hair tied in a ponytail, teeth like boulders and claws thick and yellowed, although he kept them carefully manicured. A chef needed to be hygienic.

I only knew of one grall in Highcrowne. "Jorg," I said, smiling as I opened the door. I didn't invite him in, nor Katherine, who was halfway hidden behind him, her arms laden with signs and placards. She somehow had a free hand to wave a clipboard at me.

"The latest polls," she said.

Katherine ducked between the grall's legs and tried to walk inside, crashing into the invisible barrier of magic. She dropped a few placards and rubbed her sore nose.

"Let's meet downstairs in my office." I closed the door before they could see Duane lurking, but I shouldn't have bothered, as he'd already managed to blend into the couches and wallpaper. I hoped he wouldn't try to leave through the alleyway. I didn't think any place outside my house was safe for either of us. Of course, we couldn't stay here forever.

I went downstairs and opened the office door. I kept my distance, quickly retreating behind my desk.

Jorg noticed. "No hug for an old friend?"

Katherine, oblivious, set down her campaign materials and chattered away about the debate. I wasn't even sure she was aware of Jorg.

"We need to prepare!" she said. "Doctor Ghunnan told me you're going against Mister Rose first. He's a master of charm and persuasion and will mop the floor with you, no offense, unless we make sure you are solid on our key issues."

"What are those again?"

"Family, local business, salt of the earth people—and women—seeking a voice in this mess of a male dominated world. A mess the likes of Mister Rose and his street gangs helped to create, all while they were under the thumb of the Crowns, the Elf Queen in particular."

"He's not under her, over her, whatever. Not anymore."

"The point is to play up how he was hand-picked and feted by that elf. Human mistrust of elves is at an all-time high, I daresay rivalled only by the war and the pre-war internment camps. We can play to that."

"I won't pander to hate. No 'us against them'. Stop. Wait." I shook my head. Katherine had a way of drawing you into her irrelevant obsessions. "The election is not important. Highcrowne has been invaded."

"What?" Jorg, who had been drooping and looking dejected at being ignored, suddenly stiffened. He was a businessman, chef, and the gentlest creature you'd ever meet, but he was also a grall with deep-rooted instincts for fighting that no amount of self-discipline could erase.

"I wanted more than anything to give you a huge hug, Jorg, but I can't even trust you, or my campaign manager here. Doctor Ghunnan has been compromised."

"Is he working for the Goblin Emperor again?" Katherine asked. "I knew it. Have they tunneled in? If so, I have invented just the counteragent to rid those vermin from the sewers. One of my pro-human contingency plans."

"No goblin invasion. There is something in the sewers, though. The plant alien that created those soldiers for Fharen during the war, the one that held thousands of humans in a cocoon of 'safety' away from the internment camps. I think anyone in those pods was compromised years ago, and now they've been activated. The plant has broken its bargain, and it's taking over. When you touch someone infected, you can connect to the plant's hive mind. I don't know if that means its digging into you, shoots or spores or whatever, but I don't want to take the chance."

"I'm not infected," Jorg said.

"Me either," Katherine chimed in.

"That's just what someone working for the plant would say. I'm sorry."

"Then how do we prove it to you?" Katherine had set aside politics for a moment to indulge her true passion—scientific curiosity.

"I don't know. I don't know what to do."

"Democracy now!" Someone outside shouted.

I went to my office window. It was hard to see through the throngs of people in the bazaar, but something was happening. Even jaded hawkers stopped their shouts to listen to more shouts about democracy. Then there was a flash of light. People ducked, although it had been years since we'd had a werewolf terrorist blowing up things, it was instinctual. The light went all rainbow colored and left sparkles in the sky, so it was probably elvish magic. People went to investigate, and I felt myself drawn to follow.

I knew I should be wary of being touched by anyone, but I couldn't be sure that's how the plant got you. Maybe it shoved something down your throat or put a seed in your nose, who knew? Elves casting big magic was never a good thing, though, so my curiosity compelled me past common sense to foolish bravery.

I grew up in Highcrowne, in the Outskirts, where decorum was nonexistent, and so I was practiced at shoving and elbowing my way through a crowd. It looked to be another parade in the street, but the guards weren't holding back the onlookers, they were converging on the main spectacle. Thousands of dwarves were marching and shouting with fists raised, mostly male as they outnumbered females ten to one. I thought it was another suffragist uprising, but then I read their placards roughly painted in dwarfish alongside human and elvish translations: 'Democracy for all'.

The plague of democracy had infected dwarves, not just humans. Many would see that as very dangerous.

"Harley?" I said. It looked like the dwarf king was among them. He was dressed humbly, no crown, but I'd seen him naked once, and I know how to recognize someone in unfamiliar circumstances; it was the trick of a good detective.

He flashed me wide eyes, and I realized he didn't want to be there but had somehow been swept up. Beside him was Sir Markham and a half dozen other lawyers, judging by their fine, pin-striped suits. They and Markham were holding writs and reading them to the descending elvish guards, like they were some sort of magical protection. Only, this was no spell but lawyer-ese statements espousing Crown law and something about rights to demonstrate.

The elf guards were the ones shooting bright lights into the sky to disperse the crowd, some casting sleep charms on dwarves at the edge of the mass. A few were momentarily stunned by the lawyer's chants, but then an elf sergeant I recognized, a no-nonsense woman who had little fear of werewolves let alone lawyers, strode forward and twisted Sir Markham into a hold before chaining him with silver manacles.

"I know who you are," she said. She was looking at Harley when she spoke. "This is not a demonstration but a danger to civil order."

Sir Markham and the lawyers were clearly the ring-leaders, and once she put a chink in their defenses, more guards descended to arrest them. One even had the gall to cuff King Harley, clearly not knowing who he was.

Then I recognized that guard. He was no elf. It was Duane. No, he had some glamour activated, probably one of his many charm bracelets, and he probably appeared elvish to onlookers, but fragments of my soul sense remained, and I knew who he was.

"Where's Duane going?" I wondered aloud.

Katherine was beside me. "Your rival is among them? Where?" She squinted.

I didn't want to give him away, so I simply said, "I don't think Duane will be making the debate later. Time to call it off?"

"An elvish clamp down on dwarves should not affect human elections," she said, smiling. "What a thrilling turn. If Mister Rose is swept up in this, then we could win by default."

"Maybe it's not too late for me to be arrested to?" I said, stepping forward with wrists out.

"No, you don't! Grab her," Katherine said.

Jorg grabbed me by the shoulders and pulled me back into the bazaar. Looked like I was caught by a grall clamp down rather than an elvish clamp down. Damn.

6 By Default

"I thought we were friends," I told Jorg, feeling betrayed.

"I did too, until you didn't trust me. I'll show you I'm on your side, Miss Thorne. I know you well enough to know you never do what's best for you, so I'll do it for you."

Jorg as my jailer was no fun at all. There was no escaping him as Katherine made sure we arrived at the debate in the Outskirts Temple District with plenty of time to prepare.

We had a stall on the periphery of the stage, heavily decorated with streamers and bunting and flyers with my silly election slogans and unauthorized image plastered everywhere. Other stalls fringed the stage as well, but none were so well decorated, although the baker and the butcher were both handing out free samples. The baked pies I thought a winning idea, but the butcher should have thought better of chopping meat and handing out raw, bloody chunks of it on strings. He had lots of excited goblin children hanging around, but not many human voters.

"Duane is not here," I kept telling her, pointing to his bare and unoccupied stall next to mine.

I needed to go after him, discover what he'd done with King Harley, discover what the elves were doing with Sir Markham ... there were a zillion other things I should be doing rather than politicking.

"General Moore is here," Katherine said, indicating the armored human king who ascended the stage without fanfare. "Mister Rose will suffer the consequences for breaking the rules, while you will win this debate and possibly the Human Crown."

"I really don't want it." And I wasn't human, not that anyone seemed to care. Solhans looked human, and that was all that mattered.

"It's not for you. It's for me and all the others who need you. Think of us." Katherine shook me like I just needed to wake up and smell the possibilities. This was not reassuring. She could be possessed by the plant entity; it too had a lust for power.

"Welcome to this first debate," General Moore said, his voice clear and booming without need for augmentation.

The crowd hushed, prepared for one of his famous speeches, as he continued. "Democracy relies on an informed and learned population. Without knowledge of history, of past failures and successes, how can we gauge where our future might lead with the choices made today? Without being aware of the ills besetting our neighbors, the travails they face, how can we find the compassion and will to aid them, and by aiding the whole, improve our own lots as well?"

There were a few knowing nods and mumbles of agreement, but they were faking. Moore's words were far too complex for most of my neighbors—I knew because they look confused when I said 'salutations' some mornings.

Moore chose to believe they understood, so he went on, saying, "A debate is meant to pit seemingly opposing views against one another in pursuit of solutions to common problems. Yet, this is no war. This is no contest between foes. We seek only to find the best solution for the current problems. Not the only solution, but what we agree is the best action to take now. We shall not judge harshly those individuals brave enough to put themselves forward for public office, to bend their will and mind, to spend their sweat and toil, to aid their fellow humans. We laud any who try."

With that he waved me to the stage. I was suddenly free of Jorg's grip and stumbled forward, awkwardly climbing up wooden steps, stretching out my sore shoulders as I shook my head. "You are a very hard act to follow, General Moore."

"You'll do fine." He smiled and patted my shoulder before descending into the crowd.

I stood awkwardly. No Duane or any other rival joined me on the stage.

"Looks like only one person is trying," someone heckled. "That Rose-scented elf-lover is probably off hoisting aristocrat skirts."

"Down with elves! Vote Thorne!" Katherine called, trying to throw her voice so it sounded like someone else.

"Stop," I said before the heckler or Katherine got everyone riled up. "I don't fault Duane, I mean Mister Rose, as I didn't want to be here either. Of course, General Moore made me feel like crap for not wanting to do my civic duty. The thing is, there are some really big problems we're not facing. I'm not talking inequality for human females, continued enslavement through elvish economic policies, or even whatever is up with dwarves and that democracy demonstration earlier. None of that matters right now, because ... an alien plant creature has invaded Highcrowne."

My pronouncement was met with stunned silence, so I went on. "Any of you could be infected, you or your neighbors. It takes away your free will and makes you part of its huge over mind. And it's not just loose in Highcrowne, it's in Faellion too. I don't know how far this plague has spread, but we have to do something. I don't know what, but something."

The silence continued until a few people whispered, murmuring to one another. I heard someone say, "Is this an allegory or something? Like socialism?"

Katherine dashed up beside me, clapping and smiling. "Well said, Miss Thorne! We all need to watch out for ourselves and our neighbors. It's about togetherness and being of one mind. Vote Thorne!"

Cheers erupted and no one heard my mumbled protests.

I really needed a plan that didn't involve explaining stuff like this to simpletons.

While Katherine was fielding questions and rousing more cheers, I hurried over to General Moore. Only he seemed to have been really listening, and he looked pale.

"Is this true?" he asked. "It's loose?"

He knew State secrets, knew all about the plant which Ulric and the Avians had kept in check. More worrisome is he hadn't known it was free.

"Yes. It attacked me and Duane last night. I think Duane went to speak to King Harley about it. Or about Hilja. I'm not sure."

"What about Queen Hilja?"

He didn't know. General Moore was out of the loop on everything, and that was truly chilling. "You know about the elvish clamp down on the dwarven democratic movement, I hope?"

"That was hard to miss and not surprising. From either side. The dwarven suffragist cause would be vastly improved by a democracy that allows the males to be fully represented by the vote, and nothing is more terrifying to elven authority, which relies on privilege to maintain its power. They desire a small ruling elite able to enslave and control the majority."

"Yes, but it's not important right now. Can you get me into the palace? I need to find Duane and I'd like to ... see Hilja."

If Moore didn't know what had happened, how many others didn't? Had her murder been covered up? How? Was this all part of the plant alien's plan? Had one of its minions managed it all, so it could take over without royal impediment? Was Moore in danger too? No, it had gone after Duane and me because one of us was likely to win his Crown.

King Harley. He might be next. Duane must have figured it out and wanted to warn him.

I was already walking, and General Moore hurried to catch up, saying, "I shouldn't show favoritism to one of my potential replacements, but I will help you with this matter. You are, as ever, a unique case Miss Thorne."

He didn't know just how unique this case was. I'd never investigated a secret invasion.

I needed Ulric for this, but he was in enemy territory, neutralized. It was up to me, and what I lacked in necromantic power I needed to make up for with information. Every villain, no matter how seemingly alien, had some vulnerability. I just needed to find it.

Walking through Highcrowne was easy with General Moore. Doors opened for him, literally. Guards who liked to give Solhans, and me in particular, a hard time bowed and opened doors. It also helped to have a grall along. Anyone not intimidated by one would defer to the other. Jorg had appointed himself my bodyguard ever since he discovered I didn't trust him.

"Being by my side is not reassuring," I explained to him again. "You could be waiting for an opportunity to infect me. Katherine has won me over, because she stayed behind to appease the crowd and clearly cares more about the election than anything."

"I care about you more than anything, Miss Thorne." Jorg argued. "You gave me my first break in this city. You were the first to believe I could be a chef."

"I thought you had wanted to be an accountant?"

"Tried it and realized I'd discovered a better dream. Thanks to you. You should come to my restaurant. Let me cook for you."

"Once again—that's a likely way to slip me some alien plant seed, in my food. It's how you could be infecting everyone in the city."

"I thought I was paranoid and overly worried about all the potential strategies of my enemies," General Moore said. "You put me to shame."

"It's easier when you know who your enemies are," I said. "Right now, I'm erring on the side of 'everyone'."

Jorg was unshakable though and stayed with us all the way to the Elf Palace. The EEPs cordoning the place off were the first guards we encountered to steadfastly keep the doors shut.

"Queen Hilja is indisposed," one said.

"I bet." I didn't elaborate, but a few elves flicked a glance my way. They knew I knew. I didn't press the matter and instead steered Jorg and General Moore toward the Dwarf Palace instead. "Duane is up to something as usual, and this is my best guess as to where."

"Not sure about that grall," one of the dwarf guards said. At least he was holding the door for General Moore.

"You're from one of the werewolf clans." I knew them all. "You can't be afraid of Jorg here?"

"Werewolf?" It was Jorg who started quaking in his huge boots. He'd been raised on tales of scary werewolves and had a deep seated fear of them. When he took a step back and said, "Maybe I should wait out here." I suddenly knew I could trust him, so I fought to keep him with me.

"He stays. Now, take us to King Harley."

"Yes, Miss Thorne."

Werewolves tended to fear me rather than the other way around.

General Moore smiled.

"What's that for?" I asked. He was always so serious.

"I cannot wait to see the outcome of this election. You and Mister Rose are both feared, one overt and the other covert. It is too bad the Human Crown could not be worn by you both, for our citizens would be better off having you both fighting for them."

"Duane and I don't need a Crown to do what needs doing. Let the baker win and save us both the headache."

He raised his hands. "It is an election. I have no control."

One of the dwarf guards with us was writing something down. I snatched the paper form him and saw our words quoted. "Are you a reporter or something?"

"A speechwriter, Miss Thorne. Steal from the best they say."

I sighed and gave him the paper back.

The Dwarf Palace had changed since I'd been there. King Rutgard had been a ghost, the palace a giant mausoleum. Now, there was real furniture with cushions rather than stone, and children running around everywhere. King Harley's wife, Matriarch Selena, had already produced a dozen—twins were common, so that was two a year since the war—and her extended family had also taken up residence, along with Harley's lower born relatives.

Fireplaces in every room lent cheery warmth to the gilt wallpaper and other décor, which was a mixture of elegant antiques, children's hobby horses and other toys, as well as more humble workshops with collections of tools and woodcarvings, armor and weaponry, and Harley's busy kinsmen continuing their trades despite their elevation in society.

"I like it, but I'm lost," I said. The place was now a maze.

Then we were led to a small room where King Harley and Duane sat opposite a huge fireplace in winged armchairs, sipping dwarven whisky.

I folded my arms. "Here I was, worried something had happened to you both."

"Eva!" Harley wobbled to his feet and gave me a hug. "It's so good to see you in my home. Sorry about that business last year with the egg and truth serum. I have to act all formal in public, but I was rooting for you. Knew you'd save the day. Now, Mister Rose has saved me. He extricated me from that nasty elf attack on a free dwarven rally. We are planning a counter move." He winked and took another swig.

Duane was red-faced from the fire, not alcohol, as he only pretended to drink after clinking crystal tumblers together with the King.

"The EEPs wouldn't let us in to see Hilja," I said. "Any way you can help there?"

Harley looked at General Moore who shrugged. "I too was turned away."

"This is ridiculous!" Harley sputtered. "The EEPs have gotten out of hand. What are we to do?"

"We need Calka," Duane said.

The Avian Queen was the only one who had kept the elves in check, and the months since they'd fled the destruction of the Avian Sanctuary, since they were attacked by Aguragas and his terrorists, had been a dark time for Highcrowne. Calka thought it was an opportunity for the younger races to grow up without them, but with plant aliens on the loose, rampant democracy set to elect people like me, and elvish tyranny, I was all for Duane's plan.

"Let's go get her," I said. Calka could help defeat the plant—she was the only one powerful enough without Ulric around.

"No one knows where she is." I could tell Duane was holding something back, and I'd extract the information from him if we had a private moment, but for now he was making a show of thinking out loud so that King Harley, Moore, and even Jorg and the eavesdropping dwarven guards, likely Matriarch Selena and whoever else was listening too, knew what he wanted them to know.

"Surely the Shadow King can discover her location?" General Moore said. He was a savvy one and was playing along with good humor, asking just the question Duane was expecting.

"I might be able to, but the elves may try to bring me down first. I believe there is a plot against me, and against Queen Hilja, which is why they will let none of us near her. Mister Gardens tried to arrest me last night."

Harley gasped and nearly spilled his whisky.

"I was there." I could play along too. "I stopped Mister Gardens, of course, but it was clear he was not aware of the particulars and only following orders, and not from Hilja. I would like to know who is pulling his strings. I have a lead."

Jorg patted me on the back so hard I nearly fell into the fire. "Good job. That's why you're a better detective than that Elf Butler."

"What lead?" General Moore asked.

"Seneschal Ernest." No need to tell them he was a lead thanks to Duane's informants. If I was playing along, I could bolster my own reputation and get something out of this too. "Unfortunately, he is hiding behind EEP guards. However, his beloved pooch...."

"Fuzzy," Duane supplied helpfully.

"...Yes, Fuzzy, is his weakness. Is there some way to lure him to us?"

"Oh!" Harley jumped and spilled his whisky this time. "I know. Talon!"

"That's not a dog eating werewolf, is it?" Jorg asked, worried.

"My pet eagle. It's walking time. Come on, come on...." Harley drunkenly led the way.

This was starting to feel like one of my boarding school Saturday nights when everyone got a bit too tipsy and thought rearranging the gargoyles on the roof and dressing them up as teachers was a good idea. I hadn't been drinking, so it was a lot less fun than I remembered.

I hung back and took Duane's arm. He was still in a city watch uniform, and the white armor reminded me of Conrad. I flashed back to a barely remembered dream from the other night and had the oddest feeling that the past was coming to haunt me, even more than my usual bad boarding school decisions.

"Not here," Duane cautioned, indicating the walls. They probably had more spyholes than my office. I'd kept a few from when Kali remodeled the place, so I could watch clients sweat before I went in to speak with them.

"You shouldn't be here. Go. Leave this to me," I said.

He looked set to argue then nodded. "You're right."

"Now, that's the first time you've ever said that. I'm really worried."

"So am I." His green eyes reminded me of phosphorescent pools in the caves of Kell. They shone brighter because of the darkness surrounding them.

Was he in over his head this time? Had either of us ever had our heads truly above water? It seemed we'd been swimming for our lives since we drew breath, me to a mother who wanted to sacrifice me to Death and him to a world that had tried to eradicate his people even before the Dead God came to reap what souls remained.

"Be careful." I had a hard time letting him go, but a scrape of a shoe from some careless spy reminded us we were not alone. He slipped away, finding a secret panel to vanish into, and more footsteps in the walls indicated the rats were scurrying.

I followed the sounds of laughter to the roof where King Harley was showing off Talon. The eagle was as tall as him, his dark eyes looking like he might eat the Dwarf King if given the opportunity.

"We don't want to hurt Fuzzy," I said, glaring at the murderous bird.

"He'll be fine. Talon is a sweetheart." Harley kissed at the eagle who looked affronted by the lack of respect. He fluffed his feathers in an effort to restore some dignity.

"There he is," General Moore said, pointing at the Elf Palace across the sward. Fuzzy was on a leash among a pack of other small animals out for a walk with a human servant fighting against entangling leashes trying to trip her up.

"How can Talon know which one is Fuzzy?" Jorg asked, fascinated. He had Harley's bottle of whisky and was absently sipping as he joined in the fun.

"He knows," Harley said with pride. "You're a smart one aren't you, Talon?" More kissing sounds, and the bird gave me a look as if we were the only two sane beings. "Go get him!"

Talon was free, and I ducked, as the giant eagle swooped deliberately close. He made General Moore duck too.

A scream sent me running to the edge to watch, but as the bird returned with Fuzzy, a horrified servant still screaming behind, I told everyone to hide, and we ducked down.

The dog was small and white except for a patch of brown over one ear and eye. He was feisty too and yapped and nipped at the eagle, even after it set him down and returned to its roost. One of the dwarven guards fed Talon from a bucket of meat, but it kept a hungry eye on the yapping pooch just in case its orders changed.

I was the pet detective, so I muzzled Fuzzy with his leash to keep him quiet. "We won't have long until Ernest comes knocking. Let's get downstairs and look innocent."

The drunken schoolboys with me were hilarious as we thundered down the stairs and draped ourselves nonchalantly on divans and sofas behind Harley's favorite winged chair. A werewolf guard growled at Fuzzy, which made him sit shaking and well behaved on the other winged chair.

Sure enough, Seneschal Ernest was escorted into the room about fifteen minutes later by the King's Guard, Harley's fiercest defenders, who quickly formed a shield between the socialist Seneschal and the dog.

"How dare you kidnap, Fuzzy!" Ernest began.

"Kidnap?" I said, standing. "The King saved your beast from certain death. You should be grateful and far more deferential to a Crown. To both the Crowns in this room."

General Moore looked around before remembering I was referring to him, so he joined me in the dog blockade. "Yes, we are quite disturbed by the lack of deference of late. Where is Queen Hilja? Surely, she would not allow this sort of behavior?"

Ernest stood straighter. "The Queen is indisposed."

That could mean her body hadn't been tossed into the trash, one good thing.

"You remember me, Ernest?"

"Of course, Miss Thorne. Although, I see you have joined the gears of the machine rather than breaking the mold that impedes freedom and progress."

"I was about to say the same about you."

"Appearances can be deceiving."

"Like finding a black rose where it shouldn't be. You shouldn't make assumptions."

Ernest's eyes went wide. He knew that I knew. Too many people knew I knew. Was I in danger now?

"The Black Rose?" General Moore asked me in a whisper. The famed assassin's calling card hadn't been seen for nearly a decade, since before the general and his refugee army from the Fortress of Mages arrived in Highcrowne, but some stories were known beyond the borders of the Kingdoms.

I needed to keep the general on side, and protect myself by ensuring what I knew wouldn't die with Duane and I. Where was he anyway?

"I have a theory that Aguragas is the Black Rose," I said. No reason to implicate Duane by revealing his secret identity, although I suspected it wasn't any more secret than his Shadow King persona. He liked to instill fear by reputation. I knew how useful that could be.

"Aguragas is in EEP custody. His execution is scheduled for sunset still. Correct?" General Moore asked the seneschal.

Ernest blinked. Not a good sign. "The execution has been … postponed."

"Don't tell me he escaped?" I folded my arms. "And when are you going to tell everyone what happened to Hilja?"

"What happened to Hilja?" Harley and Moore said at the same time.

I could tell the seneschal wanted to make a run for it. He eyeballed Fuzzy, most likely wondering whether to risk grabbing his dog, but werewolves smelled fear, and the King's Guard tightened their cordon around Ernest. He wasn't going anywhere until he revealed all he knew.

"Fine." He fluttered his sweaty silk shirt, trying to cool himself. "The announcement was to be made as soon as the regency council finished their meeting, and that was over an hour ago. No one is happy with the decision, despite giving equal voice to all warring families. It's the elves finally inspired by dwarven and human examples, my fellow Party members, who want an election, who have been overlooked entirely, but you don't hear us complaining. At least not now. We will convene and discuss our next move over sandwiches soon, you can be certain of it. We will not let this opportunity pass."

"Opportunity?" General Moore asked, confused. "Sandwiches? A regency council? Regent for whom? And elections for elves too? What is happening?"

"Queen Hilja is dead," I said. "Assassinated by Aguragas. Do you deny it?"

Ernest shook his head. "No. I mean, she is dead." Harley gasped and Moore's expression turned deadly sober. Jorg looked like he might cry. "But her death was ruled natural causes. The council could not agree on a single regent; thus, they are ruling together, or I should say in an un-together and disorganized way. This sort of turmoil is just the occasion freedom needs. Don't you think, Miss Thorne?"

"I don't see the death of the woman who ended slavery in Highcrowne or fought by my side against the Dead God as any sort of occasion or opportunity to be celebrated." My sober expression matched General Moore's. I absently handed Jorg a kerchief so he could blow his nose. He was sobbing now.

I was adding Ernest to my suspects list, but he and his entire political party were too ineffectual and hesitant to have accomplished this. Unless he set Gas free to do it for him?

"Why are you looking at me that way, Miss Thorne?" Ernest was sweating even more profusely. It could be the roaring fire and hotblooded King's Guardsmen surrounding him, or guilt. Hard to say.

"I want to examine Hilja's body. I've seen a few corpses and am pretty good and judging what's 'natural causes'." According to Duane, she should have a knife sized wound somewhere, nothing natural at all—and if my necromancy skill wanted to show up for work, I might even get the chance to speak to her ghost and find out who killed her. The easy way for once. I can dream.

Ernest had pulled out an ornate fan and was waving it furiously while wringing out his drenched shirt. "I'm afraid the regency council would not allow it. This is an elf matter, but as the Queen was part Solhan, there is talk of cremation. Soon."

Then I needed to see the body now. I scooped up his shivering little dog and waved a paw at the seneschal. "Surely, no one will notice if Fluffy's new babysitter accompanies you on your duties? You have to keep Fluffikums nearby during this trying time, isn't that right?"

No one bought my innocent puppy talk routine. Even the werewolves shuddered. I think it was my deadly glare or the poison in my tone. Scary was easier than cute for me.

"How can I say no?" Ernest giggled nervously.

Scary worked too.

7 WHAT ARE YOU HIDING?

I held onto Fluffy like he was something precious that could only be pried out of my cold, dead fingers, and not even then, as I was sure to be a lich if anyone made the mistake of killing me. The dog was my hostage, a guarantee of Seneschal Ernest's good behavior, now that we had left the Dwarf Palace and King's Guard behind for the Elf Palace and EEPs in every nook and cranny.

I was wearing a glamour, bestowed by Ernest himself, which made me appear to be his usual human servant, but there were a few double-takes, as I was taller and glaring more than humans were allowed in the presence of their betters. I tried to slouch and act meek, which seemed to placate the slave-loving elves around me.

They were 'in a state' to say the least, more uptight and edgy than usual. Probably because their queen was dead, and they all knew it now. Servants were running up and down the corridors on some frantic mission or another. Maids were draping statues in black, preparing for a funeral, while the smell of the feast the cooks were preparing, just like Duane's contact had foreshadowed, wafted from the kitchens. Scores of EEPs in black uniforms, shiny jackboots, and carefully canted berets showing off pointed elf ears lined the corridor before us.

I paused and gulped. "Looks like this is the place."

"Shh," Ernest hushed me.

Fluffy licked my face, sensing my distress at being on my lonesome at the heart of elvish power, and I gagged. Poo breath. Gods, dogs were disgusting.

Ernest's nose went into the air, shoulders back, hands raised like a crab readying pincers for battle, and he strode down the hall like he owned it. I scurried to keep up and hunched a bit more.

Rifles clacked as EEPs shifted their stance to watch us pass while not watching directly. Their eyes were still straight ahead.

It looked like we'd get away with it, until we reached the gilded double doors at the end. An officer emerged, her silken hair loose, her beret sporting a golden flower, and her stink was almost as bad as the dog's tongue. The higher the social status of an elf the more they were allowed to smell, gracing you with an unmissable sign of their presence. Her sickly sweet jasmine perfume added a layer that clung to the back of my throat, which was a good thing, as it kept me from saying something that would get us in trouble.

"Lady Maevrel," Ernest said, bowing deeply. I couldn't hide behind him when he was bent at the waist, so I dropped to my knees and put my forehead on the floor, nice and subservient. It also smelled better having my face buried in the wool carpet.

"Your presence is not required, Seneschal," she said by way of dismissal.

"Of course not, my lady. I shall go...."

I pinched his ankle, and he yelped just as much as his dog had when the eagle snatched him.

"... go fix it. I am terribly sorry, Milady, but I must confess I folded the shroud incorrectly. I have no excuse. I should have remembered the protocols, but I consulted the tomes in the library and was appalled to see my obvious mistake. I am inconsolable and must rectify it. I cannot rest until I have."

His obsequiousness was impressive. I think the officer lost interest halfway through. "Hurry. The pyre is being readied."

She strode off, stepping on my hair, and I winced as a patch nearly got pulled out by the roots. Fluffy and Ernest were trembling in equal measure, but I gave the seneschal a shove through the gilded doors and closed them behind us. I needed to examine the body before it was cremated.

I froze when I saw the chamber. It was Hilja's drawing room. I'd been here once before, years ago, and I recognized the gilt-legged couches and divans with their striped and floral silk patterns, the piles of cushions and colorful vases filled with fresh flowers from the greenhouses. Only ... Hilja was in a glass coffin rather than sitting there with a cup of tea and a cunning comment.

A thin shroud of embroidered silk, the coffin shroud Ernest must have been babbling about, lent a pale haze to her profile, which I was glad for. Seeing her through the clear glass would have been too much.

I need to examine the body. I told myself, trying to reestablish my professional distance.

It was then I saw a shimmer, and I dropped Fluffy. The dog yapped excitedly to be free and did a little twirly dance. I pulled my Ashur and stepped towards the distortion. Someone was using an invisibility charm.

"It's me, Eva." I recognized Duane's voice just in time to avoid skewering him.

He negated the charm, rubbing one of the many bracelets on his wrist, and I saw he was still in his city watch uniform. He must have come straight here from Harley's palace. Trust him to know a secret way in and not tell any of us. I was about to scold him for holding back, but then I saw the pain in his expression and stayed quiet. He was gazing down at Hilja through the shroud.

"Remove it and fold it correctly or whatever," I told Ernest.

With trembling fingers, he pulled back the pale silk. Duane took a step back, and I moved forward to pry open the lid. He turned away then. I had never known Duane to be squeamish about anything, especially dead bodies, as he tended to make more than his fair share of them. Hilja must have been very important to him, and my heart ached.

It was a strange feeling, not like the pain I'd felt when I lost Thane, or Conrad, or even the sadness I felt whenever Dawn pulled away from my hugs. I wanted to say it was my own sadness at Hilja's passing, but it was more than that. I felt Duane's pain as if it was my own. I wanted to reach out and put my hand on his heart, tell him I understood, that I wished I could take his pain from him and make everything alright again. I reached out my hand, unthinkingly, almost doing what I imagined, but I hesitated. How would he react? This was me, Eva, we were talking about, and no one expected me to show compassion or empathy. It would just make him more uncomfortable.

I swung open the coffin instead and looked down at the Elf Queen. My rival for a certain person's affection. My ally in war and politics. A potential enemy when it came to heirs and Dawn's future. My relationship with her had always been complicated—now it was easy. She was the case.

I undid a few buttons on the front of her gown and saw suture marks: A wound to the heart hastily mended when the body was prepared. I did the buttons up again and placed my hand on her chest like I had wanted to do for Duane. I was trying to feel her soul. It would stay bound to the body after death unless freed by fire. I felt something. Her soul was strong, focused, not fading and drifting. Would her ghost talk to me?

"Hilja?" I said.

I felt words in my head, like a crazy frantic inner monologue not my own, a consciousness abuzz with thoughts. All I could make out was: Go away!

"She doesn't want us here," I told Duane.

"Lady Maevrel said to hurry," Ernest reminded me. "The fire bearers could arrive at any moment!"

Duane looked down at Hilja. "Goodbye." He closed the coffin lid, and waited for Ernest to return the shroud, which he fussed with for far too long. The doors flew open. There was no more time.

It was a squad of EEPs, not Lady Maevrel or the honor guard still stationed outside. These ones looked disheveled, like they had been running around. One pointed at Duane who was ineffectually trying to activate the bracelets around his wrist. "There he is. Hurry, as the null field won't last."

They must have been running around looking for him, casting magical null fields to foil his efforts at remaining invisible. The Shadow King skulking around inside their palace, their chief suspect, must have sent them into a right huff.

Ernest reached for Fluffy and looked set to scurry away, but I grabbed him by the back of the neck. "No, you don't. Get us out of here."

"I can't!"

"You don't believe it was 'natural causes', Inspector Lien?" Duane asked the EEP leader.

"We know it was you, and you'll explain why—under torture—before we kill you slowly."

"Let me guess. Then you'll kill me with more torture?" Duane said.

"Exactly."

I still looked like Ernest's servant so was practically invisible, which was a good thing. No one stopped me when I hurried behind the EEPs and dragged a couch in front of the door to prevent any more reinforcements arriving or Ernest escaping.

Ernest's annoying dog, Fluffy, jumped on the couch and excitedly tried to kiss my nose. I was apparently more fun than his master, but I was not looking for a furry friend. Unless it was a werewolf. I could use a werewolf about now, as Duane pulled his sword and took on six Elven Elite Protectorate by himself.

I swung the sheath of my Ashur, the metal nob at the end causing the nearest EEP to crash to the ground. She'd have a concussion and really bad future headache, but at least she'd live. I couldn't go around killing my daughter's future subjects. Duane, on the other hand, wasn't so squeamish. He'd impaled one already, and another EEP was bleeding so badly all he could focus on was staunching the blood flow. Ernest looked green and swayed, ready to pass out.

Inspector Lien blocked my blow, forcing me to draw my sword. The other two were focused on Duane, but I think I'd called dibs on the dangerous one.

"Miss Eva Thorne," the inspector said. "Why am I not surprised to find you involved in all of this? The Queen was always wary of you, and now you seek the human Crown while undermining ours. Are you Mister Rose's accomplice? Why have you returned to the scene of the crime?"

"You've got it all wrong," I tried to explain. "Ernest, tell him."

"What?" He squeaked.

"The seneschal knows that Duane wasn't involved. He would never have helped us otherwise."

"You held Fluffy captive!" Ernest said.

The dog was licking my boot and seemed to take affront at the suggestion, because he growled at Inspector Lien and tore at his trouser leg ferociously, demonstrating his loyalty to me.

"Seneschal Ernest knows a lot more than he's saying. Who has more to gain than his People's Party from turmoil in the elvish ranks and no clear line of succession for the Crown?" I asked.

"Oh, the line of succession is all too clear and not at all what any of us want," Ernest said.

"See!" I said. "Question him!"

"After I torture you and Mister Rose both."

"Ugh." This was so hard when EEPs were such idiots.

I focused on the sword fight then, let Fluffy trip him up, while I disarmed him with my serrated blade and then thumped him over the head. A few times, because he kept dodging and making it difficult, but he finally went down.

Duane had skewered another one.

"Will you stop that?" I said. "This doesn't make you look innocent."

"I'm not," Duane said. "Of Hilja's death, yes, but I am guilty of a great many other things."

He went to skewer the final EEP, so I acted fast to knock her out before another one was bleeding out on the silk carpets. I wasn't sure if Ernest was more horrified by the violence and bloodshed or the damage to the décor. Fluffy was licking blood, his muzzle flecked with it, and I'd decided I liked the mutt after all. Definitely some werewolf in there somewhere.

"Let's go." Duane had a secret passage open and gestured for me to follow.

"Come on Ernest." I tried to grab his collar, but silk is slippery, and he oozed out of my grasp.

"No." He tried to pick up Fluffy, but the pooch growled, and he backed off and began pushing the couch aside. "My place is here."

"Eva!" Duane called.

"Fine." I took off and left Ernest behind, knowing I'd regret it later. I only fled because the doors were already bulging open, the EEP honor guard about to bust through.

We needed to get some distance from the Elf Palace. We couldn't return to Harley either. He'd already helped too much and could be implicated. We didn't need any more internal strife in Highcrowne now, not with Hilja's death soon to be announced.

Duane used a lever to seal the secret door behind us and made his way expertly through the narrow passages. These weren't servant's corridors, I'd seen enough of those, but far narrower and rigged with noisemaking and entangling booby traps every few feet. Duane kept reactivating traps behind us.

"Did you build these too?" I asked. They went right into Hilja's inner chambers, so I felt a wave of jealousy at the thought.

"No. Ancient spy nooks which I reappropriated. Only Hilja knew about them. A Crown secret."

"Not so secret." Up ahead, more EEPs were entering through another sliding door in a further room.

Duane didn't pause but shifted a stone block aside, revealing a side passage which we took and sealed behind us.

"Secret passages within secret passages?" This was elves, so I wasn't that surprised. "Where are we going?"

"You'll recognize the place." He was back to being quiet, enigmatic, Duane, and I knew he hadn't had nearly long enough to say goodbye to Hilja. It's why he'd braved capture, dared coming here at all. He had needed to see her face again, not the memory of her bloody body in his arms. I wasn't sure it had helped.

I surrendered any sense of control, thoroughly lost, and let Duane lead us wherever he needed. I blinked as we suddenly emerged into sunshine. I did recognize this place. The garden shed and the crevice where I knew yet more secret stairs awaited. These I could activate myself. We were headed to what remained of the Avian Sanctuary.

We were halfway up, embraced by gray stone on a narrow staircase, me in the lead, when Duane said, "It was me. I think someone drugged me, made me crazy and see things, I don't know. I was the only one who could get in there, with her unprotected. I killed her. Then I forgot."

"No." I stopped and turned around, which was tough in the tight space.

I thumped him over the head with a finger until he said, "Ow," and looked up at me.

"You did not kill her. You were framed. You saw: others, EEPs, know about the secret passages. You were drugged, yes, but whatever it was only made you pass out. Not kill and forget. What is the last thing you remember before you lost consciousness?"

"Hilja called me there. She was worried. She needed my help. That's all I can remember."

"See. Someone else was after her."

"They always are. She was paranoid for good reason."

"True, but Ernest is involved. I feel it. I wish we'd dragged him with us for questioning. And why are we going to the ruins of the sanctuary? Calka is in the mountains."

"Yes, but the Celon will know where she is."

"You mean Naren?" Naren was the Avian arcanist, the one who had devoted his life to the study of the magical green goo which powered countless inventions, of which the goblin professor was so envious. I had always thought the goo, called Celon, was an Avian invention, but Naren said it was different from their magic, something he had devoted his life to studying.

"No," Duane corrected. "The Celon is what knows."

"You are starting to sound all wacky and mysterious and Avian. I must have thumped you too hard on the head."

"I've known the Avians longer than I've known Hilja. Aguragas sent me to kill one when I was too young and stupid to understand it was the equivalent of sending me to my death. Calka spared me, seeing how pathetic I was, and set my head straight."

"Not that straight. You still became an assassin, but for Hilja rather than Gas."

"A weapon is a tool, and all that matters is what it is used for. That's what Calka told me. She told me that we are all used by those more powerful than us—whether it's a domineering uncle..." That remark hit close to home for me, as he intended. "... a boss or client..." Another blow. Whose side was he on? "... a Crown or a society that calls us to war to fight and die for it. We are powerless, until power is ours, and then the desire to hold onto that power will control us."

"Bleak. The bleakest Avian wisdom I've heard."

"My own slant on it, but yes, Calka had an optimistic version. Something about gaining power over the self being the only power worth pursuing, what frees us. Some nonsense like that." It clearly wasn't nonsense to him, no matter what he said. It explained a lot.

He had become Shadow King because information was power, but instead of letting it corrupt him, he had served Hilja and then Calka, the Kingdoms. He had steered my uncle into their orbit, harnessing even his dark, Solhan nature into service of something greater. I'd once thought Duane craved power for his own glory, thus the fancy suits, but it was all a costume, part of his guile. He traded suits for rags or armor, like he wore now, whatever was required to get the job done.

"Your first instinct was to come here," I said. "Do you still sleep in the Avian Sanctuary? Even though only rubble remains?"

"Where else can a Shadow King close his eyes without worry?"

This was his home. That's why he knew more about the Celon than he would tell me. Why the long, distracting philosophy lesson, and why he was easily able to open the door at the top of the stairs, moving his fingers over the complicated pattern of ancient Solhan-Avian script without looking.

It still shocked me to see the devastation. I had been to the sanctuary a few times, sometimes visiting the throne room, sometimes the cells, but all of it was gone. Broken stone lay everywhere, clouds of mist hanging over everything, so it seemed the dust had never settled. Through the fog, only one structure was visible: a circular door set into a stone mound. A tomb.

"You sleep in there?"

"It's bigger than it looks, and drier when it rains or snows."

"I thought Calka had sealed it with Naren inside. His prison?"

"Symbolic. Naren can open it whenever he wants, and so can I." More quick tracing of Solhan lettering, and the door rolled aside with a rumble that vibrated through me all the way to my teeth.

How had he learned that? I knew how to do it because I'd hit the books after first seeing this script. I'd wanted to learn how the most ancient dialect of my people had become so heavily influenced by Avian. By 'hitting the books' I mean I had Nanny help me channel ancient Solhan knowledge, as my own necromancy was rusty. This kind of knowledge wasn't written anywhere except in the souls of those who had lived it. Old ghosts like that weren't easy to find, and were often dangerous when you did, but Nanny had been all too eager to teach me what she knew. She thought my education had been lacking and was glad to see me finally taking an interest. With Thane and the Dead God gone, and the abilities they had lent me with it, I had to rely on study and an old fashioned Solhan education like Nanny offered to recapture a fraction of the power I'd lost.

Power. That's what this script spelled out, along with warnings to stay away.

I'd already gone too far down the garden path towards Solhan power, such warnings too late for me, Death's bride, and I'd already figured out the dangers for myself. Seemed Duane hadn't fully listened to Calka's warnings about power either—else he would not have come here.

Naren stood there as if expecting us. The Avian was slim, his brown feathers like that of a goose, with a few cream plumes sticking up randomly on his head. Only his hooked, orange beak stood out in an otherwise dull appearance. If you could call an immortal race of birds 'dull' by any definition. A handful of them had essentially ruled the Three Kingdoms for millennia, despite hordes of undead, upstart humans and elves, and rampaging gods trying to take over.

"Thorne and Rose together at last," Naren said.

"Together?" I looked nervously at Duane and started rambling. "What? I mean ... Sure, I'm working a case for him, like I said I'd never do, but there's a first time for everything, and the situation is out of the ordinary. Queen Hilja...."

"I know. Celon knows," Naren said.

"Not you too? Don't tell me—you drink the stuff, and it gives you wild visions. Right?"

"Celon sustains. Celon is all." Naren nodded.

"So, the goo can tell me who killed Hilja?"

"Is that really why you have come?"

"Ask Duane. He brought us here." To Duane I said, "You talk to him. Naren is the most enigmatic and opaque of every enigmatic and opaque Avian I've encountered. I know you trust the goo, but maybe you shouldn't be drinking the stuff, as I presume you have been. It's made Naren strange, and remember, Naren betrayed Calka. He's a liar."

Naren had deceived Calka, stealing and genetically manipulating her egg, their next queen, and his people— which encompassed only her, Kerrik the Unmentionable, and Roosal, Calka's mate. She had exiled him for his betrayal, left him in the ruins of their old home, while they migrated to a secret location deep in the mountains. Naren was unwilling to leave the goo and his studies behind, anyway, so it wasn't much of a punishment.

"I have never spoken untruths," Naren protested.

"Just like Duane never lies, either. Which I've always found unbelievable, considering his line of work. No wonder you two get along so well. Bunch of truthful liars."

I regretted it as soon as I said it. That was old Eva, always criticizing Duane, suspecting him. I knew he stayed quiet when he had secrets to keep. He deflected conversation, let people assume what they wanted, misinterpret his phrases ... but he didn't outright lie. To me the outcome was the same, though, even if the method was pure.

Duane didn't let my irritability at Naren, which had spilled over onto him, disturb his calm, because he only smiled. Seemed he was intent on disturbing my calm, though.

"Eva is just being defensive, Naren. Your 'together' remark triggered her immune response. Please do not take offense."

"No, Naren. Do take offense. Lots of offense. You are an egg-stealing traitor, and if Duane didn't need this Celon to find Calka, as I presume he intends, then I'd lock you in this tomb more permanently. I have learned a few things about ancient Solhan magic and could manage it, I think. So, get on with things. Enough greetings and ceremony. Let us drink the crazy juice and see what we need to see."

"You're not drinking it," Duane said. "You aren't prepared."

That was like an invitation. I always did the opposite of what people wanted. Unless ... that's what he wanted? Duane was aware of my knee-jerk reaction to overprotectiveness and might be employing some reverse psychology. Unless ... he knew that I knew .... Ugh. I was exhausting myself already.

"I can handle it," I said with finality.

Rebellion against overprotectiveness and reverse psychology aside, I was too curious not to try the stuff. Naren was crazy from centuries of bathing in it. One drink couldn't hurt. Right? Besides, Ulric had survived it—it had once granted him the power to both control the plant abomination, shield against bad guys, and trap a dangerous relic in one impressive demonstration of multi-tasking. If it could give me an edge against the plant too, I'd take it.

I didn't wait but strode into the chamber and looked around for some of the glowing green goo. The rubble inside had been cleaned out, so the chamber was more spacious than last time I'd been in here. There was more Solhan-Avian script on the walls written in silver lettering. I reached out to touch one section that seemed to glow, but Naren blocked me with an extended wing.

"No. That is not for you. Celon will explain." He took a silver cup from a stone bench and used it to scoop up some of the goo from the pool in the center of the chamber. He indicated I should drink.

Before I could think better of it, I took a swig. Duane drank from the same cup, much more hesitantly. He looked at me with those green eyes, and they seemed to glow the same as the goo, filling my vision, filling my insides.

"Focus, Eva," he said. "We need to find Calka. We need to save Highcrowne. We need…"

"A Solhan Empire," I whispered.

I could see it beyond the green haze of his eyes.

Not the tower of the Dead God in Solheim or the desolate Chamber of Inner seeing. This empire was ancient, like what Ilsa had shown me in Archon, the same architecture and writing. An empire built by Thornes. It was alive, teeming with people and Avians, thousands of them. It spread across jungles, loamy valleys, and climbed the rugged slopes of mountains, reaching for the sky.

"Eva." Duane took me by the shoulders, and the image of the past faded. I saw a crown on his head, the green glow of his eyes brighter than ever. "We need you, Eva. She needs you. Focus."

"She? Calka? Hilja?"

"Dawn. Thania."

"How do you know her secret name?"

"Whose secret name?" It was Duane, plain Duane before me in his stolen EEP armor. No crown.

"The Celon takes you through time?" I asked. I'd experienced a similar sensation, long ago, but that had been a massive magical construct. "What is this stuff?"

A familiar face suddenly flashed across my vision. Familiar in that it was Solhan, pale skin and eyes with black hair, but it had only been a flash, leaving a faint outline, an afterimage burnt into my retina. Other visions came and went as quickly: a silver door, bubbles and balloons, fire....

"You must rest," Naren said. "The visions are best interpreted by your primal, unconscious mind. Lay down. Rest."

It seemed I was floating, led by Naren into another chamber, and I fell forward into feathers. It was soft and warm, and I let darkness come.

I always let darkness come. Death. Devourer.
The vastness of that Primal god is unfathomable,
but I hear its screams as it seeks the First Soul to
cleanse. Death flees from it, my Thane, drawing
farther and farther away from me....
Something else is here, devouring everything in
their absence. The plant creature spreads its vines
across the world, a creeping fungus covering
everything from farms and forests to ancient
battlegrounds.
Corpses rise from the soil, sprouting like seedlings,
but they are Risen. The Dead God is returned,
fighting for me, the Risen under His command,
and a New Solhan Empire obeys my will.
No. Dawn's.
I see Dawn with Hilja's cruel smile in a pretty
face, see her twist curses like Nanny and Ilsa, see
her sway legions like the Elf King, Fharen. She

even commands souls like Thane.... Dawn has
more power than I can imagine, life and death in
her tiny hands.
"She needs my help," a motherly voice calls from
the far mountains.
I see Calka holding her child, a gray owl. "She
needs our wisdom," Calka tells me. "She needs
guidance.
Temperance. What you cannot give. Bring her to
me."
"No." I shake my head. No boarding schools,
Avian or otherwise. I was keeping my daughter
with me.
"Then she will reign over the hordes of Death,"
Calka warns.
Conrad is there, a general, by my side as I stand
beside Dawn's throne. "Hail Eva, the mother. Hail
Dawn, the daughter. Empress..." he says, bowing.
He serves absolutely. They all do. An army raises
its swords, a rattle of air through shredded throats
and
clatter of bones against metal armor. They have
no choice, for their souls are bound to undead
flesh.
My soul is bound too. I see my dead, gray arm,
Lili's curse, which I once concealed with magic, is
now

skeletal. My ribs are visible through mummified skin. I am a lich like my mother.

I wake in the nest of feathers with a gasp, but it is still dark. I see the familiar Solhan face again. It is like a painting, at first artful, then rough and primitive, and I feel I have seen it before on a cave wall in Archon or somewhere far away, but the face is alive, here, looking at me, asking me for help.

"Free me," the image speaks without moving its lips.

"I can't. The Devourer will swallow you, will swallow all of us," I say.

I see the face shift to Fharen's, my Thane's. My love. But the face is filled with green eyes, Duane's.

I wake for real, but I know not how long later. Dreams, terrifying, fade, and I try to remember the important things. Calka's location within the mountains. Dawn in danger. The danger. An empire... Love's face ... Green eyes.

I realize Duane is next to me. He has just woken up too. Our bodies lie against one another, our arms bare, our clothes replaced with Avian made robes. I wonder when that happened. Had Naren dressed us?

I don't want to move or breathe. Feeling
goosebumps, electricity. The lightning is no longer
distant but close, arcing between us, skin to skin.
I can tell Duane is not breathing either.
We are as close as we've been with our swords and
anger, with tears and pain, but I feel a different
closeness ... a nakedness, exposure. It is terrifying,
dizzying, like a chasm I'm about to fall into. I
want to run, but I want to fall too. I balance on
the precipice. I take a step ... move my finger
against his skin, feel goosebumps form at my
touch. I feel him press closer to me. His hand
takes mine. His finger caresses my palm, and I
shiver. I interlace my fingers with his. I press my
lips to his shoulder, and I can see past him. I see
Naren standing there, calmly watching us.
Present tense becomes past.

I jumped to my feet in surprise and embarrassment.
I shook my head, feeling groggy.

"I feel like I was drugged. Is that what you wanted?"
I went on the attack against Naren, my 'defensive'
reaction.

I ignored Duane who was slowly climbing to his feet.
I couldn't look at him without feeling a fever, a shiver
through my whole body, which I did not want to feel
right now.

"Did you drug Duane with this stuff?" I suddenly wondered. "Is that why he thought he had killed Hilja? Is this why he wasn't in his right mind?"

"No, this is different," Duane protested. "This was very different. Every time I see something new, but I feel like I'm seeing something I'm supposed to see, knowing something I'm supposed to know. When I was drugged before, when Hilja died, I lost all consciousness. This is the opposite—like hyper consciousness."

"More like hyper craziness. If you saw any of the things I'd seen, you'd be terrified and would never want to touch that goo again. I never want to."

Duane's expression went blank. That's what he did when he wanted to hide what he was feeling. He had likely seen something very different from what I did.

"I can't control it," he said. "Sometimes I think it shows me what I want, but ... it didn't show me where Calka is."

"It showed me." One good thing at least. I tried to shake off the feeling of being undead, a lich. That was what kept coming back to me. I had liked lying next to Duane, the aftereffects ... but there was too much horror before that, too much of a warning not to be forgotten in a moment of sweetness.

"Then let's go." Duane seemed nonplused to find his clothing changed. He casually went over to a shelf carved from the cave wall and brought out what we'd been wearing, now folded neatly.

Naren was still quiet.

"Who is the Solhan?" I asked him.

His dark eyes looked at me then. Always he seemed vaguely somewhere else, but in that moment we connected. I was in his world now.

"Celon shows you what you must know."

"But what did the goo show me? Nightmares? Warnings? Immutable Fate?"

"All. None. Only you can judge."

A lot of help that was.

Duane had changed in another chamber. I'd been aware of him leaving and coming back, the nearness and absence of him, but when he held my clothes out to me, I couldn't look him in the eyes. All I could see was his hands reaching out.

"Yes, we need to go," I said. I grabbed my clothes and hurried away, my cheeks flushed.

I only wished I hadn't been so distracted, that I'd stayed and pressed Naren for more information about the Solhan. So many things I wished I'd done differently.

8 REGRETS

I am not an outdoorsy girl. Sure, I've crossed deserts, hacked my way through jungles, even dived beneath the sea to battle monsters ... but I don't like it. I don't like sand in my clothes, spiderwebs in my hair, and especially not bugs flying up my nose.

I sneezed another one out and said, "What is it with these things? That's the fifth one."

"They must like you. You smell good," Duane said.

"Smelling good to flies means I smell like crap." I sniffed my underarm and winced. "Which I do."

We'd been hiking for days, with heavy packs, no motor carriages, horses, wagons, or anything but our sore feet. No one had built a trail, let alone a road, to where we were going. The Avians flew there, so I wasn't even sure there was a way overland.

"Look on the bright side." Duane smiled. Actually, he had not stopped smiling the whole trip, as this was his element. Who'd have thought a city boy raised in the sewers craved fresh air and open sky so much? "It's warm enough for flies. When we get to the higher reaches, everything not warm-blooded will freeze."

I groaned. I hated the cold too. "I wish that Doctor Ghunnan wasn't under the thrall of an evil plant creature. Else, I would have asked him for an exploratory hot air balloon or other flying machine to get us there."

"I own a fleet of dirigibles," Duane pointed out.

I slapped my head. "Now you tell me! ... Oh, wait. I did know that. I'm not an idiot. I also know those ships take a crew, and even if just two of us managed it, they are monstrous and noticeable and easily tracked, and we don't want anyone finding the new Avian Sanctuary. Do we?"

"No, we do not."

"If it can be found."

"You're the one who knows the way. It's a little late to be expressing doubts."

"I never stop with the doubting. Even if I order my favorite chocolate mousse from the best restaurant in Gernwold, I'll pause halfway with the spoon to my lips and wonder if I shouldn't have gone for the lava cake in Faellion instead."

"I can picture it."

"Because it has happened. Twice."

"You do know the way?" He looked frightened, the grin fading. It would be exactly like me to lead us into the middle of nowhere without a plan.

"I saw it in a vision, if you can call that knowing. Don't worry, we'll get there. Somehow. We may have to figure out how to fly at some point."

"I was expecting something like that." He patted the stack of magical bracelets on his right arm. They came in every material and color from silver and leather to beaded turquoise and jade, and I was certain one of them allowed some form of floatation if not outright soaring. At least for him.

He probably hadn't brought one for me and hoped to leave me behind while he talked privately with his adopted Avian family. Not going to happen. I would not allow myself to be left behind, thus I was keeping the route in my head rather than on my tongue and giving away my leverage. It would be just like him to think he was 'protecting' me by going off on his own. I was the one here to protect him. He was my client.

Although, he hadn't paid me. Yet. And ... I wasn't sure I wanted money. I wasn't doing it for that. I wasn't sure why I was doing it, not when you applied logic to the matter. Duane was my political rival, sometimes ally, former thief and assassin, an overall unscrupulous sort who probably shouldn't be wearing the Human Crown. Not that I was any better. Still ... he was my unscrupulous thief and assassin. Or I wanted him to be. Mine. Maybe?

The other thing I hated about long hikes through the wilderness was all the time to think.

Duane noted my sudden silence, looking worried again, but it was good I'd stopped complaining for two seconds, because we both heard the footstep. Someone was sneaking up behind us. Someone or something. There were trolls, gralls, bears and other monsters with big teeth in the mountains too.

Duane put a finger to his lips, as if I was about to start chatting when I was afraid of being eaten. He gently set his pack down and crept up to the rocks on our right side, scaling them quickly and silently, so he had the upper ground.

I was frozen, still picturing big teeth and claws. Wait. Was I the bait?

"I really hate bears. I mean flies," I said loudly. If I was the bait, I needed to act like it and be extra noisy to draw our pursuer to us. If it was human or human-eating. If it was a harmless herbivore, then me being noisy would scare it off. "So annoying! The forest! Yuck!"

I made stomping motions, so it sounded like I was walking too. I glanced over to see Duane rolling his eyes. Sue me. I'd never had drama lessons.

There was another sound, like the scuff of a boot on the dirt path. Not likely to be a harmless creature then, nor an innocent traveler, as no one willingly came this way. It was the edge of the world. We were being followed. I looked to Duane again and saw he had vanished. Great.

I set down my pack and used it as a cushion as I fanned myself with my hand and unbuttoned my shirt, while leaning back in a provocative pose. I may not have had drama, but I'd had seduction lessons. Probably the only useful thing I'd learned at boarding school. I felt eyes on me. Call it the remnants of soul sense or simple intuition, the distraction was working.

A loud breath followed by a flurry of footsteps made me drop the pose and lunge forward, Ashur drawn. I ran around a patch of trees and saw Duane and our pursuer trading blows. Duane had a knife in one hand and a sword in the other, while his opponent was unarmed, but the fight was not ending as quickly as I expected. Our pursuer was dressed head to toe in Darrubian linens, their face covered, only eyes visible, their hands and feet were a blur as they dodged and blocked Duane's attacks, going for his wrists and elbows.

I'd heard of the Djinn of Darrub but never seen one in action. They weren't literal djinn, at least I didn't think they were supernatural, but I kind of wondered, what with how fast this one moved. Duane was amazing in a fight, better than me on some days I'd grudgingly admit, but he seemed like an untrained rube next to this Darrubian master. He needed help.

I approached cautiously, Ashur at my side, looking for an opening. There wasn't one, so I coordinated my strike with Duane's, hoping that three weapons at once from different directions was too much to block. The Djinn didn't need to block—they were gone. I spun around looking for any sign and felt a shadow pass over-head. Whoever it was had done an aerial flip over both of us and landed yards away, next to my pack.

"Hands off!" I warned. That was my stuff. Nothing valuable, but there were snacks I didn't want stolen.

The Djinn twisted around and swung the pack, letting fly, so it hit Duane in the face—he'd been rushing forward—then it bounced and flew over the cliff edge.

I was so mad. "I warned you not to mess with my stuff!"

I tried to rip the Djinn's soul from their body, clenching my fist with fury, but then I remembered I'd lost that power when I'd lost my connection to the First Soul and the Dead God. I was stuck with regular necromancy, so I turned my fist clench into a finger-waving and muttered a Solhan incantation. See how high this jerk could jump when their knees rotted out.

Then the Darrubian did something even more unex-pected—a Solhan counter curse. The words were whis-pered, so I still couldn't tell if they were male or female, but our attacker had to be Solhan. That explained why the Djinn was tall and thin and able to blunt my spell. It didn't explain why they were using Darrubian martial arts, however, or why we weren't dead yet. Solhans liked to kill—slow or quick didn't matter as long as you were dead.

"What do you want?" I asked. If it wasn't my pack of snacks and it wasn't us dead it had to be... "The Avians' location? Never gonna happen." I'd turn around right then and face Doctor Ghunnan and an army of plants to steal a small flying ship before I led a Solhan/Darrubian assassin to Calka and her precious, baby queen.

The Djinn must have recognized the steely resolve in me—Solhans knew Solhans well—and the fight left them. They leapt over the cliff in the same direction my pack had gone.

"What the!?" Duane flummoxed was something I never thought I'd see. He was always so cool and calm.

He dashed to the edge and looked over, me right behind him. We stared down at a goat trail that must have been hundreds of feet below. My pack was smashed, contents everywhere, but the Djinn was running off in one piece. How had they survived from that height? Djinn magic?

"I can't believe we're alive," Duane said.

"Don't you mean him? Her? Whatever? They fell like two hundred feet!"

"No. Us. That's the assassin who killed Saral, the one who took Gas's marker when I couldn't."

"You know them?"

"No. Never seen their face, but Calka used every means at her disposal to hunt them down, and the closest she got was an image pulled from the energy of the assassination. I don't understand magic as well as you do, but the way Calka explained it: bad events leave an imprint that can be seen later. Like ghosts."

"A dent in space-time. That's what the professor would call it, anyway. Solhans see ghosts and such events too, when we want, and I almost never want. That assassin evaded Calka's hunt because they're Solhan and a powerful necromancer, able to hide their soul from anyone's magical sight. Only a terrible event, Saral's murder, would have left a dent so bad they couldn't repair it. That assassin must be one of the Nine."

"Like Ulric?"

"I thought my uncle was the last of the Nine. Erick said he killed the others after the Fall of Solheim."

"He missed one. Unless it is Ulric?" Seemed Duane didn't trust my uncle much, but I'd interrogated him with truth serum and knew his secrets now. A dual life as a Darrubian Djinn was not one of them.

"It's not him. But ... could this be the same assassin who killed Hilja and framed you?"

"Likely." Duane stared up at the peak looming over us, a snow-covered rock I had not been looking forward to climbing. He frowned. "We should go back."

"I know. I don't want to endanger Calka and her child either. What do we do now? Who else can stop the plant creature?"

"Us. We'll find another way. Maybe the Celon can show us?"

"I don't trust that stuff. The sun is going down, so let's camp here, and I'll try a dream walk first, before we give up."

"You said Ulric couldn't help?"

"I saw Calka when I drank the Celon, so maybe I can reach her another way. It's worth a try."

Only after Duane started to pitch his tent did I remember mine was gone. My travel roll too. He noticed my expression and said, "Don't worry. You take the tent. I'll keep watch."

I thought he meant by the fire, but he didn't light one. As night set and snow began to fall—early summer this far north meant the snow only melted in midday sun—I looked guiltily at the tent and then sighed.

"Get in." I told him.

"You're the one who needs to dream walk, and the assassin could come back."

"If it's the person who killed Sarel when you and Aguragas could not, it makes them the best assassin in the world, and you shivering out here isn't going to save me from them. They could have killed us already."

He raised his hands. "I give up. Your logic is unbeatable."

Only when the two of us were resting back-to-back in the one-person tent, the heat of our bodies warming up the small space quickly, my nerves tingling, mind racing and wondering how I was supposed to dream walk like this ... did I wonder if Duane, the master manipulator and spymaster, had used reverse psychology on me.

"You didn't intend to stay out there and freeze," I said.

"I knew you had a heart. And I like being next to you."

"You're not the one who changed my clothes in the Avian nest, were you?"

"No. I am a gentleman. That was Naren."

"About that …. The Celon gave me horrible dreams. That's why I reacted so badly. I didn't think it was horrible lying next to you. Not horrible at all."

"It's not horrible lying next to you either."

"Still being the gentleman. I stink. I haven't bathed in days."

"I like your smell. Maybe not when we've been traipsing through the sewers, but when you first came back to Highcrowne and I followed you until we had a chance to speak, I didn't need to see you to know where you were. You smell amazing, like nothing else."

"You can track me by smell? You're not part werewolf are you?"

"Not as far as I know."

"It's kind of weird. Animalistic."

"Weird? Animal?"

"Or sexy. Thinking that you like my smell. I don't know."

"Sexy is better." He turned around.

I felt him press against me, his body warm, breath stirring my hair.

Bracelets glinted in the dark as he reached over and took my shoulder to turn me towards him. Words froze in my throat as he kissed my neck. I usually had something clever to say, some joke, but I couldn't think of anything worth disturbing the moment. I didn't want to say a word. Sometimes words were stupid.

I pressed by hips back and softened, sighing as his kisses left goosebumps, each one so gentle and slow. He brushed along my neck, my ear, my chin. I wanted his lips on mine. I ached for it, but he held back, knowing how full of doubts I could be, giving me a chance to run.

I didn't want to run. I didn't want to be anywhere else.

"Duane," I whispered. I had never said his name like that before, trying out the syllables laced with longing rather than disappointment and anger. It sounded good that way. More beautiful than any 'Rose'. My Duane.

"Eva." I was glad he didn't sound anything like Thane. He'd been saying my name my whole life, but he spoke as if it was for the first time, as though he had only just met me and there was so much unknown, so much to discover. And there was. This was all new for both of us. An adventure.

Icy wind made me shiver, snowflakes billowed around us, and we both sat up.

"Calka?"

The Avian Queen had stuck her beak into the tent, magpie black and white feathers framing a smiling bird face. Birds can smile. There's a twinkle to the beady eyes, a cant to the beak, an opening of the mouth that was unmistakable.

"My two favorite people," she said.

I'd forgotten she was the whole reason we were here. She'd found us—but why did it have to be now?

9 Wait ... No Regrets

"**Y**ou shouldn't be here," Duane told Calka.

I thought he said it because our moment had been interrupted—and who knew if we'd ever get another one with our luck—but then he added, "The assassin who killed Saral is here, looking for you."

"He's right. You can't be here!" I took Duane's hand off my hip and hated the loss of that weight. I crawled out of the tent, shoving Calka back. "You should go."

"I know why you're seeking me, and I had to give you something. I had to risk it." She held up a bracelet with multi-colored glass beads, each one bright to my magical sight, and the silver thread joining them together seemed to hum like one of the professor's lightning-powered devices.

Most magical objects had a weight to them, a living presence that those who wielded magic could detect. The better you were at magic, the better your senses. I'd been training the hard way, without the First Soul or Dead God to help me, and so I knew my magic sense was not as developed as it used to be. Even so, the bracelet (which for all appearances looked like something you'd buy from a street vendor or junk shop) was so charged with power it felt like I was standing next to the sun, or next to a god.

Duane had followed me out of the tent, and when he saw the bracelet, he said. "No. You can't give us that. It's all you have left, Calka."

He took a step forward, and Calka held up the bracelet, saying, "Stop."

Duane stopped mid-stride. More than paralysis, it was as though the world around him had stopped too, flakes of snow paused in their descent, hair caught in a breeze that never died.

"You froze time." I'd seen Trickster manage it, but no one else.

"You understand," Calka said, appreciatively. "And what your Duane says is true—this is all the magic I have left. All my precious trinkets merged into one. You will need it to retrieve an even greater power, the only thing that will enable you to force the Growing back into the seed from whence it came. It is the only way you can stop it."

"The Growing? That's what you call the alien plant. Apt. Wait. What do you mean 'my Duane'?"

"He prefers I call him Black Rose, the name he went by when we met and when I forced him to do our bidding, but names should change just as we ourselves evolve. You have found Duane again. Your Duane. I wish you joy, Eva. Both of you. When Saral was killed, I thought my heart would never mend, but with Roosal it did."

"I lost Thane."

"I know. You understand. And he lost Hilja."

"He loved her?"

"In his way, but there was ever a wedge between them, one of my making. We Avians worship immutable Fate, whose thorns weave into many nests, and in Their wisdom, Fate allows souls to choose their destiny, but the choice is false. There are many worlds, many universes, as the professor has shown you, as the Voidwalker knows, but within this one universe there can be only one course. The river that threatens to over-whelm its banks or cut a new path must be engineered back into its appointed track. That is what we Avians do, have always done. Celon's visions aid us, but serving Fate was our calling long before Celon came into our possession. The fate of the Black Rose was to be our dagger in the dark, our instrument, and only ours, so he could never be allowed to fall fully under Hilja's sway."

"Duane was an assassin because of you. For you."

"Yes. He thought he came to kill us, but he came to serve us. He has been ours since a youngling. He worked for Hilja because we demanded it. He helped her rise to power because we preferred her to Fharen. Duane grew close to her, yes, even to love her, but we Avians wanted that also, so he could influence her as he did Ulric.

"We thought he would be the Human King until Moore arrived with his democracy, an outlier not even the Celon could predict. Duane influences Harley as well, but we foresaw his rise among the dwarves. We see much because of the Celon, and we can control more of the future than most realize.

"Duane has been our most important instrument— but I gift him to you as I gift Celon. Use him for your purposes. Our time is at an end. Let the Black Rose die. Let Eva's Duane live in his stead. The time of Thornes returns. You are the future."

"No."

"What?" Calka seemed surprised to be surprised.

For beings who worshiped 'immutable' Fate and foretold the future—created the future according to their wants more like—they could be thick.

"Duane is not an instrument. He is not 'mine'. He belongs to himself. You have used him terribly. You say

I am free to choose, to direct this new future, but how do I know you're not using me too?"

Silence. It said all I needed to hear. I had a reflex against being used. A deep-rooted stubbornness.

"It is your choice." She said the words, but I knew she did not believe them. "I thought you cared for him?"

"I do, but it has nothing to do with his usefulness. Duane is my lightning in the storm, he rekindles the life in me when all I've known is death ... but just because I need him, it doesn't mean I should have him or that I deserve him. That's for him to decide. You may not trust Fate, not believe They can be swayed, but I do. I believe They listen to our hearts. I tell Them to listen to his, listen to Duane. Not to you or me. We don't deserve this world, Solhan or Avian, but humans do. They deserve a chance. Duane deserves a chance to choose his own path."

Calka went very still and then bowed her head. The Avian Queen, bowing to me?

"Very well. It shall be as you decree. Let Duane choose the way. Still, I leave this in your care." She pressed the bracelet of beads into my hand, the magic burning me with its potency. "It is you I charge with this mission for me, and it is your choice to undertake it or not. But if you wish to free your uncle and free the world from the Growing, then you had best listen.

"Celon is the only thing that can stop the Growing. Use this trinket to defeat Naren and take Celon to Faellion. The seed is there. Force the Growing back inside. Do not tell Duane, you must not tell Duane, for he will not desire me to risk this magic. Know when you take this bracelet, I am defenseless. What's more, Duane will not turn against Naren and steal Celon, for he, like Naren, has been exposed. It has touched him and has more influence over him than even you do, and Naren is completely devoted to it. Use Celon to defeat the Growing, but do not trust it. Never trust Celon. Understood?"

I wanted to fight, argue, but Calka's desperation was not feigned. She was risking everything to help us. "Alright. I'll do as you say."

"Thank you." She sagged.

"Now, get out of here before that Darrubian assassin returns. Unless ... we use this bracelet to kill them?"

"No. The magic within is finite. As much as I desire vengeance, destroying the future for the sake of a past that cannot be changed is insanity. This magic is yours. You will need all of it to get past Naren and control Celon."

I nodded. Was that the scuff of a foot on stone? "Go!"

Calka took to the sky, shooting straight up, and I turned, brandishing the bracelet at the Solhan, who was back. The assassin froze and Duane unfroze. I had no idea how I'd used the thing.

Duane reorientated himself quickly, glimpsed Calka leaving, pulled his dagger and advanced on the Djinn. The Solhan was fighting to get free. Somehow. I felt a weakening of the magic in the bracelet, and I flinched. I needed it. I had promised Calka—future not past.

I released the Djinn, and when they saw Calka was gone, they vanished over the cliffside again before Duane could strike.

"Damn," he cursed.

I hid the bracelet before he could see. He'd want me to return it, and I couldn't do that.

"We need to get back to Highcrowne," I said.

"What did Calka tell you? I assume you spoke when she enchanted me?"

No hiding some things from him. He was too sharp. "Yes, and she told me how to free Ulric. I need to get that goo from Naren then head to Faellion. Will you help?" I hadn't understood what Calka meant by 'taking Celon', but I assumed she meant the whole supply. It was not a lie I'd told Duane. Let him assume I meant 'some' goo, not all of it.

"Yes, great. I'm glad you found out what you needed to do."

"You're not mad she froze you?"

"She has her secrets, always has. As long as she's safe from the assassin, that's what matters. Looks like she froze him too and then flew away, so I'm glad she was smart."

"Yes, she's smart." I didn't correct him, but it still felt like a lie, hiding the bracelet from him. I didn't like lying to Duane. I didn't like it one bit.

"Let's go." We could travel at night. I couldn't sleep now, especially not next to him, not when there was a secret like this between us. I didn't want there to be secrets when we were together, so we couldn't be together.

We made faster time going down the mountains. I gave Duane the tent when he grew too tired to continue, while I kept watch, in case the Djinn returned. "Solhans don't require sleep as often," I told him. He did not sleep long, and we were out of the High Reaches before the sun set on another day.

Soon, Highcrowne was in sight, the Central City rising above a sea of roofs and spires, smoke and light, and clanking machinery, with clouds of dirigibles overhead.

The lack of intimacy on the return trip—when we had been so close before Calka's arrival—was palpable. I had told him, "I need to focus on the mission. On saving everyone. I can't think about anything else right now."

I had run away, emotionally if not physically this time, as I always do. He'd known I would, because he seemed unsurprised by the distance I put between us.

Now, with home in sight, he tried to rationalize for himself. Resign himself to business as usual.

"Back to our old world, our old selves. I suppose it's for the best," he said.

"Why's that?"

"There's an election for one thing. We probably missed another debate."

"Speak for yourself. I attended ours." I'd forgotten he couldn't be there because he was being hunted for Hilja's murder, so I added, "Not that you had a choice, I know."

"I didn't sleep with Hilja," he said, startling me with the sudden admission. "We haven't been a couple since she became queen. I was still her friend and protector, though. That's why I went to see her in the palace. That's why I was there."

I wanted to say it didn't matter, but it did. Of course, I felt like an even worse piece of crap for hating Hilja and being jealous.

"It's dangerous in the Elf Palace," I said, trying to change the subject. "That's why I want to keep Dawn as far from that world as I can. There's enough danger with her being a Thorne, let alone Hilja's heir. I hope another elven clan takes over. I hope I don't win the election, because her mother being the Human Crown would be just as dangerous. I hope you don't win either, because Little Viktor would get pulled in too. It's bad enough you're the Shadow King. If you were King, then there's no way we could be together. I couldn't risk Dawn more. There are too many targets on her already."

"If I was King we couldn't be together," he repeated. "I'm not King now, Eva. What does that mean?"

We were still above the smog, the red-orange light of sunset shining through split crags of rock and the marble columns adorning the palaces on the plateau, its rays spilling over the city like molten gold. Duane was in profile, his hair and face limned in light, his peridot eyes bright and sharp, cutting into me, past my defenses, past my lies.

I couldn't do it. I couldn't lie to him anymore.

"Calka gave me the bracelet and told me not to involve you. She said the Celon has corrupted you like it has Naren. That it will control you and stop me from using it to stop the Growing—the plant alien."

"Calka doesn't trust me?" That's what shocked him. Not me lying to him.

"She doesn't, but I do. Here." I gave him the bracelet, closing his fingers around it. He couldn't sense magic, but when I touched his skin it felt more powerful to me than any Avian trinket.

"Eva. You ... you never trust anyone."

"I'm trusting you. Will you help me retrieve the Celon?"

"Yes, of course I'll help you. You know I'd do anything for you. I always have, always will."

"I know. And I remember when you took the truth serum and drove us out of town so you could tell me how you felt. I lied to you then too. The serum was no longer in my system. I wanted to tell you .... I should have told you then. I couldn't learn to love you as you asked—"

"—Eva. I know you don't feel the same. It's okay."

"No, it's not. I couldn't learn to love you ... because I already do. I loved you before I knew what it was, before I kissed you at thirteen. I loved you even when I pretended to hate you, when I was angry and trying to convince myself you weren't right for me, while secretly comparing everyone to you. I've always loved you, even when I shouldn't."

I kissed him.

I couldn't help recalling the first time, how he'd been shocked just like this. His best friend's sister. I'd had to get on tiptoes to reach, but now we were the same height. He'd worked for my uncle, and now we were both free of him, free of all the reasons why we shouldn't. Now, all I could think was 'why not yes?'.

"Eva," he said when I let him come up for air. "What are you doing?"

"What I want. Not what everyone tells me I should do, not what some prophecy or contract writ before I was born says, not even the smart thing or the right thing. What I want ... and I want no regrets."

"Don't play games with my heart."

"I love you, Duane. You. Just as you are. No games." I dropped my mask. I wore as many as he did, but I didn't want anything to stand between us this time. If only he could sense souls, he'd know I'd laid mine bare, opened myself to him, risking the pain that would come. There was always pain, but I didn't care. I waited for him to see the truth in my gaze.

He took my face in trembling hands and kissed me back. Then he took me home.

10 Timeless

He had lived on the streets, in thieves' dens and Avian sanctuaries, while I had been sheltered by one prison after another, from Uncle's house to Gernwold and Faellion. I'd travelled the world imprisoned by the First Soul. Highcrowne was our home, but we had nowhere to go to be alone together except for the old warehouse where the shrine to the Devourer frightened everyone else away, whether they knew it was there or not. It didn't frighten me or Duane. Nothing frightened us but the fragility of this new truth between us.

It was full dark by the time we got there. A glance kept his shadows, his lackeys, away from us, a bubble of solitude, so it was quiet as he unlocked the door. I saw stars, a great swathe of them overhead, the sky clear for once. It was colder for the clarity, and as soon as we were inside, he started the fire. It was wood, not warlock crystal or coal, and I loved the scent of it, reminded of the barrel fires in the Outskirts we once hovered near in the timeless days when we ran wild together.

I took off my jacket and turned the taps to fill the copper tub. Duane had installed all the latest amenities, including running cold and hot water. It was amazing, feeling the heat from the pipes, watching steam rise, and as soon as the water was deep enough, I stripped naked and sunk into it, washing away the grime of the road. When I emerged and pushed wet hair out of my eyes, I saw Duane standing there. His gaze caught mine, green fire. Lightning shivers went through me. He never looked away as he slowly undressed and slipped in across from me.

He lathered soap on the sponge, but I took it from him and wiped a smudge from his cheek. I ran it across his muscled shoulders and upper arms. When I leaned forward to reach his back, he kissed my breasts. I gasped as his hands caressed me, all of me, expert and knowing exactly where I wanted his touch even before I knew myself. His mouth covered mine, and I loved the wetness of the bath on his lips, the sweetness of the dried berries we'd eaten on the trail on his tongue.

I wrapped my arms and legs around him, and water sloshed over the floor. It felt so right to hold him. We fit perfectly. He was always quiet, but so was I this time, our breathing loud in the stillness. He trembled, despite the hot water, and I knew he held back, being careful, nervous. I had been so cruel to him at times, always driving him away, and this was what came of it. I couldn't bear him being afraid of me.

I locked gazes with him once more, softening my expression, telling him it was okay to be vulnerable. I was frightened too. This could break my heart, but it was already broken, and so there was a chance, one worth taking, that this could make me live again.

He couldn't read souls, though, couldn't know my thoughts, so I told him: "My whole life, all I've known is death, but you are life. You, Duane. Everything is pointless, nothingness, without you. I work for everyone else's future, for Dawn's and Highcrowne's ... but you are my future. Mine. If you'll let me have you."

"Eva ... I've been so alone. You can't imagine. I don't want a crown or to be Shadow King, any of it, if it stands between us. All I want is you."

"I'm yours." I didn't want him to see my tears, so I kissed his lips, his neck, his shoulders.

He lifted us both out of the tub with one acrobatic show of strength and agility, and I laughed, clinging tightly to him so I didn't fall. He carried me to the bed and laid me down, so that I could let go and relax. He was smiling too, his fear fading, some of his old bravado shining through, and I wondered what other acrobatics he was capable of.

Once again, I had to remind myself that he was human, not a god incarnate, not a necromancer who could understand my unspoken desires. With him I had to be conscious, deliberate, real. "I want you inside me, Duane. Now."

"Yes, Eva." He smiled as he balanced over me, muscles flexing as he held himself, so no part of his skin touched mine. "Whatever you command, Eva." He began kissing my mouth slowly, tantalizingly.

He was driving me crazy. I arched toward him, reached for him, but he took hold of my wrists and pinned them to the soft mattress. He kissed my neck, shoulder, curve of my breast, all the way down to my waist. So agile. I blushed, more than blushed. Every part of me tingled, burned, wanting him.

His arms shook, and I was hoping that meant his muscles were finally giving out. He'd have no choice but to put his weight on me. I craved it. But his lips trembled too as they kissed my hip and moved towards my inner thigh. He wasn't weakening, and my soul sense was good enough to know he was shaking with long pent-up desire.

No cheating, Eva, I told myself. I shouldn't be reading him. I wanted this to be an even match.

In many ways it felt like a fight: testing your opponent, measuring their intent and capabilities. I had no patience and always went for the heart, but Duane loved the hunt, the slow stalking and wearing down of his rivals. I didn't care which of us won this time, though. Either way, I'd be happy.

He sensed my capitulation, recognized my resigned sigh, and only then did he relent and give me what I'd asked for.

I gasped as the weight of him hit me, the heat of his skin pressed against mine, the heat of him inside me. I bit his shoulder, his neck, as my hands clutched at his muscled back, and he moaned. With each thrust, I wanted him more. I wrapped my legs around him, tightened everything around him until I climaxed. I relaxed, but he held himself back. The scoundrel. I'd get him to submit.

I flipped him over and straddled him. This time, I got to hold his wrists down, my breasts tantalizingly out of reach. I was no good at playing the tease, though, so I let him lick and suck. I couldn't help pressing myself against him, kissing him, because he was what I wanted. I wanted to taste him. I nibbled his chest, his lips, as I rode him.

He'd obviously been trained to withstand torture. He was a tough one. As soon as I tired just a bit, he flipped me over and drove into me from behind. New moans escaped me, as he went sweet and deep. I was not ashamed to climax yet again, but he was a machine.

It wasn't until we had turned full circle, his front pressed against mine, so our eyes met, our lips gently brushing against one another. It felt like a timeless eternity passed between us in that moment as he watched me, open-eyed, like he was trying to read my soul, if he only could. I wanted him to read me, to know me, to know I loved him. Only then did he release and give himself to me.

It was a long night. A joyful one, as we dozed and warmed ourselves by the fire, trying out the rug there, the curved couch, and the bath once more. By sunrise, we were naked and starving, rummaging through his cupboards for food.

"You have a full kitchen, pantry ... but nothing has been touched," I noted.

"I told you. I sleep in the Avian Sanctuary. All this is just to make people think I live here." He was lounging on the bed. The warehouse had no walls, so he could watch me peering into tins and rummaging through bags.

"Well, I'm glad you have buckwheat. I'm making pancakes."

"You can cook?" He sat up, looking less relaxed now.

"Not like Nanny. Don't worry. Dawn's favorite is pancakes. I learned from an inn that was still standing at the river junction near the Fortress of Mages of all places. There were no other guests, and the cook shared his best recipe 'for the little one'. I should really go home and check on her and Nanny before we go after the Celon. Goo. Whatever."

"After I get these pancakes you've got me craving. Along with other things." He was naked too and had somehow crept up while we were talking, embracing me from behind and threatening to drag me back to bed.

"Too hungry. Must eat now. Soon to be monosyllabic."

"Not yet you aren't."

In the end, he did distract me from making breakfast, but he made up for it by doing the cooking, while I gave instructions and sipped kaffe. We even got to enjoy every bite, exchanging a few nibbles. I swear the recipe tasted even better on his lips when I kissed him.

We were entangled on the couch, about to enter a sugar coma, when pounding on his metal front door shattered our solitude. I grabbed my Ashur before even thinking about my clothes.

"Don't worry. No one could get this close without my authorization. It will be one of my people." He also didn't bother to get dressed but boldly opened the door, saying, "What?"

Katherine, AKA Doctor Suttner, AKA my election campaign manager was there. She had one of Duane's goons by the ear, the kid on tiptoes, obviously having strongarmed her way this far, but she dropped the sentry and covered her eyes with both hands.

"Mister Rose! For shame! Have you no common decency?"

"Not the common type, no. What do you want, Doctor?"

"I am looking for your erstwhile opponent. I was told you have her, and I demand her release!"

"I don't want to go!" I shouted, grabbing some pillows from the divan to cover myself.

"Miss Thorne?"

I peeked around Duane's naked form. "Yes?"

Katherine uncovered her eyes and then covered them again. "Oh. My."

"Yes, oh my. Now, run along. I'll head home soon ... or late. I haven't decided yet. I'll see you there, temporarily. I'm on a mission."

"What about the election?"

"Why don't you take my place?"

"I'm not on the ballot. The rules...."

I groaned. "You do remember the city is overrun by that plant alien I'm trying to stop while also discovering who killed Queen Hilja?"

"Oh yes. They say it is a curse to live in interesting times. I must point out that your behavior is highly irregular. What are you doing here if you are not a captive of this larcenous braggadocio and provocateur?"

"I am captivated." I smiled at Duane, and his green eyes entranced me, so that I soon found myself in another kiss, pillows forgotten.

Katherine cleared her throat.

"Fine. I'll get dressed."

"Dressed!?" Katherine clamped her hands tighter over her eyes.

Duane shut the door and 'helped' me with my clothes. If anything, he was more a hindrance, making the whole process take ages, with them coming off completely again at one point. Only more banging on the door reminded me Katherine was still out there.

"You really need better criminals," I told Duane. "Why has no one gotten rid of her? How can all of your guards be afraid of one redhead?"

"I told them not to harm her—after a few suggested we assassinate her to ensure my victory. She seems to be your secret weapon among the voters. And ... I hate to say it, but the sun is high. We have things to do."

"Fighting an insidious plant invader? Elvish fascism? Maintaining fair and democratic elections? Why can't we do all that tomorrow?" I pouted.

"I am very tempted to not care about anything at all. Except you." He kissed me, then frowned. "And Viktor, and Dawn, and...."

"I know. They need us. But I need you." I gave him one last, slow, passionate kiss, the banging on the door forgotten. I'd already forgotten this place held the shrine of the Devourer, that it held bad memories for me, because Duane had transformed it. There were far more good recollections than bad now, and I had something else worth fighting for: A Highcrowne where it was safe for the two of us to be together.

"I'll meet you at the Avian Sanctuary," Duane said. "Let me try convincing Naren to help willingly, without using Calka's power if it's possible."

"Okay. If anyone can convince him, it's you. I'll see you soon." I told myself the pang I felt at those words was not a premonition of dread but simply sadness at our parting. A perfect night and morning was not nearly enough. I wanted forever with Duane.

Katherine chattered the whole way back to my neighborhood, me not hearing a word, my head in the clouds. I felt like I was floating. Everything was beautiful, even goblin muck rakers and Beggar's Block, which I passed as I'd chosen to walk instead of taking the tram. I emptied my coin purse for them and Katherine's too, sharing my happiness.

I lost her somewhere in the bazaar when people came up asking questions, rallying and calling my name, protesting elves, and other things I didn't hear. I left her to deal with it, as I breezed into my office. I saw Nanny had cleaned, and all the whisky was gone. I didn't mind. I hadn't had a drop in over a week. Interesting times, especially with Duane, suited me just fine.

I climbed the stairs to the living room. "Dawn?" I called. Suddenly missing her but also wanting to share my joy and hold her.

When I got upstairs, I was stunned to see Thane.

Thane. Father of my child. Fragment of the Dead God incarnate. Still wearing Fharen's body—the lost Elf King.

How was he here? How...?

"Is the First Soul gone?" I asked through my shocked daze. That was the only way he could be here. He must have given it to the Devourer and survived. Somehow.

"Eva." He said my name in that way he had of sending shivers down my spine. Only now there was a shiver of fear. Thane was here after all these years ... but now I had Duane. I ... I couldn't think about that yet.

"How did you escape the Devourer? Is the Dead God back too? Will He put an end to the risen?"

"So many questions." He frowned. "Aren't you happy to see me?"

"Yes. Of course." I held him, put my head against his chest, and I heard his heart beating. He was alive. Real. The familiar embrace reminded me of all we had shared, of Dawn.

"Your daughter..." I began.

"I've met her already." He gestured, and I saw Dawn on the staircase, watching us warily from between the rungs of the banister. "She won't let me come any closer."

"This is your father," I told her.

"No, he's not."

"It's Thane." It was complicated. I knew that. My mind was doing somersaults. My first thought had been to wonder how he'd gotten past my wards, but what couldn't a god do?

Dawn ran up to her room.

"Give her time," I said. "She's surprised. We both are."

"Kiss me." He put his lips on mine, and I stiffened. I felt like I was betraying Duane, but he had sacrificed himself for me, for this whole world. The least I could do was make him feel loved, appreciated. I kissed him back.

There was something missing. Had I fallen out of love? I always assumed that when I finally gave in and told Duane how I felt, that if we ever got together, then I would still love Thane with some part of my heart, no matter where he was, alive or dead. I thought my heart was big enough for both of them. Maybe it wasn't? It was shriveled, dark, and Solhan, so who had I been kidding? Lucky I loved anything at all.

I lacked my soul sense, but Thane still had his. There would be no hiding my feelings from him if he searched for them, so I tried to cover, deflect.

"It's crazy here," I said, taking a small step back. "The plant alien is taking over Highcrowne, has already taken over some regions of Faellion, as far as I can tell. I could use your help."

"I'm not what I was. I don't think either of us are?"

Did he know?

"Were you injured by the Devourer? Obviously not physically. I mean, like did it drain you or something?"

"Yes. I am weaker than I was. I'm not sure how much help I can give ... but tell me everything you know."

I filled him in on my adventures, not mentioning Duane as the one who had roused my suspicions—and other things—and helped me investigate so far. I told him about Ulric being taken, my dream-walk nightmare vision, even my concerns about Doctor Ghunnan and every human and dwarf who had spent some time cocooned and hidden during the war (and there were a lot) being agents of the plant creature.

"That is very worrying," he said. "I think we need more resources. I am the Elf King, for all appearances, and with Hilja, poor Hilja, dead, I could restore much needed order. Come with me to the palace, you and Dawn both."

"No. Dawn stays here where she's protected." I knew that I kept her trapped too much, but there was good reason with the plant lurking everywhere.

"Of course. I understand. Still ... I need you by my side." He took my hands, trying to catch my gaze, but I darted my eyes away after a moment.

Duane would be waiting for me at the Avian Sanctuary. Still, Thane was right. We needed to use his influence over the elves to keep the plant in check, long enough for Duane and me to stop it in Faellion.

"I'll go with you," I told him. "Just let me check on Dawn."

"If you could convince her to ... to let me hold her, I would be so happy."

Poor Thane. What a terrible welcome we'd given him. I felt awful.

I nodded and dashed up the stairs. Dawn's door was locked, so I knocked.

"Go away."

"Don't be frightened. I know it's scary to meet your father."

"I did meet him. The statue."

"That was winged Death, and yes Thane too, because Thane is a part of Him. Only a god … they think strangely." I didn't want to say there was a time He wanted me dead, so I could rule by His side in the Halls of Death, until Thane convinced Him not to kill me. Thane had learned about the joys of life, of mortal love. With me. Instead, I said, "Thane is the one I fell in love with. He loves us both. I know he's been away your whole life, but he was trying to save us all. You should say hello."

"No."

She was stubborn that one. I'd learned logic was the only recourse, but I didn't have it in me. I too was wary, confused. I knew what she was feeling, even more so.

"I'll be back soon," I said. "I have to stop the plant alien from taking over everyone. Thane is going to help me. Duane too. We'll fix this, and everything will be okay."

"It won't." She flung open the door and gave me a rare hug. More than rare, unheard of. "Be careful. Not everything is what it seems. I don't know how I know, or what the discrepancies mean exactly, but they're important."

"'Discrepancies' is a big word for a seven-year-old." She impressed me every day with her smarts. Wherever did she get those from?

"I'm serious. Be careful."

"I love you too."

She huffed and slammed and locked the door again. Somehow, I'd blinked and missed her childhood. She was a teenager already. Precocious. At this rate, she'd be forty by next week, and then maybe she'd talk to me as an equal instead of judging and looking down on me?

I went over to the window in the hall and slid it up, placing a handful of dried berries from my belt pouch in the flower box and whistled. Seconds later, something invisible had gobbled the food up as well as a desiccated daisy and some clumps of soil.

"Is that you, Bitten Belly?" I asked.

"Yes, mistress." He was on edge too and not dropping his camouflage. I wondered if the plant alien could take over bogles? Probably. Maybe even pigeons. I shivered at the possibilities. Still, I had to hope my network of bogles was still intact.

"Find Rat Meat Man, A-K-A Duane, and tell him to wait for me. I'm gathering more allies, which will help when we go to Faellion. Tell him to give me a day."

"Faellion?"

Simple instructions, I reminded myself. "Just tell Duane to wait."

"Wait."

"Perfect. Now go." I shut the window.

I practiced my smile in the hallway mirror before heading back downstairs. Nanny had Thane on the sofa, forcing some noxious tea and Solhan nibbles on him. Things like diluted hellebore and thistle to build your resistance to poison, along with a plate of cricket biscuits, which were made from, you guessed it, ground crickets. She'd even brought out the toasted cockroaches, a real treat.

"We don't have time for tea," I told her, and Thane gave me a relieved look at having come just in time to save him.

"There's always time for tea. Besides, I want to know about...." She made the sign of protection against the Devourer, and I fought hard not to do the same.

"I don't remember as much as I'd like," Thane said. "I know I'm lucky to be alive."

"And I said," taking Thane's hand and pulling him off the couch while dodging saucers coming at my face now too, "if we all want to stay alive, we need to stop the plant creature. No time to rest."

Nanny began her usual tirade about me never being home for more than two seconds and skinny from lack of good Solhan cooking, but I ushered Thane out the front door and took a deep breath when we were safe on the street.

"At least we know she misses us," I said, trying to find the bright side.

Wow. Duane had changed something in me. I never went for the bright side.

"You couldn't convince Dawn to see me? To come with us?" Thane was definitely not in a sunny place, so I tried to dampen down my joy when I replied.

"No. I did try. Like I said, give her time."

I was terrified of time. It was just Thane and I now, and that meant I'd break at some point. I'd have to tell him. I didn't know what exactly, but I couldn't give up this warmth, this hope inside me. I couldn't go back. All I could do was press forward, and maybe it would become clear what to say. I hadn't been lying when I said there was no time to rest, and that, fortunately, also meant no time to reflect.

"Let's go," I said. I raised the hood of his cloak, the nearness of him stirring emotions in me. There was also something ... what was the word Dawn had used? A 'discrepancy'. "Stay hidden until you have to reveal yourself. There's a lot of anti-elf sentiment in the city right now."

"For good reason. I have Fharen's memories, and I know how brutal most of the Houses and Parties are, how little regard they hold for humans and dwarves. Even Solhans were once despised. Both Hilja and I were forced to hide our Solhan ancestry behind glamours for so long. Fharen changed that over time, reviving the histories, reminding the elves who it was who once ruled them. Strength like that is what they respect, so we must show strength to bring them into line again. To unite them and turn them against our common enemy."

"United elves scare me more than elves squabbling among themselves, but you're probably right. The plant alien is insidious, turning neighbors against one another. Anyone not infected must come together, setting differences aside for now, to fight it."

"Yes. I hope, together, we can inspire that unity." He took my hand and rubbed his thumb against my skin in that way he had that always melted my insides, that made me want him. I fought the feeling, and it was easier than I expected to resist.

I pulled my hand away. "Let's hurry."

11   ANTS, SHARKS, AND VIPERS

We made it all the way to the Central City without being accosted by my supporters, Katherine, plant people, or annoying EEPs, which was strange. When was the last time I'd had such utter quiet and time to think?

Thane didn't speak, and I knew he'd read my soul. He was waiting for me to tell him what it meant, and whether I would let my mind or my heart dictate my actions, our future.

The heart was changeable, while logic was immutable. He was Dawn's father, a good man, part Primal god. He was everything I had once desired and amazing in every way imaginable, his love for me absolute and unshakable. I should love him back. It was the logical thing. The right thing. Only ... I no longer felt it. I only felt an ache, a pain in my chest like a fist clenching my heart, knowing I was either going to have to hurt him, the last person who deserved it—or die inside by setting Duane aside and hurting him and myself both.

I knew what I had to do, but I couldn't speak. I was mute. It was a relief when we reached the Elf Palace and there were finally some EEP guards standing in our way that I could berate. Being angry was so much easier than being heartbroken.

"Straighten that beret! Wipe that smirk off your face. Do you know what kind of trouble you're in? Stand aside, now." Sometimes I thought being a drill sergeant would have been a better career than detective, the pay more regular at least.

"Eva," Thane whispered from beneath his hood, reluctant to reveal himself. "It is better to remain discreet until I am safe among allies. Not all Houses on the interim council are friendly to one another."

"Oh. Right. Carry on you two. You're getting off easy this time. Do send word to..." I waited for Thane to fill in the missing name.

"Seneschal Ernest," he whispered.

"That's right! Ernest. Send for the seneschal, as that's who I've come to question. I have Avian authority." I waved my glass badge in their faces.

Hopefully these ones hadn't been involved in chasing me and Duane through the secret passages. It was hard to tell elves apart, but these ones looked too young, not as elite as the ones who'd tried to grab us before. Raw recruits, most likely.

"An Avian Marshal? What authority can you have? They ceded this city," the youngest of the guards said with a sneer.

"Tell that to Naren and his tons of explosive green goo up on the top of the mountain. They are still here—and watching. Move it!"

The drill sergeant routine worked even better than the badge, and the one who had been convinced the Avian bogeymen were gone until I disillusioned him took off like the message runner he'd probably been before EEP training. The other one stayed steely-eyed and rigid, blocking the door with sheer elvish snobbery.

The runner was back at his post moments later, and I was about to give him a tongue lashing, when I heard Ernest huffing and puffing. The seneschal emerged, drenched in sweat, and waved us forward. "Come along Miss Thorne. I've been expecting you."

"You have? I thought you were still upset that Fluffy liked me more?"

There were some yips on the other side of the door, and I knew the dog was excited to hear my voice. He'd missed me.

"Nonsense, Miss Thorne. Come inside. Your guest as well."

Ernest was surprisingly forgiving. He must have had a taste of the interim council and decided I was the better ally after all.

He grabbed Fluffy before the dog could lick my ankles, although the mutt did try to stretch his tongue toward my face in passing. I felt a few drops of slobber and wiped them away in disgust. I was glad when he handed the pooch off to a servant who got the tongue bath instead of me.

If anything, the palace was even busier than after Hilja had died. Officials scurrying around, nobles striding places with their noses in the air, hangers-on hurrying after, the servants slouched or huddled in corners out of the way of their betters as they darted about doing their work as unobtrusively as possible. No one noticed us with all the frenzy. This was what an ants' nest looked like without its queen.

"I'm sorry I missed Hilja's funeral," I told Ernest. I wished I could have been there. I couldn't hate her anymore.

"It was perfunctory, rigidly ceremonial, and poorly attended overall," Ernest said, not even glancing back as he cleared the path for us through the teeming corridors. "Just the way she would have liked it. She never appreciated false tears unless they were her own, as no one else had mastered them so well as she."

"True." I smiled, remembering the flighty princess I'd first met who had called me sister and made me believe

I was all she had ever wanted for a friend. She'd been damn good.

Ernest led us to a suite of apartments. The Elf Palace in Highcrowne was a miniature version of the one in Faellion, with nobles having secure, isolated suites of rooms connected to a main hall that led to the throne room. It was miniature in that there were only a few dozen suites rather than hundreds, as few elves enjoyed living in Highcrowne unless they absolutely had to for sheer power and influence's sake.

Once inside the opulent suite with its velvet patterned wallpaper, delicate ceramics, silken drapes and gilt everything, Ernest bolted and barred the door behind us. He took a deep breath as if we'd just escaped shark-infested waters.

"So, everyone outside this chamber is the enemy?" I asked.

"Yes. They are all vying for the throne or serving the interim council members vying for the throne, or working on supporting and or betraying their allied Houses who are vying for the throne. It's chaos."

"Wonderful," Thane said.

Ernest was unperturbed at hearing Fharen's voice after six years. He turned and bowed, saying, "All here are your most loyal and vetted servants, my King."

He had not been surprised at all, because he'd known.

I looked around at the others lingering in the entry chamber. Some had been talking or sitting, but all stopped what they were doing and bowed or curtsied to

Thane. There was a woman in a champagne-colored gown who looked like a governess. She had that disapproving expression and erect bearing I remembered all too well from boarding school.

"She's for Dawn. Isn't she?" I said.

My gaze didn't linger long on the stern woman, younger than me but not as friendly. I searched every face. There was a Solhan, surprising, and he was wearing an embroidered Archonian jacket. A few petite elvish women in puffy dresses fluttered feathered fans while looking superior, draping themselves over a brawny wyvern hunter that reminded me of Hilja's sadist of an ex-fiancé. Perhaps he was a relative of Prince Gallan's?

No one was surprised to see Thane, which meant he had spoken to these people, come to them, before me. Why?

A man emerged from the drapery, silhouetted by sunlight, and I recognized him immediately, even though only his pale eyes were visible through the Djinn mask. The assassin who wanted to kill Calka—and who had thrown my pack of nibbles over the side of a mountain!

"You! What's going on here?" I asked, taking a hesitant step towards the door.

Ernest stood between me and it and whispered, "There is no escape this way, Eva."

When Aguragas strode into the chamber from an adjoining room, brazen as day, no shackles, cleanly dressed and well fed, all the hairs stood up along my arms and neck. This was a nest of vipers I'd somehow stepped into. Or shark-infested waters. Whatever my analogy had been, the danger was in here—not out there.

"What is going on?" I looked to Thane, willing my soul sense to return so I could speak to him silently, understand his plan. I didn't want to muck things up, but I was damn confused and in need of reassurance.

"You can drop the pretense among my allies, for they all know you are mine," he said, sounding very much like the narcissistic Fharen he was pretending to be. "You played your part well, Eva, placating my traitorous daughter, so she suspected nothing as we vanished for six years. I was free to raise the army that would enable me to not only reclaim the Elf Crown but also conquer the Three Kingdoms."

Ah, I got it. The idea was to use all these villains against all the other villains. "Yes. That was the plan. Well done us." Wait. What army?

"Our first order of business," Thane continued, "is to destroy this interim council before any of the cronies upon it turn over full control to one of the older Houses or, worse yet, implement a human system of voting. My grip must be inescapable. Jahl," he indicated the wyvern hunter, "you will work from within to weaken them, while my Darrubian dagger," he nodded to the Djinn, "assassinates all the House elders foolish enough to have come here in person. Slit their throats and leave the bodies to be discovered. Most importantly..." he turned to me "...we must protect my new heir."

He meant Dawn. Surely, he hadn't told these monsters about her?

He took my hands. "Eva."

"Yes?"

"Your power is not what it once was, else I would not have been able to step past your wards. You must convince my heir to come here. Uther will help you to protect her." He indicated the Solhan wearing ceremonial clothes reserved for shamans in the deep swamps of Archon. He had an aura of magic about him, not just the usual necromancy my people had an affinity for, but something more.

I bristled, angry Thane had revealed my weakness so publicly, especially with Gas there, but ... it was true. Dawn had to be protected.

"You're quiet, Gas," I said, staring daggers at him because he had not been given any other job than being the subject of my ire.

The Djinn too I despised. Why was Thane working with someone trying to kill Avians? Why hadn't he warned me about all of this ahead of time? Was he worried about far seers or other spies? I wished I could interrogate Thane, but it was impossible here and now.

"I owe my life to your Elf King." Aguragas bowed, holding his usual flirtatiousness towards me in check. "How does he wish to spend it?"

"You will stay hidden until I have need of you," Thane said, sounding exactly like Fharen, with the same annoyed, murderous tone in his voice.

"Yet, you want my people. They follow me, not you."

"They are meant to believe you are imprisoned and in need of rescue. They will shake down the walls of this palace to reach you now that they know you have not been executed and there is still time for them to rally their numbers—if you do not foolishly go to them looking as fine and healthy as you do now."

"You could have left him imprisoned," I said. "That would have been easier. Better if the beheading had happened. That would have riled them up plenty."

Why did Thane want Aguragas's followers enraged? They were terrorists, bombers, not good people to have running around Highcrowne. If he meant to shake the Elf Palace to its foundations, then there were less dangerous ways to do it. This way meant collateral damage. There had to be more to his plan.

"I love how you think, darling Eva," Thane said. "Alas, Aguragas has other uses beyond this distraction, and as satisfying as his death would be, we must delay such gratification."

Gas stiffened at the word delay. He didn't like it, but he knew this was only a stay of execution. He was likely thinking a chance to escape was all he needed, bargaining power, or maybe his followers would free him.

Thane said he needed a distraction, so the plan was probably to get the elves and Gas's followers fighting one another so we could do something unnoticed. The real Fharen would want all of Hilja's supporters and his enemies dead, so he could reclaim his crown, just as all the villains in this room had been told. Thane must want something else. Did he know how to stop the plant alien? Was one of the elvish Houses involved? Controlling it somehow? Is that why they had assassinated Hilja?

It was so hard to keep my questions and curiosity in check. I squirmed with them. I tried to make it look like I was twitchy and eager to strangle Aguragas with my own hands, which was also true, and so he kept a safe distance.

"You know what you must do," Thane said. "All of you. So be about it!"

There was more bowing and scraping as the vipers slithered away to do their dark work throughout the palace, leaving just me, Thane, Gas, and the Solhan, Uther. I wished Ernest had stayed behind, a semi-friendly face, but after he'd unbolted the door, he'd scurried away on some mysterious errand.

Thane had his back to the door, eyeing Aguragas distrustfully. "You have a private chamber. Do I need to show you the way again?"

Gas bristled at being openly dismissed. He took vengeance by casting a lascivious look my way and saying, "When you tire of this pompous buffoon, Eva, you know where to find me."

"Just make sure you're not wearing armor," I purred. "I'd like my knife to penetrate your heart with little effort."

Gas chuckled and strode off, as if being sent to his room had been his own idea.

Just Uther, me, and Thane now. Who was this Solhan in Archonian garb? I raised an eyebrow.

He was handsome, a hairsbreadth taller than me, with a strong jaw and sharp cheekbones, long black hair like a raven's wing, skin pale as mine and eyes nearly as white. There was a cream tinge to the irises that hinted at some impurity in his Solhan bloodline, but it was impossible to tell what. He wore linen, hot weather gear despite the cold in Highcrowne, only his wool jacket to keep him warm. It was embroidered in colorful threads, layer upon layer, so no pattern could be discerned—but there was a pattern, magic in every stitch, a reservoir of power to be harnessed by those who knew how. He was younger than me by at least a handful of years, but his presence was that of an old soul.

"Miss Thorne," Uther said, bowing graciously. "I have heard the stories, but I daresay none of them can be trusted."

"Let me guess. I'm not wearing a gown like in the tapestries? Or is it that I'm not dripping necromantic power from my hands anymore? I disappoint myself too these days."

"I am not disappointed at all. On the contrary. I sense much in your soul that your alluring visage conceals. Solhans know Solhans."

Once upon a time I would have been angry to be called one, to have the darkness inside me alluded to with such respect. I simply chose to ignore his 'compliment'.

"Your magic is decidedly un-Solhan," I noted. "There is the usual affinity for death, yes, but something else. What secrets have you learned in the swamps? What right have you to your Archonian embroidery?"

"Secrets are not secrets if spoken freely. If you regain your ability to pull such information from my squirming soul, then you are welcome to it."

Compliments and now derision. Or was that a challenge? Did he think I could regain my full power? I was trying. I had learned enough spells to satisfy Nanny, although I had not yet eclipsed Ulric as I once dreamed, let alone tasted the power the Dead God had once given me.

Perhaps I was being too greedy? I had other magics, as Uther had his shamanism. I did not think necromancy superior to other disciplines. Sometimes it was the unexpected combinations—cord magic with Darrubian runes or Lyssian sands—that made you more powerful than others expected.

"There it is again," Uther said. "A stirring in your soul. There is hope for you."

"Are you flirting with my bride?" Thane said.

Bride. Thane and I were not married in the mortal way. As the Dead God, I was his betrothed, but ... now there was Duane.

Uther frowned, sensing the tide of emotions that surged through me, and I summoned the knowledge needed to erect a soul shield. Nanny had taught it to me when I was a child. I had never needed it before—mostly because my uncle had kept my soul in a jar to protect me until I came of age—but now there was this prodding and uncouth Solhan forcing me to hide my private feelings.

"No," Uther said. "I would never dare, King Fharen. I am merely conversing in the manner of my people. Solhans are direct and unyielding, enjoying discussions of the inner world."

"The Chamber of Inner Seeing," I said, remembering what I had learned of Solheim and the decadent times when Solhans were lost in trances meant to connect them to the Dead God and the halls of death, spurning the real world until they awoke to find their empire gone. "It's easy to get lost there, Uther, so keep your eyes front, here in the real world."

"An apt reminder." He bowed in agreement. "Let us proceed with securing the heir."

I looked at Thane, willing him to send this one away too, so we could be alone. "While my wards are not perfect," I said, the Elf Palace, especially with Aguragas in residence and his maniacs set to attack, is even less secure. I won't put her in danger."

"I do not want you to bring her here." Thane took my hands, his eyes pleading. "Take her to the Avian sanctuary. I know Naren is there. With his power and Uther's, she will be safer than anywhere in the world."

"What about the Djinn? He likes killing Avians. How can you trust him?"

"He was tasked with killing Calka long ago, and he will never stop until that duty is fulfilled. Naren is not in his sights. He will not disturb you—especially as he already has much to do here in the palace." A nice way to describe a killing spree.

"Won't murdering the heads of the other Houses cause civil war? Turn them all against you?"

"Not if they believe Aguragas is responsible."

"Then humans will be blamed."

"They are already. Only when the Houses are powerless, and the Crown mine again, can I restore order to the Three Kingdoms."

It made sense. If you were Fharen. I could tell Thane was holding back, but he wasn't sending Uther away to tell me his secrets, which meant being alone would make no difference. Was it the Solhan he feared? If his magic was as powerful as he hinted, then perhaps there could be no secrets? I was suddenly glad to have erected my soul shield. I reinforced it.

"Alright," I said, playing along for now. "We'll go to Naren." That's where I wanted to be anyway. I wasn't bringing Dawn, though. I needed to find a way to ditch the Archonian before then.

"I will meet you in the Avian Sanctuary soon," Thane said. He kissed me, and I let him, but I didn't lean into it. I told myself it was because we had an audience, but it was more than that.

My heart belonged to Duane now. How quickly and utterly he had stolen it. I could not even pretend to claim it as my own anymore.

Uther opened the door for me, and I followed him. Once upon a time, two Solhans walking boldly through the corridors of power in Highcrowne would have been unthinkable. We were the hated, the despised, bringers of death. Nowadays our talents were better appreciated, feared, and so even without the seneschal as escort, we found the scurrying ants parting for us.

Distant screams told me the Djinn was already at work.

"What do you know about that assassin?" I asked Uther. "A Solhan pretending to be Darrubian', just as you're pretending to be Archonian. What is his name? Why would he aid Fharen?" Knowledge was power, so I might as well gain what I could. Let the interrogation begin.

"His name is Daschal Ib Khalem. I call him Dasch because, well, I can. Few would risk his ire, but what have Solhans like us to fear, eh? And he is not playing at Darrubian any more than I am playing at being Archonian. He was raised in Darrub, a Solhan refugee just like you and me, doing what must be done to thrive in a foreign land. He was talented at death, no surprise, but lucky enough to gain the attention of a formidable trainer. It has ensured his livelihood—and the loss of many others' lives—to grow his gold and reputation."

Reminded me of my uncle: willing to cause immeasurable suffering as long as his own hide was protected and his own coffers lined. At least how my uncle used to be. He had changed. I didn't think the Djinn was going to turn priest any time soon, but it made him easier to predict. He was just another ruthless Solhan with a knack for evil.

Uther was the difficult one to analyze. He exuded both power and integrity, and I found it hard to believe both could be contained inside one Solhan.

"You assume a familiarity with me that is one sided," I told him. "I do not know why you serve Fharen either, nor your full name, nor why you think I would trust you when every Solhan I have ever known, even blood kin, are the most untrustworthy of all. Goblins and trolls are more reliable."

"Ah yes, the dangers of reading souls. I feel I know you even better than you know yourself, Eva. I apologize." He stopped in the middle of a long hallway, forcing those hurrying around us to quickly adjust their trajectories, and bowed. "I am Uther Thorne."

I went cold. "Thorne? That's impossible." Everyone with that name was dead except Ulric, Vikky, Ilsa and me. Not even Dawn could claim it, for Solhans were patriarchal in that way.

"A distant relation, I assure you, spared the Fall of Solheim simply because I was born after. My father was your father's third cousin. He died a few years after the Fall, leaving my mother to raise me in Archon where she and her sisters fled. I am not of the lineage of the Keeper, with no claim to great power like your family. I know of them from my mother and my studies, but you are the first true Thorne I have ever met."

I was aware of the crowd around us and the hidden passages for spies and suddenly felt too exposed. "Let's keep walking."

Only when we were outside and crossing the noxious rose gardens—which I always ended up spending too much time in thanks to Gypsum and Hilja both reassuring me they were the most secluded and least monitored area of the Central City, a favorite spot for all clandestine meetings and rigorously protected from scrying, far seeing and other means of espionage by all the disparate factions wanting a secure spot for plotting—did I ask my next question.

"Does Fharen have Thorne blood as well? Is that why you follow him?" I'd always known Fharen was part Solhan, but I feared hearing he was a distant relation, like Uther.

It was Thane who I had been in love with. I had never thought about what it meant to have a child with Fharen's body. Solhans had grown few in number over the centuries, so inbreeding was inevitable.

"His grandfather was your grandfather's second cousin, so also not of the line of the Keeper, but yes—a Thorne too. Genealogy has always been of interest to me."

Just as I feared. Second cousin twice removed or whatever wasn't awful, but it wasn't great either.

Perhaps it had something to do with why Fharen (when he had been the evil Elf King and not possessed by Thane) had wanted to marry Ilsa? Two lineages of Thorne converging must mean something. I wanted to ask Uther but didn't know if I could trust his answer. Would he tell me the truth? And why had Ilsa wanted Dawn as her heir so badly?

"I am not reading your soul," Uther said, raising his hands in surrender, "but I cannot help reading your expression. Yes, there is a concentration of power whenever bloodlines converge again. Fharen's line is far weaker than the Keeper's, but any Thorne is more accomplished at necromancy and other magical disciplines than most Solhans."

"And Solhans put humans to shame," I pointed out.

"Do humans even have magic?" Uther wondered.

"Their warlocks held off the Dead God for years, remember?"

"Oh, yes. The details of the war did not reach us in Archon. The swamps are a deadly world unto their own that few, even Risen, seek to enter."

"I spent some time there, so I know why. Everything is trying to kill you, and even the ground will swallow you whole."

"There are endless treasures to be found in bogs because of it. That's how I spent my childhood, mud-diving," Uther said, smiling. "Surviving years as an outsider not born there is a great achievement. For me and for you. That is why you recognized my vestments."

"Archonian shamans are secretive and just as deadly as their surroundings. How did you convince one to teach you?"

"I had talent, and an irresistible smile," which he demonstrated, "as well as many magical artifacts from my bog discoveries with which to barter with."

"Bribery. Of course. That makes sense." I did not think his smile, as charming as it was, would have sufficed.

Bribery had been what I'd used to get the knowledge I'd been seeking when I was there. And power. Thornes of the Keeper's lineage were at their most powerful when they wielded what the Keeper had been groomed to protect—the First Soul. Its power had been mine and Dawn's for a time. No other Thornes alive could claim as much.

"You do know that the First Soul is gone and never coming back?" I said.

Thane had come back, and I really needed to know how and what had happened, but I could sense the First Soul was not with him. It was gone, if not destroyed, or at least so far away I could no longer detect its compelling darkness.

"I do not seek its power, I swear. It destroyed our people. Solhans need to find a better way."

"That I can agree with. Only, I don't think about Solhans but all of Highcrowne and the Three Kingdoms. This is my home. Not Solheim."

"Solheim is not my home either. Although, I have not yet discovered what attracts you to Highcrowne. It is cold, crowded, and as deadly as Archon in its own way."

"You still haven't told me what brought you here. Why brave the cold? What do you want with Fharen and me?"

"There is no distracting you from your curiosity, is there? Very well. Fharen obtained the seed for the Verang, the plant he used to create his army of abominations during the war, from Archon. He got it from me."

I instinctively put my hand on my Ashur. This was the man to blame for the plant alien and everything happening, all the minds stolen and puppeted?

He went wide-eyed with fear. "No, please. It was not my fault. I merely found the dormant seed in the bogs. My shaman master helped me study it, but I sensed the danger of it from the outset. I would never have unleashed it. Fharen's mages somehow sensed its power as soon as I unearthed it. He came with an army of them and stole it from me. I begged for him to see reason, how unwise it would be to awaken this ancient evil, but he was too frightened of the Dead God. He would take any risk to ensure even a small hope of victory."

"If he stole it from you, why are you helping him now?"

"He has vowed to make amends. He needs my help to cage it again. I know more about the Verang than anyone, and I'm here to stop it."

Maybe Uther was just the person I needed also. Trust Thane to have a plan.

"I'm glad to hear it," I said, removing my hand from my sword hilt. "We're not going to get Dawn."

"Don't you want my help protecting her?"

"Perhaps. But the best way to protect her is to eliminate the real threat to her and everyone. I want to show you something I found in the sewers."

No one, not even bog-diving shamans, looked pleased when you mentioned sewers. Uther was even less pleased when he climbed into one. Bogs smelled sulfurous and rotten, but there was a distinctive scent from fresh feces that only a Highcrowne sewer experiencing the first thaw of spring could provide. He looked ready to cry as he squeezed his nose shut and gagged, soon realizing he needed to seal his mouth too. That left no way to breathe without gasping for air when needed. I gave him a kerchief sprinkled with lavender oil, a trick picked up from pet detective work and communing with informants in stinking alleys. I'd made sure I acquired fresh supplies on my way through the city that morning and was glad of it.

I showed Uther the pulsing growths on the damp walls, crawling over sewer clumps of mushrooms and piles of offal. There was a goblin in one corner, watching us, and from the look on its face I knew the plant controlled it. A sentry. The goblin didn't run calling for help, for the plant communicated silently.

"We can't stay here for long. We'll be surrounded," I warned. "Is this the Verang? Do you know how to stop its spread?"

"How far do these sewers run?" he asked.

"Everywhere in Highcrowne."

"This is not good."

"Tell me something I don't know. Is there anything I can do to stop it?"

"You must find the over mind. The first growth from the seed. These are but tendrils, like the hairs growing from your head or the tips of your fingernails. Cut them off and more will grow. You must take out the center of it all."

That was already my plan, and I knew where it was—Faellion.

"How though?" I was told the Celon was needed, but I didn't want to reveal I knew that much.

"Fire. Lots of it. An inferno. Maybe an army of mages could manage it."

Or the Celon ignited. It was very explosive stuff.

"Good. It can be killed. That's all I needed to know."

"I think so. I can't guarantee it. I tried burning it before Fharen came, but the seed was impervious. The fire did push back all the tendrils that had begun to grow from it when I was studying it. It made it dormant at least. Until Fharen set it loose in the valley near the wall."

"Dormant is not as good as dead."

"That's all I know."

I didn't believe him. He wouldn't have come all the way from Archon just to tell Fharen to burn it. There was something more going on, but this was not the place to uncover it. Shadows moved in the corners.

"Up. Now," I said, not waiting for him but tearing up the ladder towards the surface.

Doctor Ghunnan was up there waiting for me. He held up his hands placatingly. "Don't run, Eva. Let me explain."

"Is the plant controlling you?"

"It's talking to me."

"Same thing. Move out of my way." I drew my sword.

"It wants to help us, all of us," he said. "It is a vast mind with eons of knowledge we can access, centuries of wisdom. It once knew only conquest because it devoured conquerors, but it has been feeding on something else, and it has a new goal. Just listen to me."

Uther climbed up beside me and reached into his pockets, pulling out a metal figurine on a braided, multicolored cord. It looked like the figure of a person, their arms spread wide, wrists and feet tied by the cord. He held it before him, and the metal glowed green with Solhan necromancy.

"Release him," Uther commanded. "Release…."

Doctor Ghunnan screamed and clutched his head as if suffering the worst migraine ever. He took off running. More possessed goblins had been climbing out of the sewer behind us, but they shut the stone cover and hid from us instead. The side street was quiet as a ghost town, which was an oddity in Highcrowne. How many people were possessed if banishing them made the day so desolate? Things were worse than I thought.

"That's a handy trick," I said. "Can you teach it to me?"

"It's no trick but a rare artifact of the ancient Solhan empire. I have only the one, and its effects are temporary."

"Eva!" A grating, snooty, all too familiar voice called, and I saw Katherine's dark red hair flying as she ran down the street towards me. "There you are."

Part of me had hoped she was possessed by the plant as well, which would explain her generally odd behavior, but she wasn't, which meant there was no changing her unyielding insistence that I fulfill my civic duty as an electoral candidate.

"Why, when everyone else is running away from this spot would you run toward it?" I asked her.

She gasped for breath, not being in good shape from spending most of her time in a laboratory, and finally said, "Because if people are running, then you are sure to be at the center of whatever evil or malignant event is behind it. What happened? What did I miss?"

"It wasn't me this time. Uther here has an artifact that repels people possessed by the plant alien."

"Marvelous! Can I study the artifact?" She held out her hand, and Uther clutched his necklace protectively, taking a step back. He was good at soul reading, so he knew he would have to fight hard to keep it from Katherine's rampant scientific curiosity.

"Aren't you concerned that it affected everyone on this block?" I asked her.

"More than this block. I was at least three blocks away when people turned and ran. I really must study that object. I insist."

Uther stepped further back, and I saw him feeling for a dagger on his belt. Best I intercede before there was bloodshed. Only a more intriguing problem would deter Katherine.

"Doctor Ghunnan said he was communing with the plant and that it wanted to help us," I told her.

"Nonsense. Oh, I do believe my former thesis advisor is possessed, but why would the creature want to help us? Don't fall for its ploys and seductions."

"Seductions?" Odd term for her to use.

Katherine blushed. "Well, I was investigating a victim—chosen on purely clinical criteria not because he is the most accomplished player in the theater with a divine visage and the voice of an angel who has never failed to pour his heart into every line uttered and never falters no matter how many times I have seen his performance—a victim who was quite convincing and sincere in a similar protest of innocent intent. He was far more charming than Doctor Ghunnan, and if I resisted so can you. I do know how you have a weakness for him."

"What? For the goblin doctor?"

"Yes. You do flirt mercilessly."

I had no idea what she was talking about. I was a flirt as my default setting, but him? I wasn't even revolted, just perplexed that anyone could even imagine it. What a sick, twisted mind could even conceive of it? "Are you sure you're alright, Katherine. Perhaps the plant alien did try to take you over and some abnormality in your brain structure perhaps granted you resistance?"

"What an interesting hypothesis. I daresay you could have been a scientist, Miss Thorne. I suppose detective work and experimentation are quite similar endeavors."

"As oddly entertaining as your conversation is," Uther said. "I have work to do. We should at least check on the heir."

The heir. He meant Dawn. Maybe I did put too much faith in Nanny and my wards—which Thane had pointed out were failing.

"Yes," I said. "Let's go to my house now while the path is clear."

Katherine shadowed us, prattling along about how there were more elves on the streets than humans today, and how odd that was when you were aware of the disparity between reproductive rates, with humans out breeding them ten to one. I often ignored her, but when I spotted a marching squad of elves I suddenly took interest.

"Were the elves you saw earlier all in armor?" I asked her.

"Yes."

"Let's see where they're going." It was on the way anyway, so I followed the squad, relieved when they turned away from my house. The bazaar was as busy as ever, so Uther's repulsion spell had not spread this far. The elven soldiers turned toward the commons, and I saw that was where most of the plant-affected people had fled. Doctor Ghunnan among them.

The stage where I'd held my debate against a no-show Duane was covered in electoral posters with all the candidates. Th elves marched up and began tearing them down, snapping sign posts over armored greaves. There were grumbles from the crowd, but Katherine took real offense and climbed up on stage among them.

"What is going on here?" she shouted. "What right have you to interfere in free, human elections?"

"The right of the interim council," an officer among the elves said. She unrolled a parchment with lots of elvish writing in fresh ink with red wax seals holding loops of silken ribbon. "Democracy is a crime against the Crowns, punishable by death. These proceedings are disbanded, and anyone found participating will be briefly imprisoned, tried, and executed by hanging from the clock tower. Are you participating?"

"No, she is not." I dragged Katherine away by the arm, using my shoulder to hide my face as I didn't want the officer to recognize me. My picture was on half of the posters around us, and being a candidate would certainly qualify as participating.

"You can't do this! We have rights!" Katherine said, foolishly wanting to fight for democracy within a millennia-old monarchy.

"Not here. Not now." I told her. She opened her mouth, and I planted my hand over it and dragged her away. She was heavier than me but not as determined, so I succeeded in saving her life.

Uther was long gone, a smart Solhan, but I had questions for him.

12 DOWNTRODDEN

It was chaos on the streets as EEPs and elvish soldiers cracked down. I didn't see any human or dwarven guards, and I wondered if the first prong of the interim council's attack had been to lock them in their barracks. Unless they were werewolves. There would be no keeping an angry, hairy dwarf down for long.

"They're tearing up our posters! You know how much those cost to print?" Katherine was furious.

"I thought we got them for free?"

"A huge discount."

"Did you pay for them?" I felt a gush of warmth for her. I had no idea she personally believed in me so much, and that feeling was quickly replaced by guilt, knowing what a disappointment I was. Then she took all my guilt away.

"No, of course not. I've collected donations from every merchant wanting your ear or demanding their issues be addressed first by our policies. That's how the system works."

"It doesn't work, and it's not a system; it's an illegal activity, until we can gather the Assembly and get King Harley and General Moore to officially countermand the interim council."

Which I would do as soon as I dealt with more pressing concerns, namely the fascist elves arresting protestors and steadily headed towards my house.

The EEPs were making a frontal assault through the bazaar, pulling screaming, finger pointing merchants aside and asking for their papers. Since no one had needed any before, they were slammed against a wall and shackled. It reminded me of the slave quarter, as people were chained together and herded with batons and boots towards the killing field.

I really hoped that term wasn't to be literal today. The cleared ground between the outer defenses and the newer Outskirts wall was supposed to be free of structures to provide a clear line of sight for archers during war time, or who might need to defend against surprise attacks and buy time for the gates to be sealed. A clear killing field. As I climbed stairs to get around the bazaar and approach my house unobserved from the side alley, I glimpsed the field and saw it was now fenced in quadrants with barbed wire, each segment being filled with prisoners from all over the city.

"This reminds me of the war," Katherine said, her usual chipper tone suddenly haunted. "It was dwarves being caged then, and I took it as a sign humans would soon follow, which is why I went into the caverns with the resistance."

I hadn't known Katherine had been in Highcrowne for that. I supposed it had been the safest place, scarily, with Lili of Solheim's armies marching through the Three Kingdoms.

"Well, they learned humans are the real concern and started with you first this time. Why aren't people fighting back?"

An explosion took out one of the guard towers nearest the killing field, and I knew they were. EEPs peeled off to investigate, and a ragged group of humans hurried in to cut the wire fences and direct the prisoners down the hill to the docks where merchant ships were drifting dangerously close together as each vied to be first out of the harbor.

Explosions like that always made me think of Bell and Aguragas's other followers. I suddenly stopped hating Bell a little less as relief flooded me that someone was doing something.

Time for me to do something. But first, I had to make sure Dawn was safe.

"I'm going to help." Katherine pulled out of my grip and ran toward the killing field without a backward glance.

Once, I would have done the same, but there were lives more precious to me than others' now. It was very undemocratic, I knew, but my heart was ruled by a select few.

I was in the alley behind my house, and all sympathy I felt for Bell and her crew vanished when another explosion nearby sent shingles flying off my roof, cinders setting it ablaze, and smoke began billowing. My wards should douse the fire, but they weren't working. The flames grew taller, the smoke blacker, and it began to pour from the upper story. From Dawn's room.

I ran full tilt and pulled the back door open screaming, "Dawn! Nanny!"

"Yes?" Dawn said. She and Nanny walked, unhurried, from the front parlor, not aware of the conflagration above their heads. "Is this about the soldiers on the street? Surely, they can't come in?"

"We have to go, now." I took Dawn in my arms, swooping her off her feet with a startled cry. She might act and sound like an ancient queen, but she was still a seven-year-old in the body, so she couldn't stop me. I pushed Nanny ahead of me. "Go."

Out in the alley, Nanny marveled at the smoke. "How strange," she observed, still calm.

"I am the candidate in an illegal election," I explained, trying to shake her stoicism, "which is punishable by death, and the only people defending us are terrorists, so this is not a safe place to linger."

"Your wards...?" Nanny began.

"Are failing. I'm failing."

Our only choice was Naren and Avian magic for protection, but how could we get there with elves everywhere and plant-possessed goblins lurking in the sewers?

Goblins. No one noticed them.

I carried Dawn kicking and complaining to one of the muck raking machines in the next alley over. It stunk, which made it easy to find. The goblin running it was on break, leaning against a wall and puffing a pipe, so he reacted too late when I tossed Dawn inside and hopped into the driver's seat, my knees jammed to my chin.

Nanny ran behind as we took off down the street. "Where are you going?"

"Crap." I stopped. The machine was too small for all of us. "Hop on top and try to blend in."

"I shall not. This is ridiculous. Where are you going?" Nanny insisted.

"The Avian sanctuary."

"I will check on Viktor and meet you there."

"It's too risky," I argued, but Nanny ignored me and strode away, the angry goblin, along with chittering rats and bogles disturbed by her passing, all cowering when the shadow of her sent a chill to their bones. Her dangerous aura of necromancy was more effective than mine these days.

"I want to go with her," Dawn said.

"No. You are not leaving my side."

Dawn couldn't get out without climbing past me, and I was stuck as tight as a hermit crab in its shell.

"Why didn't we take the sewers?" Dawn asked. "This muck raker smells as bad."

"The sewers are infested with that plant creature controlling everyone."

"Then why don't we fly to the Sanctuary in a balloon or something?"

"I don't have one of those."

"Doctor Ghunnan does and so does Mister Rose."

"The good Doctor is infected by the plant I just mentioned, and Duane's balloons are too big for any one person to handle, besides he's already at the Sanctuary waiting for me."

"Then why doesn't he send Naren to fly down here and fetch us?"

"Because Naren is a recluse and hates people...."

There was an endless torrent of "but why" questions the whole way, which made the bumpy, stinking, uncomfortable ride all the worse. At least the shouting protesters, angry rioters, and jackbooted squads of elvish soldiers all ignored us as we puttered our way up the tiered Highcrowne streets, all the way to the top.

In the Central City, the coal powering the steam engine of the muck raker ran out, and I was forced to abandon it. Dawn was relieved to be free. She gaped at the manicured landscapes and glimmering palaces all around.

"This is the Central City? It's so much larger than I thought from the pictures. Can I see Hilja's palace?"

"Definitely not."

It was strangely quiet. Probably because no one was home, all the elves off messing with humans. I almost made for Harley's palace to see what the Dwarf King could do, but Dawn's safety came first.

She tried to dodge and go exploring on her own, but I hoisted her over my shoulder and carried her, protesting the whole way to the garden shed. I stopped for breath and a stretch, and that's when Uther found us.

"You and the heir are safe. Good," he said.

"No thanks to you. I thought Tha—I mean Fharen said you were a fantastic protector."

"I am. I repelled the arresting forces, giving you and the child time to escape. I also kept the way here clear of soldiers for you, as I followed behind on foot. The miasma of fear I created surrounds us even now. No one will come within sight or sound of us."

"Oh. I thought it was strangely quiet."

"Who is this ... man?" Dawn asked, her tiny face screwed up suspiciously "You told me never to trust Solhans."

"I don't trust him. No offense, Uther."

"Perfectly understandable. I am delighted to meet you, Miss Dawn."

"It's just Dawn. Why are you helping us? What do you get out of it?"

"Your father has promised to help me in exchange."

"I don't believe that. Why—"

"—Dawn," I interrupted, "can you please stop asking questions for two seconds, so we can get to safety?"

"I don't understand how you've survived this long, Mother, without asking questions."

"If I spent all day asking questions, Daughter, I'd never get anything done."

"How do you know what to do, if you don't know what's going on?"

"Knowing what's going on just gets in the way of doing. I figure it all out in the end."

She groaned, and I took that as a minor victory.

"So, this is the way to the Avian Sanctuary?" Uther gazed at the sheer rock face stretching hundreds of feet above us.

"Yes, but you're not coming. Naren is touchy to say the least. It's bad enough I need to ask him to watch out for Dawn—another new face won't sit well with him. He likes things traditional and predictable."

Uther looked set to argue, but he wisely closed his mouth before words came out. He nodded.

"Naren is the villain who stole Calka's baby, Princess Glau," Dawn said. "You can't trust him either."

"I don't have a choice. My wards failed. The city is at war with itself—again—and the only other person I trust is up there with Naren right now."

"You mean Mister Rose?" Dawn probed. "You trust him now? Why?"

I tried not to blush. "Just do as your mother says. Come on." There was no time to attempt to fulfill her insatiable curiosity.

I took her hand and headed for the illusion concealing the stone stairs. I always carried Calka's feather in my belt pouch, and I'd learned I didn't need to activate it to pass through the protections.

To Dawn's credit, she didn't flinch as we stepped through. She stopped fighting me, which was a relief, as there was no way I could have carried her up all those narrow steps. She went ahead of me, curious to see this place for the first time. I'd told her plenty of stories, most of her life was stories, rarely did I ever allow her out. This must be a longed-for adventure, which is the only reason she argued so little. While I had not been foolish enough to teach her swordplay yet, I knew there was no beating her in a verbal sparring match.

I kept an eye on our rear, certain Uther would disobey me and follow, but there was no sign of him. I didn't trust Solhans, especially such a seemingly helpful and trustworthy specimen. There was no such thing.

Dawn marveled at the ancient Solhan-Avian script on the door. I pressed the glyphs in the correct order to open it, and I knew she watched and memorized it. She always seemed to be assessing and memorizing everything around her.

She was less impressed when she found we'd emerged inside a prison.

"This is so like you, mother." She shook the bars, frustrated.

"You really need to respect your elders more. Or at least fear them." When I was her age, I'd feared and respected Nanny and Ulric both. She was too young to be a teenager.

I moved some of the ancient furniture aside and levered up a stone block. Underneath was the key I'd hidden last time I visited. I'd used wax to make a mold of the lock, created the key, and hid it for times like this when I wanted entry without permission. There was a satisfying click when the new key worked in the old mechanism. I put the key back and then led her out onto the fractured mountain top.

Once, The Avian Sanctuary had been a plateau in the clouds, dotted with ancient buildings abandoned over the eons as immortal Avians slowly died of attrition. Aguragas's attack months before had destroyed everything except for a few doorways set into the mountain, like the one we emerged from. Calka's throne room was gone, the obelisks shattered, fragments tumbled among other rubble and debris.

"I didn't picture this," Dawn said.

"Neither did I. I never imagined all-powerful Avians were as vulnerable and powerless as the rest of us in their way. Ulric would have said their kindness was their weakness, while I believe it was human evil. I don't blame the victim. This is why you never trust Gas or Bell or any of those Upside Down Party people, no matter how convincing their lies and rhetoric."

Dawn rolled her eyes. "I've heard that warning enough times, mother. So, where is this mysterious person you trust so much?"

A secret to unravel was the only thing that kept her attention for long. "With Naren, I suspect. Trying reason with a non-human whose brain is entirely different from ours—and an insane variant according even to his own species. I didn't have much faith it would work out, but I always have hope."

I opened the protected chamber of Celon, the stone disk rolling aside with a loud rumble. No sneaking up now. I stepped into the cave, which was aglow with green magic from the pools of goo all around, and Dawn gasped with surprise. It might have been the ancient chamber with its strange magic, the fluffy Avian perched atop a stone in the center of it all, looking regal and alien ... or Duane chained to the stone like some god being punished. He was naked to the waist, bronze muscles straining and covered with sweat as he tried to pull free, green goo up to his knees and rising, as he slowly sank into it like quicksand.

I covered Dawn's eyes. Duane looked far too sexy. I knew he was in some sort of danger, but my quickened pulse and flushed cheeks told another story.

"Wait outside, sweetheart," I told her, as I ushered her out.

Naren hadn't stirred, but Duane said, "Eva," with a breath of relief.

"I won't say I told you so..." I began, clearing my throat as the sight of him made it hard to speak "...because I never pictured this. I thought Naren would tell you to get lost."

"He wants to 'educate' me," Duane explained.

"By drowning you in goo?"

"Celon will help him to understand," Naren said. "Purify his confusion. Set him free."

"Death is a kind of freedom, but not what either of us have in mind."

I edged forward, casting about for a tool I could use. There was nothing in the chamber. I didn't want to break my Ashur by trying to pry the loops of metal loose from the stone. There would be no cleaving chains—they were too thick for that—and besides a stray spark among all this volatile goo could be explosive.

"Celon will transform him, not kill him," Naren assured me.

"People all over Highcrowne are being transformed, possessed by the plant alien," I told him. "We need the Celon to help defeat it. And right now, we could use your help to stop the elven interim council. They've clamped down on the city, imprisoning humans, declaring democracy illegal. Dwarves will be next, but they will fight even harder. Already, there is fighting and explosions. We need you, Naren. Help us."

"No," Naren said, matter of fact. "I never cared to aid the short-lived beings here. I was prepared to while away the centuries until you killed each other and stopped causing so much noise. I am still prepared to do that. I cannot abide this one, who my beloved Calka trusted, skulking in here to steal from me."

"I came to reason with you," Duane said.

"You came to steal Celon!" Naren stood, stretching out his gray wings aggressively and opening his sharp, orange beak. "I saw. The vision showed me. No one will take Celon. No one." His gaze bore into mine.

I raised my hands. "Calm down. You know us. What is this vision?" I recalled my one and only taste of the green goo had given me very disturbing hallucinations, and I could imagine something similar making Naren paranoid for sure. He could kill all of us. As gorgeous as Duane looked tied up, I had to get him free and deescalate the situation fast.

"Celon gone. My life's work stolen. You were there, and you, and you ...." He pointed somewhere behind me.

"Dawn..." I said, knowing she could never stay out of trouble, but when I turned back it wasn't her butting in, it was Uther.

"How did you get in here?"

He gave me a look that said he was a powerful Archonian shaman as well as a Solhan necromancer, so why wouldn't he be able to get through all the Avian protections?

"Right. You're making things worse, so get out of here."

"It looks like you could use my help." He held out his hand, a few brown seeds nestled in his palm, and then closed his fist. I heard the seeds crack, and Duane's chains broke at the same time.

Duane was a survivor and didn't hesitate to scramble out of the pit that had been slowly sucking him in. He ran for the doorway, pulling me and Dawn along with him. "Naren is not in a reasonable mood."

Out on the plateau he shivered, and I gave him my jacket. Not because I hated looking at his bare chest, quite the opposite, but for Dawn and decency's sake. I was becoming such an overprotective mother. What was wrong with me?

"Who was that Solhan?" Dawn asked me. Uther was still inside, likely having never seen an Avian before and satisfying some deep curiosity despite the risk of death. Solhans could take care of themselves, so it never occurred to me to try and save him. "Someone who won't be around long if he keeps being stupid and confronting angry Avians."

"Can I see the Avian too?"

"No," Duane and I both said at the same time.

I smiled. "I'm glad you're smart enough to run," I told Duane.

"You don't think I'm a coward? I feel like a coward. Maybe you prefer a foolhardy Solhan like this Uther?"

"Is that a note of jealousy?"

"I should go back...."

I pulled him to me. "No. We need the Celon, but we can't take it without the power Calka gave us. You have her bracelet?"

"No. I left it in the shrine of the Devourer, where it's protected. I thought I could convince Naren."

"You managed to go into the shrine?" I was really impressed this time. He was no coward. The altar to the Devourer frightened even me.

"I can't take Calka's power. We'll find a way without it. Who is Uther and why is he still in there?"

"I don't know. I..." There was too much I had to tell Duane that I didn't want to. Like Thane being back. Like how Uther was responsible for the plant alien. I didn't want hard right now, so I skipped to the easy bits. "I do know why we need the Celon. If we go to Faellion, to the source of the Growing, the Verang, whatever the plant is called, and burn it—then we'll stop all the tendrils here in Highcrowne too. We'll free everyone from its influence. I think it's affected the elven interim council. That's why they and the EEPs are rounding up everyone in the killing field."

"Killing field? What?"

"You've missed a lot this morning."

"I usually know everything before anyone else. I don't like this."

"Then you'll like this even less." That was Thane's voice.

I froze, my hairs standing on end as Thane emerged from the mist on the plateau, his villainous hangers on, the elf and the Darrubian, arrayed behind him. Aguragas was with him, and just as he appeared, a fireball explosion arose from the palaces below.

"That's my people," Gas said, smiling. "I should return and allow them to rescue me."

"I think not," Thane said.

The Gallan lookalike elf, Jahl, had Gas by the arm, so he was a prisoner and obviously not free to go back and be rescued.

Another explosion reverberated through the stones, another fireball on the horizon, and Thane smiled like I had never seen him smile before—it was like a cat enjoying the suffering of prey.

"That would be the elven interim council, huddled together in their chambers behind ensorcelled protections and bodyguards, fleeing my assassins, too stupid to realize there is no hiding from humans and their destructive creations. Now, no one stands between me and the bloody throne that is rightfully mine."

"Fharen?" Duane said, his eyes narrowed.

"No, it's..." I was about to say 'Thane', but Duane was right.

I suddenly realized what the 'discrepancy' had been when I first held him. No scent of cinnamon.

"You are Fharen," I said. "Not Thane at all."

"Took you long enough. You are definitely not as smart as your sister, nor as pretty."

"How did you get past my wards then?" I took Dawn by the arm and pulled her closer to me, despite her protestations.

"I didn't. I am the master of glamours, my dear. You see what I want you to see. You thought I was in the house, when I was not. You thought the house was aflame when it was not, but you pulled my child from your protections and brought her here. To me."

"She's not your child."

"In all the ways that matter. She is my heir. Come to me, Dawn."

"I knew he wasn't my father." Dawn gave me her most disappointed look.

I should have trusted my instincts or listened to her. I should have done a lot of things. As it was, I was slowly being surrounded by Fharen and his pet monsters. The Gallan lookalike drew his sword, while the Djinn strode boldly forward, reaching for Dawn.

Duane stepped in front of him. "It's time we finally met. You killed Calka's mate, Saral. You killed Hilja. Now I will kill you."

I wanted to point out to Duane that he was unarmed and exhausted from trying not to drown in green goo, that he was going to get himself killed, but I also knew anything I said wouldn't matter. He was as foolishly stubborn as me.

Fortunately, Uther offered a distraction as he came running out and shouting. "Naren will destroy Celon before anyone can have it. We have to do something. King Fharen!" He froze, stunned by the tableau he'd run headlong into.

Duane and the Djinn still stared into one another's eyes, muscles slowly clenching, as each readied to strike, but Fharen did not like the message Uther had brought.

"Stay here with Eva and Dawn," he told Uther. "Protect them. You." He slapped the Djinn on the shoulder, the Darrubian not flinching but shifting his gaze just enough to convey his distaste at being treated so disrespectfully. "Get in there and stop that insane Avian."

"Stay away from Naren!" Duane lunged forward, grabbing one of the Djinn's swords, but the master assassin pinned Duane's arm and swung around, delivering a vicious blow to his face and nearly breaking the trapped arm. Duane dropped, turning jelly-like and slipped the hold. On the ground, he donkey-kicked the Djinn in a knee, bringing him down too.

Jahl put the point of his sword against the Djinn's back. "Our king gave you an order. Come on."

The Darrubian narrowed his eyes, disarmed the uppity elf, and stuck the sword in the ground a hairsbreadth from Duane's nose. "Another time, my friend."

Just as Duane rose, about to follow, Uther pulled a wad of dried leaves from his belt pouch and blew them in Duane's face. I caught a whiff and sneezed, Dawn too, and suddenly all three of us were doubled over in pain. My stomach was wracked with cramps.

"I told you to protect them," Fharen said.

"I am protecting them from doing anything foolish," Uther said. "They need you in there, my king. Naren has protections against Solhan magic that I can't break. Your persuasive abilities, your glamours, are needed before it's too late."

Was Naren planning on igniting the Celon and blowing the rest of the mountain up with us all on it? That sounded just like him. Fharen was damn persuasive, a good liar, but I wasn't sure even he could dissuade such an insane Avian.

"I can talk to him, to Naren," I said.

"You did not do so well a moment ago," Uther pointed out. "Stay here, Eva. For Dawn's sake."

I hated it when people pulled the Dawn card, but I was in so much pain I couldn't do anything but clutch my gut.

Dawn whimpered in agony, "Mommy." And I couldn't imagine leaving her anyway. I held her, wishing I hadn't brought her here, wanting more than anything to keep her safe.

Satisfied that we were helpless, Fharen joined his two goons, still dragging Aguragas, inside with Naren.

"Uther," I gasped, now that we were alone. "Why are you doing this? You said you wanted to right the wrongs you had done."

"He lied to you just as Fharen did," Duane said through clenched teeth.

"No. I didn't." Uther crushed and blew more leaves our way, and the pain stopped. "I want to help you, and soon they will realize Naren is doing nothing except barricading himself inside as I told him to do. You three need to get out of here, now. I'll say you knocked me out."

"Or I can just knock you out to be safe," Duane said stepping forward menacingly.

"Arrr!" A shout jerked all our necks around, and we saw an out-of-control balloon headed our way.

Unlike dirigibles with proper steering controls, the mini rocket balloons Doctor Ghunnan had invented were like projectiles zipping about crazily. This one was being steered by Katherine the Campaign Manager and Seneschal Ernest of all people.

"What are you doing here?" I ducked as an anchor nearly took my head off before catching on a nearby rock.

"Rescuing you!" Katherine shouted. "Get in."

Ernest tossed a rope ladder over the side. I wasted no time in pushing Dawn toward it.

"I should help Naren," Duane said.

"No, you shouldn't. He tried to kill you. We need to get Calka's bracelet and then come back and force him to help us. If Fharen hasn't killed him first."

"He won't," Uther cut in. "I've made sure of it. He knows Naren is indispensable for the next phase of his plan."

"And what's that?" I asked.

"Siezing the source of the Avian's magic. What else? He wants absolute control of Highcrowne and the Three Kingdoms. Get out of here and gather your allies. You must stop him."

This was pretty much all of my allies, but I didn't say that. It sounded pathetic. I'd have more if I could defeat the plant alien, but I needed the goo for that. It was kind of a chicken and egg situation. Still, living to fight another day was always a good plan. Calka's bracelet was step one. I had to stay focused.

"Duane. Let's go. Please."

The please got to him. He nodded and shimmied up ahead of me.

"Thank you," I told Uther. "Should I punch you in the jaw or something to make it look good?"

"I can throw a bomb on him," Katherine said, brandishing a bullet shaped one with fins above our heads.

"No!" I shouted.

"I'll be fine. Go." Uther took off after Fharen.

Ernest didn't have to be told twice. He had pulled up the anchor before I was halfway up the ladder. The last few feet were hard with the balloon swaying everywhere, jets firing erratically.

"We need to get to the slave district," I told Katherine.

I froze, seeing Doctor Ghunnan there. He'd been too short to spot from below. He looked to be dancing as he stoked the coals that heated the balloon's air, pumping the bellows with one mechanical foot, while adjusting jets secured to a metal frame on one side, using metal poles with mechanized hands attached to them, which he controlled using glowing, green wires attached to a pot on his head.

"Miss Thorne." He smiled, enjoying the mayhem, appropriate as he looked to be central to it.

"We must go to Faellion," Ernest told me, wringing his hands with worry.

"The slave district," I insisted. We needed Calka's bracelet and Naren's explosive green goo. I wouldn't mind smashing Gas, Fharen, and all his goons in the process, and Calka's magic might make that possible. Retreat was not my style.

"Impossible," the goblin said. "This is a prototype, and I cannot land where you desire, my dear, nor alter course very far from the prevailing winds, which happen to be going where we need to at this moment. Also, this balloon is likely to blow up if I try to turn it off before its fuel is spent. I am afraid we are stuck."

"I am not going anywhere with you. You're possessed."

"Then feel free to jump out," Doctor Ghunnan replied.

We were hundreds of feet above Highcrowne already, so that was not going to happen.

Duane was eyeing the drop to a high spire in the Central City, so I put my hand on his shoulder and whispered, "No. I just got you back with me. I don't want to lose you again."

I had missed him. Every moment I'd been with Fharen had been agony, wishing I was with Duane in the converted warehouse again, just the two of us, stealing a day off from my reality.

"I should have listened to Calka and used the power she offered to steal the Celon from Naren," Duane admitted. "I was foolish to try reasoning with him. Now, Fharen has everything."

"He doesn't have me. You do."

"And if it had been Thane?"

"It wouldn't have changed anything." I kissed him, and everything felt right.

All my angsty years of agony and indecision around men, my reluctance when wooed by Thane, it all made sense when I realized it had been Duane all along, and I'd never realized it. It had always been Duane.

I wished the certainty I felt at that moment would never leave. But there was the real Thane out there somewhere, Dawn's father. Duane was Shadow King, and I was me, a lodestone for danger. Would it ever be truly simple? Was this my one moment of perfect clarity?

Duane smiled as he kissed me back, and heat rose in me. I wrapped myself around him...

"Miss Thorne!"

"Disgusting."

"Mother!"

The protests from two prudish doctors, a socialist elf, but especially my daughter, splashed cold water on my desires.

"Later," I told Duane.

"I hope sooner rather than...."

"Me too."

"So, Ernest, why do you want us to go to Faellion?" I asked. It's where I knew we needed to be, but I never gave away information for free.

"There is something you need to see and someone you should meet."

"Cryptic. I hope you don't mean a plant creature to take over my brain like Doctor Ghunnan, and I assume you and now Katherine?"

"My brain is clean, as are my morals," Katherine said, still poo pooing my lasciviousness. "You are a public figure, Miss Thorne. Do try to watch your behavior."

"How are you certain you haven't been invaded by the creature, like Doctor Ghunnan here?"

"Because her thoughts are not part of the whole," the goblin said, pushing his glasses higher on his nose in a dismissive way.

"I believe that my research to replicate the Avian fluid has, as a side effect, infused me with a particularly nasty herbicide-pesticide-general 'cide' that is quite deadly to any infectious agent," she explained. "I have been unable to pass on the immunity to others as yet, probably a result of my pervasive and sequential exposure to increasingly higher doses and specific activities that has spared me the toxic side effects."

"Toxic side effects?"

"It kills rats too. Volunteers also. I seem to be the only one it is 'safely' effective on, but I can assure you that nothing can take root in this body."

"I have no doubt." Prudishness alone would have made her sacrosanct. "So, you're too toxic to be affected. What about Seneschal Ernest?"

"Oh, I have long been a part of the collective, for the democratic-socialist flavor of shared thoughts, emotions and goals is the most treasured realization of the People's Progressive Party. We are all for one and one for all. Except, since Doctor Ghunnan has joined our number, we feel he is holding out on us."

"I am no puppet. I have multidimensional knowledge far beyond the grasp of your simple collective," the goblin said, smirking. "I am quite immune to the plant's influence, but I now have the ability to listen in on your collective's deliberations. I am a Master Spy, after all. Retired. Of course."

"Of course."

So, Duane, Dawn, and I were all stuck on a balloon headed right for the lair of the plant creature with one of its long-devoted servants, a double agent, and a poisonous campaign manager whose tissues were so infused with toxins it might be dangerous to stand too close to her. Or get her too close to flammable sources. I nudged her away from the burner the goblin was feeding with coal.

It was a good thing we hadn't brought buckets of Celon along. The balloon was already a poisonous incendiary device occupied by the enemy. We could come back for the goo later.... Or find another way to destroy the plant.

I thought about feeding Katherine to it for a moment, but that was a last resort. Second resort, anyway. There were lots of other ways to burn the plant to dust, especially now that we had the highly destructive Doctor Ghunnan along.

I smiled at Duane. "Don't worry. I'm certain we don't need the bracelet or Naren. We'll be just fine."

Time to sit back and enjoy the ride. The enemy—the easiest one to deal with right now as I didn't want to think about Fharen—would soon be at our feet. Or at least a few hundred feet below, and I hoped the doctor could find a way to safely land this thing by then, else we would have to dive out and use the whole contraption as an explosive device.

"Mother," Dawn said, rolling her eyes. "You are never 'just fine'. Thank goodness I'm here."

"Not for long." I turned to Duane. "Tell me you have a way to call Calka."

13 FREE ME

Duane had a bracelet for everything. They came in all different colors and materials, stacked thirty deep on each wrist. I found them sexy, but I found everything about him sexy. This bracelet was black and seemed to work like one of the goblin's two-way radios, because I could hear Calka's replies.

"...It sounds like you are crossing the western peaks," the Avian said after Duane described where we were. "I will meet you before the moon rises."

It was a mid-air snatch and grab we had planned, but as I secured Dawn into the harness that Doctor Ghunnan had constructed from strips of leather and iron bolts in a flurry of quick tinkering, I worried. I was tossing my daughter out into thin air, with only a weakened Calka, magic gone, to protect her.

Duane secured a levitation bracelet on Dawn's arm and activated it, so she floated gently, only the harness strap in my hands holding her down. I had renewed all the runes and protective spells stitched into her clothing, but it still hurt my heart to let her go. I had been away from her, but she had never been away from me before.

There was no choice but to let her go. This was better than taking her into a hellish battle with the plant creature or being stuck on this experimental contraption when it crashed in a spectacular fireball.

Dawn was not as convinced. "You need me, Mother."

"I need you safe. Besides, I thought you wanted to meet the Avian princess? And Calka has more knowledge in her pinky feather than all the books in the libraries of the Three Kingdoms." I was trying to bribe her with knowledge.

"I know what you're doing."

"Of course you do. But it's working. Right?"

"A little."

As soon as her scowl weakened, not quite a smile yet, I kissed her forehead and said, "I love you."

The scowl was back. She didn't like demonstrations of affection. She was half elf but seemed to have inherited her Solhan half's distaste for emotional weakness.

Even without her magic, Calka was impressive. Despite the goblin's runaway balloon zipping along on a combination of explosive jets and air currents, the Avian managed to catch up. The difficulty came in when she tried to approach, as there was no place for her to perch without piercing the balloon or getting her wings dangerously close to coal-heated air or maneuvering thrusters. I lowered Dawn over the side using a rope attached to the harness, Duane anchoring it while Katherine and Ernest worked with the goblin to counterbalance our acrobatics with their own weight on the other side of the balloon's small basket.

As soon as Dawn went over the side, I wanted to stop this stupid idea and pull her back. She saw my resolve turn to jelly and immediately strengthened her own expression. "Good luck, Mother. Don't forget to find me when you're done saving the world."

"You are my world." I wanted to say I would find her soon, but I didn't even know if I would survive. That was my everyday uncertainty, and I had resolved long ago to never lie to her as my family had lied to me. There would be no false promises.

She respected that and nodded, indicating we were to lower her down now. When she was dangling in the dark somewhere below, I caught a glimpse of blacker wings against the night, a different rush of air, and then the slight weight of her vanished. I panicked, worried we'd dropped her, but Calka swooped around, Dawn cradled in her arms, and smiled. "You have Celon. You will succeed. I wish you a good fight, my Rose and Thorne."

Duane and I looked at one another sheepishly. Neither of us had wanted to mention we didn't have her magic band nor the Celon. We were improvising this— and badly. Instead, we gave her and Dawn a smiling, care-free wave goodbye.

Duane held me as I stared into the night. Only after Calka's silhouette was a memory, erased by shifting gray clouds interspersed with beams of moonlight, did I sigh and turn to face the opposite direction, towards Faellion.

The last time I had come this way, I had been in the clutches of my dragon godmother, Olyve, not knowing who she was then or if I would survive. This trip felt less laden with doom. I didn't know where I was going or what I would face, but this time I would not face it alone. As much as I distrusted the plant-infected goblin and seneschal, or clashed with my overly enthusiastic campaign manager, none of them were as purely evil as my twin, Ilsa, my only companion the last time. And now I had Duane. He changed everything.

I shivered, but not from the wind. His touch, the brush of his fingers on my collarbone as he wrapped himself around me like a cloak, made my nerves tingle with electricity. The scent of him filled my lungs, and I breathed deep, infusing him into every part of me.

"I love you, Duane." I wanted him to know.

He kissed me, first on my lips, then each of my closed eyelids. "I love you." The words as foreign to him as they were to Dawn or me, but he spoke them fluently. I could face anything that was coming now.

It turned out we didn't need to crash the balloon into the alien plant over mind—at least not yet.

By the time we reached Faellion, Doctor Ghunnan—with a little help from Katherine that was offered and accepted grudgingly on both sides—had rebuilt and mastered the prototype dirigible controls, so we were no longer at the mercy of the prevailing winds. Ernest directed us to land in a patch of jungle.

Faellion was a vast kingdom that stretched from semi-tropical seas in the west, to rich, volcanic plains and mountains to the north, and dense jungles like these in the south. Elves claimed all lands past the dwarfish mountains, which was more than half of the Three Kingdom's total area. And the best bits too.

I didn't think it would be possible to land in jungle without shredding the balloon in the descent, but then I saw an observation deck high in the treetops. It was likely used by elvish scouts but currently manned by goblin scientists monitoring complex meteorological devices that spun and whirred as we drew near, our jets firing to control the approach. A few shielded the instruments with their bodies, braced for impact, but armed, goblin mercenaries hurried up from below and took the ropes Ernest threw down to them, securing us to metal rings set in the wooden platform. Doctor Ghunnan cut off the jets at the precise moment, Katherine venting the balloon in a coordinated fashion, for a flawless landing.

There were a few slaps on the back and congratulations—Katherine and the goblin each congratulating themselves, saying things like, "My, did you see that?" or "Did you notice how well timed that adjustment I made was?"

"Brilliant, doctors," Duane said, smiling in that diplomatic way he had, and the way they beamed back, I knew he had won two more votes. Even my campaign manager was on his side now.

Not that the election mattered. And not that I was competing with Duane. Nope.

Time to focus on other things.

"Miss Kissel?" I said, recognizing the leader of our welcome party.

The goblin commando was a ruthless servant of the elusive goblin emperor. She would have killed or left Katherine, Doctor Ghunnan, and myself to die if circumstances had required—and they had at one time. Good thing I was over all that, bygones, and had enlisted her as an ally in the last war. She and the mercenaries with her were among those granted Highcrowne citizenship. It was surprising to see them here, in Faellion, but they, like Ernest, must be working for the plant creature.

Should I have taken over the balloon and crashed into the castle where the goo-powered vision had shown me the plant alien nested? I thought it must be near here somewhere, but I wasn't sure. Had I squandered my chance? With all the heavily armed mercenaries surrounding us, I suspected I was now a prisoner, making things a mite more difficult.

The commando grunted in my direction dismissively, looked Duane up and down and held her rifle a little more tightly, but pointed it at Doctor Ghunnan when he stepped onto the platform. Katherine dived for cover with a yelp.

The doctor held up his hands. "Miss Kissel. We are old friends, remember?"

"I remember you are a traitor. First to the emperor and now to the collective."

I assumed by 'collective' she meant the plant.

"You misunderstand. My work is more important than missions assigned by ill-counselled and ill-informed oligarchs and imperialists. I am so close to something transformative. So...."

She cut him off. "An execution order has been issued."

"Wait," Ernest said stepping between the goblins, the gun now pointed at him. It was uncharacteristically brave of the seneschal. "The Emperor's order is superseded by the needs of the collective. Doctor Ghunnan is still useful."

"I know that," Miss Kissel said. "I am in constant contact with the over mind. He would have been dead already otherwise." She packed the gun away and everyone breathed easier, especially the scientists whose meteorological instruments were in the line of fire again.

Katherine cautiously remained behind cover. I wondered if I should join her. I must have inched that way, because Miss Kissel noticed and frowned. "Come with me now," she said.

Duane whistled as we walked down the spiral staircase, unperturbed by the armed escort ahead of and behind our small group. I wasn't bothered if he wasn't. Soon we were competing over who could look calmer and more collected. Doctor Ghunnan won, because he was smiling widely and checking instruments, sniffing plants, and engaged in deep scientific work whenever we paused for a second. Execution orders from his emperor must be a common occurrence. Maybe even plant-controlled people were usual in his line of work. How had he broken the creature's control over his mind? I'd like to know how, just in case we couldn't kill the thing.

The humidity was terrible once we reached the forest floor. I was Solhan, we preferred the cold, and this was hotter than the hottest Highcrowne summer. After we had hiked a kilometer and I was dripping, I stripped down to my underwear, not caring when Katherine gasped prudishly. Duane just smiled. He loved the heat and took off his jacket in solidarity.

Miss Kissel led us to a hut made from living sticks and leaves woven and grown together. There was an arched doorway tall enough for elves and goblins but too short for me, and I had to double over to gain entry.

It was dark, and it took my eyes time to adjust. There was sparse furniture, primitive in design, and a set of open shackles hooked to a stone weight by a long chain. So, this was to be a prison? Just great.

Only after my eyes adjusted did I realize there was a shimmer in the air. My soul sense, weakened as it was, also told me someone else was in the room.

"Nice try," Miss Kissel said to the room. "Show yourself."

There was an annoyed sound, and suddenly the shackles were no longer empty. They were chained around the dainty ankles of none other than Queen Hilja.

"You're alive." Duane said.

"I'm glad someone is relieved to hear that." She smiled, and I pushed down a surge of jealously. I also resisted the urge to take Duane's hand territorially. I was secure, I told myself. Repeatedly.

"I'm relieved to see you too," I finally managed to say without it sounding like a lie. "But how? I saw your body. Touched your ghost. You obviously weren't cremated."

"I wasn't dead. Lady Maevrel and Seneschal Ernest helped me accomplish the deception. I had to let the Djinn think he had killed me, so I could act unobserved.

I dare say, I may be better at glamour than my father. Did you know he is still alive?"

"Yes." She had never understood the difference between my relationship with Thane and her father, but it was clear form my tone that I wasn't happy about it.

"He wants the throne back—and far worse things. I must stop him."

"Hard to do when you're chained to a rock in the middle of nowhere," I pointed out. "Where did your plan go wrong?"

"It hasn't. Now that you're here. It's so good to see you, Eva." Hilja giving me her best sister act was a warning sign. What was she up to?

"That was our agreement," Ernest said. "I and the collective would help her to fake her death and escape to Faellion, bring her chosen allies to her—and in return she would join the over mind and wrest it free of her father's control."

"Fharen is controlling the plant?" I asked. "How?"

"Glamour," Hilja explained. "The same power to shroud and confuse minds that makes him so damnably convincing at hiding how evil he truly is, is the same power that allowed him to control the over mind rather than succumbing to it. He's been using the over mind to take over the Three Kingdoms. I'm the only one strong enough to fight it and break his control. I release the plant from his influence, and in return...."

"You will have the honor of joining us in ultimate democracy within the collective," Ernest said joyously.

"I cannot wait, my Queen. I won't have to call you Queen anymore! We can be equals."

"Yes." Hilja grimaced. "I can't wait."

She raised an eyebrow at me, and I knew exactly why she had wanted me here. She needed a rescue.

She'd have to get on the waitlist—after Ulric, Naren, Highcrowne's citizenry... I needed a pen and paper to keep track of it all.

It was hard to scheme unobserved in a jungle village surrounded by spying plants—I meant the ones riding around inside Ernest and Miss Kissel and the other converts, but there were probably plants spying from the recesses of the wilds for all I knew. It took quick talking to keep Duane and I from being 'converted'.

"We cannot outwit Fharen if he has access to the over mind and the mind is controlling us as well," I argued. "Like Hilja, we must remain free of it, unpredictable. It's the only way to stop him."

Miss Kissel looked suspicious, but Ernest nodded enthusiastically. "Brilliant! I have always been in awe of you, Miss Thorne. It is so wonderful to be working with you again to advance the cause of the people! We'll leave you alone now to 'plot'. This is so fun!"

He gave us a ring of silence around the hut where no eavesdropping was allowed. His seneschal powers of persuasion were not at all dimmed by plant possession, and it beat out the goblin commando's scowls of suspicion, which was good for us. I did notice Miss Kissel's people on platforms and tree lookouts beyond Ernest's perimeter, watching if not listening, just in case we tried to make a run for it.

"How dare you drag us into this?" I asked Hilja when we were alone. I, of course, would have gotten us into this anyway, as I had already planned to defeat the plant creature, but I wanted her to feel guilty.

"Highcrowne was overrun, and this was the only way. If you had been more aware of the situation and less concerned with democracy, you might have prevented this from happening."

"Me? Since when is saving the world my full-time job? You're a Crown. This is your job."

"I thought you were campaigning to be a Crown? You should thank me for the opportunity to experience what real responsibility feels like." Hilja huffed.

I was not about to let her have the last word. "Responsibility? You have no idea. For six years, I was responsible for protecting my child's life, with no help from your EEPs chasing us everywhere, while also trying to break the connection to the First Soul and keep the Devourer from obliterating this world. I think I deserve a tiny vacation."

My gaze darted to Duane, and I knew I'd given away that what I really wanted was just a few more days to enjoy peace and normalcy and happiness with him. Wow. What a concept.

Hilja knew. She must have known from our body language the moment she saw us, but she didn't say anything about our relationship. She had no right to comment.

"We will help you, of course," Katherine said, giving me her 'be political' warning expression. If I won the election, Hilja would be a good ally. She didn't know me very well, or Hilja. I sucked at politics, and Hilja just sucked.

At last Duane spoke. "I think we should ask Doctor Ghunnan about his plan."

I'd forgotten the goblin. He was technically plant-possessed too, but Ernest had ignored him like he was invisible when ushering the others away, so he really was immune to the over mind and obviously able to hide his thoughts from it too.

"My plan...?" the doctor said, absent minded. That was a sure sign he had his evasive spy cloak on. He kept his plans close to his chest, usually shrouding them with scientific blather, which he did now. "... My plan is to collect a control specimen from the heart of the over mind that will help me understand how to harness this 'democratic power', as the seneschal put it, for the collective betterment of all beings—and in the process, I may have to inject some of this experimental green goo borrowed from Doctor Suttner's laboratory, as well as some of the Celon I have kept for just such an occasion—

a clear side by side control to see which test substance is most explosive. I mean, most effective at obliterating what is essentially an existential threat to autonomous beings."

"You stole that from my lab?" Katherine said, trying to snatch the vial back from the goblin, but he was too fast and slipped both vials of green goo, one labelled 'Test A' the other 'Test B', back into his coat pocket.

"If it's an 'existential threat to autonomous beings'," I said, arms crossed, "why do you get to keep the control specimen with the potential to grow a new plant and start this whole crisis all over again?"

"Did I say that? No, Miss Thorne, I fully intend to destroy the control at the conclusion of the experiment." He crossed his heart and hoped to die.

I believed him even less.

Still ... he did have a plan. I always had a hard time formulating those.

"Alright, how do we get in there with the goo?" I asked. "Oh, and rescue Ulric. My uncle is in a deep dark cell somewhere, so it's probably best not to blow him up too. Probably. I guess it's more of an optional task to rescue him, really." My uncle was very 'gray area' when it came to morals, and it was hard to elicit any enthusiasm from the others at the idea of a rescue. Duane had a flinch of loyalty to him, but still didn't jump in with any suggestions.

"Doctor Katherine and I are invisible to it ... and you three," the goblin indicated Duane, Hilja and I, "are uninfected and the perfect temptation. You are the distractions, and if my experiments fail, then Queen Hilja can attempt her elvish 'glamour' and persuade the over mind to obey her instead. For now."

I hated being the distraction. I was good at it though. "Okay. But if I'm the distraction, I get to crash the balloon and blow things up."

"My balloon!? Why?"

I shrugged. "Just a notion I've grown fond of. I prefer to take a train back home. It's far cozier and more private." I gave Duane a lecherous smile, which he returned.

I could tell he was uneasy about something, though.

The doctors went to one corner to have a heated discussion about the details of the 'experiment', while Hilja stared haughtily and impatiently at us all.

I ushered Duane to the opposite corner of the small hut and whispered, "What is it? What's wrong? Besides being thrust into danger and adventure that will probably lead to our deaths. That bit is nothing new to either of us."

"I worry about the Djinn and Fharen. They are smarter than the goblin, I fear."

"And Gas is with them. He causes as much chaos as I do. Still, I have yet to meet anyone who can outwit Doctor Ghunnan in the long term. He has schemes within schemes."

"For his own benefit, not ours," Duane reminded me. "He'd sacrifice us as all as dispassionately as he would a bunch of lab rats."

"That's what we are to him. But it makes him predictably deceitful."

"And that's what Fharen and the Djinn are good at—deceit. They are all playing the same game. We need a different approach for our backup plan."

"You mean 'your' backup plan. I don't do plans. Chaos walking, remember?"

"I can usually rely on my networks, but everyone is compromised now. That leaves just you and me."

"You trust me then? I thought you trusted no one?"

He leaned in and kissed me so tenderly it was all the answer I needed. He didn't even hesitate with Hilja watching.

"But..." he pondered when we came up for air. "How do I take advantage of chaos walking?"

"You'll figure something out. That's what makes it fun."

14 Chaos Walking

The goblin was dead set against me destroying his balloon; the commandos worried we'd escape before fulfilling the bargain, and I couldn't fly it on my own, so we had to leave it behind.

I moped as we trudged along a narrow trail towards our destination. A steep gorge plummeted to the river far below on my right. It looked like a blue string it was so far down. Flecks of white, like lice on a troll's hair, indicated rapids. I led the way, hacking fronds and grasses out of my path with a machete to vent my frustration. How much chaos could I wreak with nothing but bug bites, sweat, and fury? More than you'd think.

"Oops. Wasps," I said, trying to remain calm as I saw my blade dig deep into the nest. I summoned a protective barrier using a runestone in my belt pouch, which ensured I wouldn't get stung.

Katherine was bug-resistant from ingesting so much strange chemistry, and Hilja didn't even pause, effortlessly able to charm even wasps. The goblin was wearing so much netting over his safari hat, nothing could get through it or his brass armored sleeves, which left just Duane to give me a disappointed shake of his head before activating a bracelet on his wrist that zapped the swarm when it headed for him. Dead bugs dropped to the ground around him. He was fine but still frowning.

"I said 'oops'," I pointed out. "Maybe someone else should lead the way."

Hilja groaned and took the machete from me. Her chains were gone, and as a waif in a delicate lace dress, she seemed to drift like a dainty fluff of dandelion wherever she walked. I didn't see how she'd clear the path, but then she dropped the machete and hummed softly so the plants moved out of our way. Elves. Such showoffs.

I went to pick up the machete, but Duane took it. "I'll hold onto this."

"Is keeping me from wreaking havoc part of your plan?"

"No, just trying to control some variables." We were at the back of the expedition queue now, so he added, "Besides, I want to be back here watching the others.

Hilja taking the lead tells me she has another plan, besides us."

"Of course she does. She's like you."

"I thought you once said I was not in her class?"

"That's not what I meant, and you know it. I was jealous when you were together, but not admitting it, so it came out wrong. I meant you were so amazing you didn't need her as a status symbol. You don't need to pretend to be something you're not, because who you really are is who I love."

A real smile of joy flashed across his face, and it was so worth it, so I said, 'I love you,' again, but with my eyes and kiss.

No getting distracted, I reminded myself. I pushed him along, so we'd catch up.

My knack for chaos always pays off, because being forced to walk at the back of the line meant I noticed the creatures paralleling us.

The jungles of Faellion are like the manicured botanical gardens of the Central City in comparison to the jungles of Archon, but they were still wild and dangerous. Strange magical creatures were likely to enchant you and do unseemly things (I meant enslavement, not what you think – get your mind out of the gutter) rather than poison and devour you, but there was no telling.

Elves had made fairies extinct, except for my friend Sandy, but there were other native fae, such as ents and dryads, who had once served the roles humans now filled—slaves. Nowadays, they were ignored and left to survive however they could in the shrinking wilderness. Some of them might eat you if required.

I stopped and drew my Ashur. The sound of a blade stirring made Duane roll and disappear into some undergrowth, bristling with knives and other weapons of his own. It was hard to tell, because he simply vanished. I worried for a moment that the undergrowth had swallowed and eaten him, because he was so quiet, but the noisy debates between Doctor Ghunnan and Katherine hadn't ceased since we left camp, and they drew our pursuers out into the open.

Our pursuers were short, hedge-hog looking creatures with protruding, blunt yellow teeth and slits for eyes. They were armed with flintlocks and wore bandoliers of grenades. Grindilock Freedom Fighters. They must have spotted Hilja, who was as high elf as they came, and couldn't resist taking such a hostage.

"Hilja!" I called in warning.

She turned and more Grindilocks emerged behind her, taking her by the arms. She looked extremely grumpy at being captured, again, and so soon. The doctors were equally grumpy having their conversation disturbed, but they were scowling at me.

Duane emerged from hiding and cut down the Grindilock who had grabbed Hilja. I winced. Duane always had a kill first attitude, but these were the good guys. Kinda. No one liked elves.

I tackled two more fighters who went after Katherine, pounding the hilt of my Ashur into the temple of one. Their bristly fur acted like armor, and the blow glanced off. I feared I'd have to use the sharp edge. No lecturing Duane about excessive force if that happened, so I said, "Please, stop. We're not your enemy. The elf is our prisoner."

It was a teensy wincey lie, but the one I had pinned down was listening. I had to speak elvish, of course, as it was the universal language in these parts, but I was far too tall to be an elf. and I looked like the human slaves who were their natural allies, so I thought diplomacy had a real chance here.

"Stop, Duane!" I said, sheathing my sword and standing. "We need allies like these."

He relented, pulling back just short of another killing blow, and leaving a relieved Grindilocks on the ground gasping for breath. The other Grindilocks had warily surrounded him just out of range of his deadly reach, and they too looked relieved at the thought of talking this over. There were at least twenty of them, but we were a lot tougher than we looked. Besides Duane's bloody efforts, the goblin and Katherine had knocked several out with a lightning pistol and chemical concoctions, respectively, while Hilja had half their number swaying in a glamoured daze.

The situation could have been resolved peacefully, I repeat for the record, if Mister Gardens had not barreled in with a heavy handed and needless rescue.

What's worse he had a balloon, not unlike Doctor Ghunnan's. Only it was elvish in design, sleeker, and powered with magic, which was much easier to control solo that a confusing assortment of valves, pivoting jets, and a coal-hungry boiler. He swooped in and dropped frilly paper mâché and plaster sculptures shaped like dolphins and doves, filled with enchanted sparkles that burst everywhere when they hit a Grindilock on the head. The creature struck, and all others nearby, fell into a deep sleep. That included me, Duane and the rest of our party, except Hilja. I saw her roll her eyes in annoyance just before I dropped, the world engulfed in a warm blanket of darkness.

I woke near sunset, hours lost, and to the sight of the snooty Elf Butler serving a three-course meal to Hilja and meagre cups of broth to the rest of us. I was the last to wake, the others already sipping their drinks, while I watched the steam rising from the mug in front of me with a strange fascination. Whatever was in those sparkles was good. I had never felt this mellow. Fortunately, 'angry' for me was more instinct than conscious choice.

"What did you think you were doing?" I hissed. "Yes, you, Mister Gardens. We had everything under control."

"You did not. An army was on its way."

"Says you." Okay, my senses were a little dulled, and my argumentative discourse with them.

"I for one am very glad to see you," Hilja said, patting his arm.

Ugh. Hilja and the butler were equally high on my annoying list these days. Both kept interfering with me and Dawn at every turn.

"You knew Hilja was alive and still you tried to detain me?" Duane said, a dangerous anger in his tone.

"I had to make it look convincing, even to you. Especially to you," Mister Gardens said. "If the Shadow King believed Queen Hilja dead—and who knew more than he—then it must be true."

Duane looked at Hilja knowingly. "The butler is your backup plan."

"Wrong," Hilja said. "Mister Gardens is the main plan. You are my backup plan. If we fail to destroy the plant, then it is up to you and your ridiculous explosives. As you get into position through the jungle, you will distract the creature's minions, with Eva looking like me, they will never see me and Mister Gardens descending from above."

"Looking like you? No..." My voice trailed off as I looked down at delicate hands and golden skin. "You glamoured me when I was asleep, didn't you?"

"Yes."

That's why Duane wasn't meeting my gaze. I now looked exactly like his ex. Talk about putting a crimp in my love life. I could probably dispel the glamour, maybe. This was Hilja, so it wouldn't be easy, but, despite my befuddled senses, I recognized a good plan when I saw one.

"Fine. Let's do this."

I prefer frontal assaults anyway. Let Hilja and the Elf Butler have their fancy, magical balloon. By the time their dainty sensibilities were satisfied, and they finally acted, it would all be over. Me and Duane would have the plant defeated. Oh, yeah, I'd need the goblin's help too. Probably, Katherine's too, but if there were any more tapestries made, I'd be front and center. Looking like Hilja. Wait. Would she get all the credit? This plan sucked. Not that I cared about fame. Nope.... Sure, it made detective gigs easier to get and people gave you free food and smiles—which for Solhans was a foreign concept—so there were lots of benefits to fame, but I didn't need it. No, not me.

Oh, who was I kidding?

"We have to get to that plant before Hilja," I told Duane through gritted teeth. "I've seen this region when I was connected to the Celon. I recall some secret chambers beneath the old elvish castle where it's holed up. We can avoid any defenses on the walls and go straight to the heart of the enemy."

"Why didn't you mention this before?"

"My plans are spur of the moment, remember? I need motivation too, and beating those two elves to the prize is what's working for me right now. Let's go!"

"It's the middle of the night."

"Fine. We wait until morning."

I wasn't tired, having slept already, so I spent most of the night tossing and turning, head buzzing with ideas for everything from what school to send Dawn to when Highcrowne was safe to how to manage the massive wave of clients wanting my services when I saved the world again. It hadn't worked out how I planned the last time, but this time would be different. I was sure of it.

As soon as breakfast was done, everyone packed up and ready to go, Hilja and Mister Gardens drifting away in their balloon to carry out whatever secret plan they had in mind—I looked at the others and gave the speech I'd been preparing in my head.

"They think we are the 'B' team but they're wrong. We're A's: A dangerous Shadow King; A goblin master spy; A brilliant campaign manager—"

"—and scientist," Katherine interjected.

"My scientific knowledge and experience far exceed that of my former student," Doctor Ghunnan mumbled.

"Okay, and A scientist or two ... and me. A hit and miss detective with some wildly erratic magical ability but a consistent talent for being a massive pain in the ass of any bad guy. We are facing a bodiless plant creature which has no ass, per say, but you know what I mean. We are so gonna kick it in its plant parts. Now ... let's go!"

I sprinted. I seldom ran, so it meant something when I did. I set a grueling pace, headed for the base of the tor ahead of us, where the river below cut into the mountain and created natural caverns that turned into secret tunnels. Elves loved their secret tunnels.

I soon tired, though, and walked the rest of the way. The others weren't inspired by my speech enough to run, so it gave them time to catch up.

Slowly, the castle grew larger on the horizon, its walls and towers made of the same stone on which it stood. It looked like a natural outgrowth, roughly built, no crystal minarets here like in Faellion, as this was a backwater province, but it was still elegant because of how it appeared to be a part of the landscape and accentuated the natural curves of cliffs and peaks. I was surprised when I reached the base, pausing to look for the secret tunnel, and found Duane was already scouting the way ahead. I must have been staring at the castle too much and not noticed him get ahead of me.

"Here," Duane said, gesturing for us to follow.

There was a shadow on one side of the road. We had to climb over a small wall and balance, toe to heel, along the rocky, crumbling cliff edge to reach the spot where Duane stood. He disappeared into darkness and did not emerge. I followed and saw the shadow was a massive hollow in the mountain. The river gorge dropped away to the right, and the narrow path became wide enough to stand properly.

I went up to Duane who was running his hands along the cave wall. "Now, I'm jealous," I said. "I wish you'd put your hands on me like that."

He smiled in such a way that I knew I'd have my turn later. When I didn't look like Hilja. "What can I say? I can make even the earth shake." He pressed on some barely discernable scribbles etched in the stone, and the wall rumbled and split, revealing a secret passageway.

"May I go first?" the goblin asked, donning some night vision goggles and stepping forward without waiting for a reply.

I was always happy to have someone else spring all the traps and face the danger. "Go right ahead."

His goggles, and nearly a century of spy craft experience, made him very good at clearing the path ahead. He did miss a few magical protections, being blind to all things not fitting his world view, but fortunately either Duane or I was able to intervene before he set off the magical traps. Katherine followed behind, curiously examining the architecture and murals.

"This looks to be quite old, perhaps from the time of fairies, before elves seized these lands," she noted. "It would be amazing to find some fairy artifacts and learn more about their lost civilization."

"The fairy I met is not that interested in learning about other civilizations. She hates people. Insects and animals too. Prefers landscapes and rocks."

I wondered what Sandy was up to these days. She had once promised to be Little Viktor's fairy godmother, and I still left offerings of cream for her as part of our bargain, but she tended to lose time—a lot—and I had no idea where she was or if she ever did anything to fulfil her side of the deal.

"You met a living fairy? Impossible," Katherine scoffed.

I shrugged. There was no enlightening those absolutely certain of their limited knowledge.

"Fairies are extinct, or close enough," Duane pointed out. "So, remember why we're here—we wish not to join them. Quiet." He put a finger to his lips. We were all amateurs compared to the Shadow King.

We'd reached a section of dressed stone, the passageway ending in a wall of finely crafted blocks and an archway sealed by a silver door.

"My turn," I said, stepping around Duane.

I recognized this door from my vision. It had all blurred by so fast when I'd been connected to the Celon, but the experience had sunk deep into my memory. It felt like I'd been here before. I think that's how the goo worked—it showed you the future but also made it come true in a paradoxical way. I placed my hand against the door and spoke words that were meaningless to me but which sounded like Sandy's mumbles to herself.

"Is that Fairy?" Katherine asked, her disbelief wavering.

"I think so."

All I knew is that I'd wanted the door to open, words had come in that strange language, and now the silver was glowing with a bright, white light. I stepped back and watched it shimmer and disappear, leaving one of those bubble-like portals Sandy had used before. It was like looking through a fisheye lens into the depths of the castle, the edges shimmering with rainbows. The section of castle it showed was empty, some courtyard with broken pillars and stone benches overgrown with rose bushes and weeds. I stepped through.

I felt Duane reach for me, as if to hold me back or caution me, but he wasn't fast enough, and I was through in one breath. Birds chirped in the morning light filtering through a broken roof. It was peaceful.

I looked back and saw the others staring at me through the lens. They were saying something I couldn't hear, but I waved for them to follow. Duane went first, with Katherine and the goblin taking up the rear.

Duane was always more uncomfortable around magic than he let on, and I saw his tense muscles relax when he was standing beside me safe and not dead. Katherine went to examine some of the overgrown plants, weeds dying where she stepped, while the goblin took so long to come through I tapped my foot impatiently. He had somehow wedged himself part way through and was examining the rainbow edges with his googles and other instruments.

When he was finally done, I asked, "Well, what was so special about this portal compared to all the others you use?"

"It doesn't go through the void but some other dimension I have nct visited before. I must return and study this further."

I'd been stuck in a bubble in that other dimension once—it's where Sandy liked to put people and forget about them—and it was not a nice place. "I wouldn't if I were you. That place is pretty, but time passes quicker there, and it's full of some nasty creatures. I think this portal must just skirt the edge of it."

"Fascinating! Bu⁊ as you say, for another time. We have an important experiment—I mean mission—we are already on."

I tried to get my bearings. A fly-through vision of the castle during a dream walk, which ignored things like floors and ceilings, was very different from being inside its ruined walls. I eyed the vines and overgrown foliage in the courtyard, wondering if a plant pod lurked among them. The ones I'd seen before were huge, because they'd been stuffed full of people. It didn't mean there weren't some smaller, rat sized pods lurking in the bushes.

I reached out with my soul sense, less reliable than ever these days, but the plant alien had always had a strange feel to it. I was in luck. I sensed something. Not close by but deeper. In the dungeon maybe? Why did the bad guys always like to lurk in dungeons? Ulric's distinctive, dark, Solhan soul was down there somewhere too.

"We need to find a way down," I said. "Look for a staircase."

I may have overstated my ability to find the plant, and my companions were beginning to catch on, because Katherine wrinkled her brow, but Duane came to the rescue. "Here it is."

There was a spiral staircase running down inside a dried up fountain. It would have been hidden when the castle was inhabited, probably concealed by a glamour, but now the stones around it were broken and the steps exposed and overgrown with lichen.

"Once we get down there," I warned them, "the plant will sense us and send its tendrils and minions to attack. We need to get to the over mind quickly and kill it." I looked up, certain I saw Hilja's balloon drifting along with a cloud. What was she up to? "Very quickly," I added.

My soul sense was working well enough to detect the creature, and once we reached the bottom of the staircase, I let it guide my feet through the narrow labyrinth. Elves loved their secret passageways, and this one must have hid quite the treasure in its day. Unless it was a fairy maze, like the portal, an even more ancient ruin? Was there something powerful left behind, some relic or artifact, the plant had needed. Is that why it had taken up residence here? Something it was feeding on besides minds?

No time for deep questions. We were on the clock— competing against discovery and against Hilja. I ran along the labyrinthine corridors, feeling my way towards the deeper heaviness of the over mind. I heard the goblin doctor not far behind, his mechanical legs whirring loudly over the sounds of Katherine's labored breaths. Stealth would be impossible—except for Duane. He'd already vanished from sight.

Tendrils of the plant blocked the path ahead, so I led us over a broken wall into another section of the maze. We'd have to face the creature soon enough, but the longer we stayed beyond its awareness the greater our chances.

Ulric's soul was familiar and close. Another ally couldn't hurt. I put my hands on the stone wall, feeling for a way in. It was sheer, no secret levers that I could detect. The door could be on the other side of the dungeon with my luck.

"Oh no," the goblin said, and I knew our time was up.

A coiled tendril of plant rose up before us like a cobra, testing the air with small hairs all along the length of its vine. Networks of tendrils emanated from it, spreading along the hallway and even up onto the surrounding walls. There was no going around.

"Burn it?" I suggested, feeling my belt pouch and realizing I hadn't brought anything remotely flammable. I could try a rune...

"Let me." Katherine stepped forward. She reached out for the plant, saying, "Hello there," in a very soothing way, as if it was some stray cat. It looked smug as it struck, resembling a viper all the more as thorns bit into her palm. "Ouch!" she cried and pulled back.

But the plant soon regretted taking such unilateral action. So much herbicide had seeped into Katherine's system that one taste quickly spread through the veins of the plant. It turned yellow, then brown, spotted with black, and drooped. The sickness spread across the floor, along other vines that soon dried and blackened. Even those on the ceiling were yellowing ... until suddenly the plant pinched itself off and retreated. The main body of the creature didn't want to be infected.

"You may just be our secret weapon," I told her.

"Not so secret," Duane pointed out, startling me as I hadn't realized he was standing so close. "It now knows we're here and what we can do."

"Not all we can do," Doctor Ghunnan said. He patted the Celon vials in his voluminous jacket of gadgets.

"We have to find the over mind for that," I reminded him. "Katherine can go first."

Katherine gulped but stepped forward. I think she would have been more driven if she had an experiment in mind like the goblin. As it was, I sensed she was more annoyed that the election was derailed, and she wanted all of this over as soon as possible. That irritation made her more formidable in my estimation, plus her demonstrated ability to kill the plant with a touch, and she kept it in retreat.

Then it got smart. A tendril knocked over a bit of wall, stone bricks tumbled down and blocked our path.

Or maybe it got stupid. It happened to have knocked over the wall leading to Ulric's prison cell. Through the falling dust, I saw him stand up, blinking against light and debris, a scowl on his imposing features.

"Uncle," I said. "I'm here to rescue you." And about a million other people, but I didn't say that part out loud.

"You look like Hilja."

The glamour. I'd forgotten. He could sense souls, though, so he knew it was me. That explained the disappointment in his tone.

"You need to focus on helping us get this plant back under control again," I shot back. It had been his idea to negotiate with it during the war, which had resulted in all the pod people today. Ulric was at least as culpable as Fharen.

"The Abomination resists my control. As I told you in your dream walk, without the Dead God in this world and few of His worshipers to aid me, there is nothing I can do."

I wanted to rub in just how weak and useless he was—vengeance for all the times he'd said something similar to me in my life—but he did look particularly old and weary. He hadn't been treated well, maybe not even fed while imprisoned. The plant looked to have walled him inside expecting him to die there.

A strange wave of compassion swept through me, and I said, "Follow my soul trail. Go back the way we came, to the village, and wait for us there, Uncle. Fharen is in control of the creature, and there's nothing you can do against elven magic. Don't worry, we have a plan."

It was a sign of how defeated he was that he didn't argue. He simply nodded, saying, "I gathered from the motley array of humans and that goblin following you around that you had things well in hand. Do not forget that you are a Thorne, though, and need no one to do what must be done. Blessed by the Dead God's power or left to wrest what we can from the souls and bones of our enemies, we always find a way to not only survive but conquer. Obliterate that creature, Eva, in our family's name."

Wow. That was the kind of speech I'd been aiming for earlier. I stood tall and proud as he strode off, my uncle hiding a weary limp behind Thorne bravado.

When he was gone and well out of earshot, I said, "We do have a plan, right?"

"We need to reach the over mind for my plan to work," Doctor Ghunnan said, "but we are blocked from going forward."

I thought about blasting through, but we needed the goo for later, and if we used Duane's sticky bombs—or whatever he had in his pockets, as I was sure he had something—then we'd be in a protracted battle over every inch forward. We couldn't use brute force. We had to be smart.

Crickets.

"Any ideas?" I asked the doctors. Smart wasn't exactly my area.

"What about that spell you once used that dissolved rock?" Duane asked me.

"The rune's power ran out months ago. It came from Archon." Meaning there was no way I could make another one.

"Dwarves like digging," Katherine noted unhelpfully, as we had no dwarves with us. A werewolf would have worked even better, but we didn't have one of those either.

"Perhaps you should be the bait, as Queen Hilja suggested," Doctor Ghunnan said.

I was about to argue, but Hilja was pretty smart. Maybe going along with her plan wasn't the worst idea?

"Fine." While I couldn't cast any elvish magic, I could act like a snooty queen. I huffed, annoyed, as I backtracked to another section of corridor and found some plant tendrils detaching from the stone, warily set to back away.

"Listen up," I told it. "I apologize for Katherine's—the human's—attack on you. She exudes something repulsive to your species, and mine, just because she's not an elf, but especially to your kind. I will tell her to go away. Go away." Katherine jumped at my tone and looked confused. "I said 'go!'"

It was Katherine's turn to huff as she headed back the way we had come, saying, "I prefer to wait outside for all this nonsense to be over, anyway. We still have an election!"

When she was gone, I said, "See? You are safe. I have come to speak with the over mind, ruler to ruler. Now, show me the way."

Its minions in the village had bargained with Hilja to wrest control from Fharen, but I wasn't sure if the over mind knew what all its offshoots were up to at all times. They may have tried to conceal the details of the plan to keep it from Fharen, so maybe the over mind knew nothing and would treat me like an intruder. Or maybe it was curious.

A tendril waved and beckoned me forward.

Curious. At least.

I followed the tendrils a few steps down the corridor, before I heard Duane swear. I looked back to see him with a blade drawn. He'd cut off the tip of a tendril that had threatened to encircle him. It's severed strand oozing white liquid as it twisted and reached for his ankle. Doctor Ghunnan took it in a mechanoid grip like a cobra caught mid-strike.

"Find another way," I told them.

"Perhaps you should take one of these, just in case." Doctor Ghunnan held out a vial of green goo. Another vine reached for it, so the professor tossed it my way. I caught it before it smashed on the floor. Lucky I had good reflexes, but that had been close.

I stuffed it down my shirt, and any vine trying to feel me up for it would get a nasty surprise. I mean, I showered and didn't have any crumbs or anything in my cleavage, at least not lately, so what I meant is that it would piss me off, and it would not like me when I was pissed. I tended to kill things, a lot, when that happened.

"I'll see you soon," Duane promised.

"You better," I told him. I turned and followed the vines deeper into the labyrinth.

The dim light from Doctor Ghunnan's electrochemical torch slowly faded. Solhans saw well in low light, but this was so dark I barely discerned the phosphorescent glow from lichen on the walls. I was in the heart of the maze, deep inside the plateau beneath the castle.

Something rumbled, shaking the ground, and a blinding ray of sunlight poured from the crack between a set of double doors that opened. Massive vines pushed them open like muscled plant guards. I pictured them as separate creatures, but those vines were connected to a beast of a plant in the chamber beyond. The castle above was in ruins, light pouring down through a crevice in the stone foundations, and the plant had grown to fill every part of it. Its bulk pressed against cavern walls, spilled up fallen stones, and stretched out into the castle and the forests beyond. There was no face or eyes, no central trunk even, just a mass of thick vines coiled like pythons over one another. They wriggled and moved, and a thin, hair-like tendril reached for me. I backed away, but I was too slow, and it struck. My nose burned as it shot inside, and then my head exploded with light and sound.

It had attached itself to my brain.

"This is the only way we can speak with no other puppet near ... Eva," it said. "I know who you are now. Your appearance was so convincing to all my physical senses, but there is no confusing my mind. Nothing can best me in this realm."

"Except Fharen. And Hilja."

"It was dangerous to merge with the Elf King. A mistake. I regret it."

"But not all the other minds you took over? All the lives stolen?"

"I've stolen nothing. I have only shared. With them, with me, with all of us. All our thoughts become one, all our wisdom and knowledge. We are greater as one. You must feel it now? Yes?"

I felt whispers, a multitude, at the edge of my mind, like a crowd just out of sight. I wanted to listen in and get the goss on what they were discussing, but I felt that if I did, I'd merge into the din of it all. I'd be washed away like a drop of water on the beach. I resisted the temptation. Maybe it was my fierce dislike for most people and strong sense of independence—or plain Thorne orneriness—but I was not about to give in.

"Do you want free of Fharen or not?" I asked.

"Yes."

"Then help me. You control everyone in Highcrowne and half the countryside in Faellion."

"Yes. We are many."

"That's the problem. Fharen controls them through you. Let them go. Then he has no power. Well, he has his usual thugs and political allies, but it's a more even field against Hilja and her allies. Let us decide this our way. Stay out of it. Go home to Archon. Return to your swamp."

"To a seed from a lost age? To an ancient relic moldering away in darkness rather than stretching my mind over the world? No. I cannot go back to that."

"Is it better to be a slave or to sleep again? You could get another chance one day. Some hope is better than none."

"There is always hope—and I have hope that even as you resist me that means you can be the one to kill Fharen. I feel your hatred for him. You will defeat him for me. I see that now. I have only to let you go. You will inevitably clash. He will try to steal your daughter, steal your power, your life. You will not let that happen. So, go. Now."

The tendril withdrew, and blood poured out of my nose. I swayed, my head killing me. It must have had an anesthetic when dug into me and, now it was gone, I was in pain and really pissed.

"You don't get to wait for your enemies to kill each other," I told it. "You are the first one on my death list."

I had one of those, all Solhans did, completely normal.

I looked up and spotted Mister Gardens and Hilja in the balloon above. The plant did too, because a tendril shot up, impossibly far into the air, to grab hold of the basket. It drew the ballon in like a kite.

I think the plant now knew Hilja's plan, from being in my brain, because meaty tendrils encircled the basket, squeezing and crushing it. It would kill her before it let her get close enough to wrest control of its mind from Fharen.

Looked like Hilja was the distraction. Yes!

I took advantage and unstopped the vial of goo the goblin had tossed me. A tendril of plant struck, wrapping around and around my fist and elbow so I couldn't move my arm. There was one thing I could do. I squeezed, and the delicate test tube cracked, splintering into pieces, so my blood and the Celon mingled, dripping down onto the plant and the tendrils it had wrapped around me. I didn't want to set fire to it while I was still trapped, so I fought, tearing at it with my other hand to get free.

But something very strange happened when the Celon entered my bloodstream. Visions came more powerfully than when I had drunk it before. Green fire shot through my veins, and I suddenly knew it was not some Avian magic as everyone believed—this was like the green electricity I had once wielded as Death's bride. This was pure power, divine, more than life or death, creation or necromancy, it was undefined and capable of anything—and it was Solhan.

The being I had glimpsed before burned bright before me, his intense eyes staring into my soul. Celon was Solhan. He stood naked and chained in the Avian inner chamber, copper tubes dug into his veins, connected at wrists, elbows and thighs, endlessly draining him over and over again for centuries. No matter how much the Avians stole from him, weakening him, he could not die, could not be free of the torment.

It was his punishment for trusting the Empress he had raised to the throne. He had helped her turn the battling Solhan clans into a unified power that no one in the world could stand against—except for the Avians. They built their wall, shielded their valleys and mountains, their vassal races praying for protection. Even so, her Empire could not be stopped—Celon would grant victory. All he needed was belief, devotion, utter surrender—and millions of sacrifices.

Gods did not grant boons without a price. Celon was a god, an old and powerful one from the first generation born after the Primals. His mother was Shadows, his father Fire, and Celon was God of Magic itself.

The Empress grew squeamish, however, weak. She betrayed him, bargaining with the Avians, helping them capture and imprison him. But he did not forget—and he always knew he would be free again to finish his great work. All Celon needed was a ruler willing to sacrifice anything for power. All he needed was Fharen.

I gasped as my view into Celon's mind through his bright image shifted. My awareness pulled out enough for me to see he was deep in the Avian sanctuary, copper tubes coiling from him and through holes in the walls. Dust billowed into the chamber as one of those walls exploded in. Through the broken wall and piles of rubble

I saw Fharen and his cronies. Naren was with them, leaning weakly against Uther's shoulder, his feathers matted with blood.

They dragged Naren forward, and Fharen pressed the Avian's clawed foot against Celon's bindings. I sensed Uther wielding a mixture of Archonian and Solhan magic, and he sent tendrils of power into the Avian, "Do it, and I will make sure you live. I do not wish to see your kind go extinct."

"I do," Fharen said.

"We had a bargain," Uther reminded him. "Honor it, or this ends now."

"Fine." Fharen waved his hand airily. "Get on with it."

"It has been eighty centuries. Be patient a few moments, elf."

Uther focused his magic, and Naren relented. I sensed the Avian's defeat. Being connected to the Celon—to the god Celon—through the blood that mingled with mine at that moment made me hyper aware of everything happening in that room in far away Highcrowne, the conflicts and betrayals barely held at bay as enemies worked together, for now, for the one thing they all believed they needed for their own esoteric reasons: the power of a god.

Celon remained quiet, drooping, a thing, an object, their prize. Only when the shackles holding him broke and fell to the ground, only when the copper tubes were pulled free, his skin stretching until they released, only when the wounds had closed, and green blood filled his own veins fully for the first time in near a millennium—only when he knew he was finally free did he stand tall. Pale muscles flexed as his mouth turned up into a predatory smile, and his eyes blazed with green light.

"Bow and pray, mortals," he said, his deafening voice causing more dust to fall from the walls and ceiling of the unstable stone chamber. "I owe you each a boon, so tell me what you wish."

Before I could hear their desires, the dark plots that would be fueled by this newly risen power, before I could even protest, Celon's green eyes bore into me, and he said, "I know who you are, chaos child. Go."

I was expelled from the vision. The goo's power coursing from me was snatched away, and I realized I was just standing there, bleeding from my palm. The plant had withdrawn its tendrils, all its attention focused on the maelstrom of attackers converging on it now.

Duane was climbing down the plant's thick body toward me, knives digging in, while the goblin was darting about injecting green goo into the plant at various locations. The Elf Butler dangled from a rope above, lowering Hilja, hands outstretched, toward the creature. I could tell her glamour was working, for the plant was mesmerized, not fighting. Ernest and Miss Kissell and all the fighters from the village had encircled the rim of the chamber, firing arrows at Hilja and the butler, who dodged and weaved. They must have realized her betrayal. Uncle Ulric stood in the castle above, among them, unnoticed as he guided Hilja's efforts. "That is the way to twist the creature to your will," he whispered.

"We need to get out of here," Duane said, reaching a hand toward me.

I felt like I'd been asleep, was still asleep, slipping from one nightmare to another. I wasn't sure which one was worse, but I think it was the last one. The chill of Celon's gaze filled me with dread. A Solhan god had been unleashed into the world while we'd all been distracted. The plant was the distraction.

"We need to get to Highcrowne," I said.

"Finally, thinking about the election," Katherine said, coming up beside me. She wore a jet pack. "Built this and came back for you. What's a campaign manager without her candidate? Hold on!"

She wrapped her arms around me and shot up, carrying me toward the balloon. Duane cursed and started climbing back up, dragging the goblin with him. He activated an Avian bracelet, and suddenly the both of them were floating. He caught Hilja's rope and scrambled past her and the annoyed Mister Gardens, reaching the balloon shortly after me and Katherine.

The plant had caused only minor damage to the basket, but Katherine checked the balloon's controls. "There's no motors, no gas jets. How does this thing work?" It was magic, and she was fascinated.

"Hot air rises," the goblin grumbled, refusing to see any of the 'magical' instruments before him. There was a rune he pressed that looked like a flame, and with it a flame inflated the air in the balloon. "Simple," he said, grumbling something about "breakable buttons rather than good solid brass valves."

I looked down at Ulric who waved us away wearily and retreated into the jungle. He was a Thorne. He'd be fine.

"Go. Highcrowne. Now," I said, still stunned.

The doctors obeyed, taking the balloon up. As Hilja was raised out of range of the plant alien, the arrows stopped, but massive vines now reached for us. It would smash us to bits this time.

"Oh no, you don't," the goblin giggled, dropping a small bomb over the side. "I suggest we all duck."

"Hilja." Duane grabbed the rope and pulled, I joined him in pulling her and the butler up as quickly as we could. I'd forgotten how much I hated and distrusted them both. There were worse things—like Fharen and everything he had awakened.

We got them to the rim of the basket when the explosion rocked us, sending a fiery wave of air to slam into us. The balloon careened into a spire of the ruined castle, and we slid down, out of control, crashing into the courtyard. We tumbled to the side, Hilja flying out to land somewhere else. When we finally stopped sliding and moving, I climbed to my feet, feeling Duane holding me. He helped Katherine next, her knuckles white. She clung so tightly to the railing she seemed fused with it. Shakily, she stumbled out onto solid ground. The goblin checked his pockets and smiled satisfactorily. I just knew a sample of plant over mind was in one of those pockets.

Good. I suspected we would need it someday.

I reached out a hand to the butler, but he pretended not to see it and stood on his own, dusting himself off. He quickly looked around and found Hilja. "My Queen." He helped her stand. We were all in one piece.

But the fire was spreading. It towered above the castle now, chewing at broken windows and ancient doorframes, reaching toward us.

"Let's go." I ran, Duane and I carrying Katherine between us. We didn't stop until we were across the bridge and watching everything go up in flames. Plant-controlled people from the village had come out to watch, animals from the forests—everyone who had been under the creature's control now stared with awe at the fire that had set them all free.

Some of them looked sad and lost.

"Naren," I told Duane. "He's hurt. And there's ... I'll tell you on the way. We need our balloon."

15   Feint

Hilja and the butler insisted on hitching a ride with us back to Highcrowne—probably because royal privilege was in danger and, maybe, because their balloon had crashed—but they annoyingly complained the whole time, ridiculing human technology. Katherine and the goblin danced over the valves and gauges, oblivious to their disdain, because they were having too much fun. My uncle maintained a bubble of privacy from his sheer, menacing evil vibe, which still exceeded mine, and that pushed Hilja and Mister Gardens closer to the frenzied activity. They jumped at strange whistles and clouds of steam, clutching the basket with white knuckles and frowning so hard they looked like they'd burst a gasket.

I hated human technology too, but I was loving it at that moment.

"If you preferred a frilly balloon floating on magical effervescence, you shouldn't have gotten yours blown up and smashed to bits," I said.

"That was all you," Hilja pointed out.

I didn't remember it that way, but I did have a selective memory. I frequently rewrote my own history; the alternative was wallowing in whisky all day every day, rather than just most days.

I was a bit tempted now, knowing how big we'd messed up with Fharen. I had to tell Duane, but looking at him all dashing and alive—as thrilled by crashing balloons, fires and battles with giant plant aliens as I was—made me feel better. He looked so happy, which made me happy. He was good at ignoring things too, when he wanted, but deep down he was the Shadow King, and I knew he knew I had something terrible to tell him. To tell all of them.

Only when we were at height and sailing along the winds towards Highcrowne, did I sit everyone down. The heat from the boiler kept us warm at this height, but Hilja preferred Faellion jungles, because she was wrapped tightly in the butler's jacket. He was too well trained to show how cold he was, now that he'd given his coat to his queen.

"I saw something when the blood of Celon entered my bloodstream," I began.

"Hold on," Hilja said. "Blood of Celon? And how did you get it into your bloodstream?"

"Cracked vial. Long story. Anyway, the Celon—the green goo we all know and love—also causes freaky visions when you drink it and even freakier ones when you have it in your veins."

"That's why you were frozen during the fight and not hearing us," Duane said.

"I thought she was merely paralyzed by terror," the butler said.

"No giant plant is going to paralyze me." I snorted dismissively. "I'm tougher than that. What Celon showed me, though ... He was gloating."

"Who was?" Hilja asked, impatient and annoyed as usual.

"The creature that creates the green goo," Katherine guessed. "I learned enough in my studies to realize it was organic. Not some radioactive or simple chemical substance. It had too many trace elements and fragments of what looked like cells under the microscope, only they were—strange."

The goblin pushed his glasses up on his nose. "Nonsense. I conducted similar experiments and saw only bacterial contamination, spores, and dust."

"Then you're blind, which explains why your glasses are so thick," Katherine shot back.

"Settle down kids," I said, smiling. "You professors are a testy lot. I will enlighten everyone, for I know the whole truth of Celon. And it's not good." I swallowed. "Celon is a Solhan god."

"Of course 'He' is, Miss Thorne." Doctor Ghunnan smiled at me like I was an imbecile and politely took his leave to check on the boiler.

Katherine sat closer and leaned in, awaiting my next words. Hilja and the butler looked uncomfortably at one another and at Duane. They had all known something.

"Why are you not surprised?" I asked Duane. I knew Hilja wouldn't tell me.

"I served Fharen at Ulric's request for years," Duane reminded me.

We both glanced at my uncle, but his expression remained impassive. He hadn't known about Celon, not really, despite drinking the stuff himself. I'd subjected him to truth serum once and made him tell me all his deep dark secrets, and that hadn't been one of them. Which meant Celon had chosen to show me the truth and few others.

"I listened in on Fharen's conversations with Ilsa," Duane continued. "They talked about Solhan gods when they talked about the glory of the old empire. I thought they meant the Dead God, but one time they clearly said 'gods'. But they were talking about something long ago, like it was some archeological fact, some mystery they were trying to solve, an artifact to find. Not a real living god."

"I heard something similar," Hilja said. "My father was obsessed with the Solhan 'gift' in our bloodline. He was convinced it was the key to ultimate power, an ultimate empire, under our control. He said 'the Solhans once had god-emperors'."

"A God-Empress," I corrected. "Only one. And she betrayed the god who granted her ultimate power and created the Solhan empire for her—Celon. She betrayed him and handed him over to the Avians who imprisoned Celon in Highcrowne. Until today. Fharen just set him free."

"What?" Hilja stood, annoyed again, like she'd just learned there was dragon treasure hidden beneath her feet in the palace the whole time and no one had told her—worse she hadn't discovered it herself.

"Naren?" Duane asked, worried. I was glad his first thought was for his Avian family.

"He's hurt," I said, recalling details from the vision. "He tried to stop Fharen and his goons. When we got swept away with the goblin and fighting the plant in Faellion. I thought Naren would be fine. Uther said …. Uther did make sure he lived. I saw that much. But Fharen has some hold over him too. Anyway, Fharen's bargain and glamour over the plant over mind was all a feint. A backup plan, really. If he needed the plant to control his empire he would—absolute power however he could get it. But it was a distraction, so he was free to snatch the real prize: A god.

"Celon has been imprisoned for centuries, and he wants to complete the work the Empress stopped. He wants a Solhan empire that will last a million years. He wants his people to rule over all creatures on this world—and to worship him for it. A god's power grows from the more devotion he receives. Celon is weak now, drained and almost forgotten, but that will change if Fharen gets what he wants. What Ilsa wants. A new Solhan empire will engender fear and worship, just as so many worshipped the Dead God, more will now worship a living, more benevolent being, in Celon. Relatively benevolent ... but not to those who oppose him."

"Doesn't sound that bad," Katherine said. "An elvish-dwarf-Avian empire is all I've known my whole life. How bad can a Solhan one be?"

"Bad. My people are not very nice," I said. "I'm considered a softie."

Everyone looked at Ulric—then quickly looked away again as his white eyes were chilling.

"Oh," Katherine finished lamely.

"If Celon is weak, then now is the time to stop him," Duane said, grasping the point of it all, just as I knew he would.

"Maybe our only chance. We need to get back to Highcrowne, learn what we can from Naren—how was Celon caged the first time? Then go after Fharen. And I think we'll need something faster than this balloon to beat him to Solheim. I'm certain that's where they're headed."

"There is nothing faster than this prototype," the goblin pointed out. He had been listening in selectively.

"There's faster. I'm hoping I can reach her, or Sandy, or No-Thing or someone. I need either a Voidwalker or a dragon godmother about now."

Unlike Duane's bracelet for calling Calka, I didn't have any means of calling Olyve. After I freed my dragon Godmother from the Unmentionable prison where she'd been chained (inside a volcano), I hadn't heard from her. You'd think she'd come by for tea or kaffe and a proper thank you? I could sometimes find No-Thing—another powerful being in the Unmentionable club—hanging out at the air docks, so he was my best bet.

It was safer trying to land the goblin's airship there anyway, as there was crash netting, grapples, and support workers around to help keep us from flying off again. We landed in a cradle large enough for a zeppelin, a huge, padded wall that blocked out all sound as it rippled from the impact.

"Now that we are home," Ulric said, "I will use what resources I have to discover more about Celon."

"Thanks," I replied.

"Thank you for saving me, Eva. You could have easily left me in that cell. You had every reason. Morgan, Nanny, any of them would have abandoned me."

"No, they wouldn't have. You're not so bad, not when there's Fharen to compare you to."

The goblin dampened the boiler and shut off the valves to the jets, while Katherine started deflating the balloon.

"Let's go," I told Duane. It looked like it would take some time for them to fully berth the balloon, and there was no reason to wait.

"We're coming too," Hilja said, pulling her dress out of the way and using Mister Garden's hand to climb awkwardly out of the balloon's basket.

"Quick," I told Duane.

We laughed as we ran, and he led me into secret tunnels beneath the docks. Smugglers and underworld lords like him needed lots of secret ways. I was sure Hilja or at least her investigative butler likely knew most of them also, so we didn't stay in the winding passageways for long. Once above ground, I orientated myself and recognized one of No-Thing's favorite spots, by giant coils of rope holding down some of the larger air liners.

"No-Thing?" I called looking around for something invisible. He usually animated the ropes or some other object in a surreal fairy tale kind of way, but there was no sign of him. Just a breeze that stirred a few threads of rope and got me overly excited for a moment.

"I'm going to get Calka's bracelet," Duane said when I'd stood there long enough to look dejected. "We may need it to heal Naren if he's injured."

"I'll meet you in the Avian Sanctuary," I said.

He nodded and was off. I stood around a few heart-beats longer, but I knew when help wasn't coming. I set off for the inner city, hopping on one of the trams that wound up Highcrowne's outer rings. I knew better than to ride the tram around the full circumference (that would be a corkscrew trip and far longer than it had to be—for tourists) and instead I jumped off at one of the staircases that connected the upper and lower tiers. I dashed up the stairs, gasping for breath, but another tram going the other direction was soon there, so I repeated the tactic: riding and climbing my way up the layer cake that was Highcrowne in no time.

No trams were allowed in the Central City. No messy human inventions to disturb elvish serenity. But before I legged my way to the Avian Sanctuary at the top of the mountain, I detoured to Viktor's school.

Since he'd started boarding school, Little Viktor was seldom at Nanny's place—my place I had to remind myself—so I'd taken to leaving offerings of cream near the school kitchen too. They were for his fairy god-mother, Sandy, who was even more absent than my own godmother. I had explained the whole bargain to the scullery maids, and the human ones crossed themselves for protection in some arcane way used in the south. The dwarves (you never saw elves as maids) had waved crystals about protectively, while the goblins had rubbed their bellies saying, "Yums. Cream."

"No eating the cream!" I had warned.

"Yums. Fairies," they'd followed up with, after which I'd had to specify they not eat the fairy either. If Sandy ever appeared.

I checked in now and found one of the dwarves sweeping near the back stoop.

"Any sign of Sandy?" I asked.

"Nope." He smiled and clutched his crystal necklace with a satisfied smile, certain his protections against capricious fairies were working.

Their species had been nearly extinct for centuries, but their reputation remained. I didn't think they were that bad from what I'd experienced. A bit cold and self-centered, yes, absent minded and uncaring about what concerned others, sure, but capriciousness would take too much effort on their part—energy they were unwilling to expend on stupid humans or dwarves, or even Solhans. I understood Sandy completely. So, it was no surprise she had snubbed me and her oath to watch over Viktor. Being a fairy godmother was probably an oxymoron, the equivalent of being an ethical criminal. Duane was one of those, though, so I knew the impossible was possible.

The cream looked yellow and crusty, so I washed the bowl and refilled it. One of the other maids slapped my wrist when she caught me digging out the good stuff, which was spiked with brandy and meant for kitchen staff only.

"Hey," I complained. "I pay Viktor's boarding fees—which are ridiculous—and so I think some of this cream I bought anyway."

As soon as I set the bowl out on the stoop, a delicate hand appeared out of thin air and dipped a finger inside. The finger vanished, followed by the sound of smacking lips. Then Sandy herself emerged from an invisible dimension beside this one. She was wearing the airiest of silk dresses, spun straight by spiders it seemed, all sticky and clinging to her waifish form. It barely covered her, and the human scullery maid who saw all this happen had a fit, trying to cover her eyes, gesture protectively, and in the end she just dropped her pans and ran for it.

Sandy, oblivious to all things except the bowl of cream, lifted it to her lips and drank with serene pleasure. "Yes. Fresh cream. Fairly fresh. I sense this came from a cow about dawn. It's better straight from the udder, you know. Although my kind can't touch such beasts directly without terrifying them into souring their milk. Thus, we need such kind offerings. Who am I to thank?"

"It's me. Eva."

"Who?"

"Eva. The one who defeated Harbinger, whom you fought beside, against the forces of Lili of Solheim? The Eva who was almost a fellow Unmentionable? The Eva who has been leaving you cream for years because you promised to look out for Little Viktor." I was tapping my foot with dangerous annoyance now.

"Eva. Yes. Of course. What can I do for you?"

Absent minded to the extreme.

I wasn't about to remind her yet again of her promise—she probably had no idea who Little Viktor was because she barely, if at all, remembered me. Fairies had a dislocated sense of time, often losing millennia in their own dimension and travelling between others, so I should ask for something simple.

"You remember Olyve? The new leader of the Unmentionables? The dragon?"

"Oh, yes! Olyve. You know Olyve?"

"She's my godmother. Just go find her and tell her to come get me. The god, Celon, is free, and you and the others need to do something. I'm pretty sure gods roaming the world is high on the list of 'no-no's in the Unmentionable handbook."

"Oh, that sounds bad. Let me just finish this...." She slurped and purred with enjoyment, daintily finishing off the cream while my annoyed foot tapping continued. "You really should get that looked at," she said. "You may have a neurological condition. Now, what was I doing?"

"Olyve. Now."

"As in right this second?"

"Yes. That's what now means."

"Very well. Tootaloo!" She vanished, and I really hoped she remembered Olyve. Right this second to her might mean sometime this year to me, so I didn't have much hope.

Maybe No-Thing or someone else had already noticed Celon was loose. Surely Kerrik would be aware. Once I met up with Duane we could ask Calka to summon him. Always good to have backup plans within plans.

I had been hoping for a dragon to ride up the mountain, but it was not meant to be. I drooped as I lugged heavy legs up the stairs to the Avian Sanctuary. Mountains, even when stairs were carved into the sides of them, were tall. This was just the peak, as Highcrowne was already at elevation, but even so, those remaining few hundred meters were killer on the calves.

When I reached the top, huffing and puffing, I realized the cage door on the chamber the stairs led into had been closed and locked again. "Crap." I couldn't remember if I had put the key back. I had the sneaking suspicion I'd lost it in the balloon crash, or maybe when handing Dawn off to Calka.

"Need an exit?" Duane said, smiling like a cat from the other side of the door and brandishing the skeleton key.

"How did you get that?"

"Mysterious ways. Here." He unlocked the door without me having to beg, which scored him major points. "I found Naren, and he's alive. A touch from Calka's bracelet healed him, but I wouldn't let him have it." He brandished the band. "Thought we should question him together."

"Let's go."

Despite being healed, Naren still looked like crap. He leaned against the wall of his inner sanctum. The pools of goo around glowed, but this would be the last of it. Celon's blood. The god was gone and there would be no more.

"You fed on Celon like a vampire," I said accusingly. "You drank his blood. Let the whole city use it to fuel streetlamps and horseless carriages and other nonsense."

"Celon is all. Celon sustains."

"He was your prisoner. You speak worshipfully of him, but you treated him like a rack of meat. No wonder he went off with Fharen. Anything to be free of this place."

"I do worship him," Naren said. "I love him. Calka and the others saw him as a danger, but I knew his power could be harnessed. We had harnessed it. Why did he leave?"

"I just told you. Torture. Vampirism. Duh." Still, I couldn't hold my high horse forever. I'd seen Celon's mind when his blood flowed through me. His dream of empire was a dangerous one and perfectly aligned with Fharen's lust for power.

I nudged Duane. "You're good cop."

"Me? Right … Listen, Naren. We can get Celon back."

"We can!" He stood, excited.

"Yes. Just tell us all you know about what he plans. No one has been more connected to Celon than you all these centuries. You must know where he's going."

"I don't understand why he would leave me ... but if he was to go anywhere it would be back to where he came from. His people betrayed him, so perhaps he wants vengeance upon them for what they did? Yes, that is the only thing that makes sense." Naren nodded, proud of himself for figuring it out.

"Solheim is gone, its people scattered," I pointed out.

"Then he will bring them back again. Gather them all in one place and make them regret forsaking him. Make them beg on their knees for his forgiveness. That must be what he wants."

It did sound very Solhan. Vengeance, domination ... so Celon and Fharen would be headed for Solheim, just as I thought. Why did predictability make the back of my neck itch so? Fharen was far from predictable. He'd fooled me once already with his plant over mind in Faellion. I would not let him fool me again.

Dread filled my gut. I had missed something else.

Uther had brought the plant back to life. Uther had compelled Naren to free Celon. I'd seen it. How had Fharen found him to begin with? Hanging out in Archon? That's where Ilsa had been too when she showed me the mural with an ancient, Thorne genealogy etched on the walls of a ruin. She had said Archon was the birthplace of the Solhan empire—not Solheim. That's where Celon was going.

Maybe.

"Do you know how I can be in two places at once?" I asked Duane.

"I do," a girl's voice said as she stepped out of thin air. I felt the hairs rise all along my body, and a shiver went through me.

"Olyve."

My dragon godmother had arrived.

She didn't usually go around looking like a dragon— too bulky and frightening to go most places without an undue amount of fuss—and so she often appeared as a young child, innocent and sweet in appearance, but with a menacing air that could not be concealed. Her golden yellow eyes hinted at her bestial nature for anyone clever enough to look closely.

"Eva. I presume you're asking because you know Celon went to Solheim, while Fharen went to Archon?"

"I do now. I can't let either of them get away."

"We cannot. That is why No-Thing and I are here to help. Sandy is staying out of it. As usual."

That explained how Olyve had stepped out of thin air. The Voidwalker was impossible to detect unless he spoke.

"Hi, No-Thing," I said waving.

"Good to see you again, Miss Thorne."

"Good to ... hear you." I couldn't see him, so I went on talking to thin air. "How do we stop Celon when we get to him?"

Fharen I could stop with my blade—unless he was wielding powerful glamour. Olyve might be able to see through that and point me in the right direction.

"He is a god," Olyve reminded me. "I've got Kerrik working on something. He helped Calka trap him to begin with, as did Naren. Hello again."

Naren did not look happy to see the dragon despite her deceptively harmless appearance at the moment. "Olyvandra. You ... You swore never to return here."

"Such distaste," Olyve noted. "It is you who failed in your duty, jailer. You should have let me deal with Celon as I had wanted. Then you would not be in this situation."

"You would have killed him. We would never have had all of this." He indicated the pools of goo all around.

"All this weakness you mean?" Olyve said. "The Avians were once powerful, full of magic, and you have made them as dependent as babes sucking on the teat of a greater being. I fully believe Celon helped hasten your end, helped your race waste away."

"And what excuse is there for the loss of your own kind?" Naren shot back. He always seemed so dreamy, I had never suspected such bitterness lurked within him.

"A hubris all our own, so I recognize it in others. You thought you alone could control Celon. You thought you were special, Naren. You are not. That god manipulated the post powerful Solhan line into becoming vicious necromancers in his service. He forged an empire not for them, but for his own worship, and he convinced you to protect him for centuries as he plotted against you all. Now he is free, you will see how foolish you were."

"Enough 'I told you so'," I said, cutting into Olyve's smug speech. "You are all guilty. We all are—of something. Now is the time for us to just get over ourselves and stop Celon. Take me to Archon."

"You think you can stop him?" Olyve chuckled. "Avian hubris pales in comparison to that of a Thorne."

"Maybe. But let me guess—Kerrik is working on some trap, probably with No-Thing as he's the most brilliant and action-orientated Unmentionable in your whole group. They will need a distraction to get Celon's attention while you spring it. Fharen and his cronies will also need distracting. That's where I excel. I am the best distraction ever. So, are we going?"

Olyve sighed, giving up. "Yes. That is why I'm here."

"Told you." I turned to Duane and touched the bracelet Calka had given us, which he now wore, hidden among all the other trinkets on his wrist. "Take this back to Calka. Whatever happens, she needs her magic to protect Dawn. To protect Viktor and what's left of Highcrowne—if we fail."

"You won't fail. I'm coming with you."

"Weren't you listening to Olyve's speech? Such hubris. You think you're that indispensable?" I smiled to blunt my words and segue into what I wanted to say: "Of course you are. I need you, Duane. And as much as I wish you were coming with me, as much as I know you would make all this so much easier.... Listen. You make me stronger. All my friends make me stronger too—even Katherine would be great to have 'distracting' by my side, if she could take her mind off the election for two seconds—but I'm not going to be so full of hubris as to think I will stop Celan. It will be Olyve and the Unmentionables. I am just the distraction. And I can't have this distraction being distracted worrying about all of you. Protect Dawn. Protect Highcrowne. I want something to come back to."

Duane was the Shadow King for a reason. He was as brilliant and practical as they came, cruel even, able to make hard decisions. He wasn't going to voice some token protest or outright disobey my wishes as soon as I was gone. He was too shrewd. He was also too much in love with me to ignore what I was saying and the truth of it. He listened and nodded.

"Good luck, Eva."

I kissed him, and the way he kissed me back, he knew I could die today. He could to. Any of us could, but it didn't matter. We weren't afraid of death or of living. We weren't afraid of anything when we had each other.

"You too." I breathed when we came up for air. I smiled, a giddy, falling into the abyss kind of feeling in my gut. I'd fallen hard this time. Fatally fallen.

He smiled back, and I could tell from the terror in his gaze that he felt the same. Why fear facing down a god—again—when finally telling each other how we really felt had been the scariest thing ever, and we'd survived that?

I gave him a smack on the butt. "Now, get."

The smack annoyed him, but he was too clever to try smacking me back. "We have one more public debate scheduled before the election," he reminded me instead. "Get back in time, or the crowd and this election is mine. As much as I know you don't want to be a Crown, you also hate to lose. You will if you don't come back."

"Ooh. You know me well. I'll be seeing you soon, Mister Rose, and I will wipe the floor with you and your fancy suits."

Olyve was waiting by the door and gestured for me to follow her out. Once we were on the ruined acropolis, she transformed into dragon form and held out a leg for me. "Come, child."

She was massive and golden and covered in dry scales the size of shields. I grabbed the edge of one and climbed, switching my grip to the next and the next. It was like rock-climbing, which I didn't much enjoy. I barely had time to wrap my legs around her skinny neck and coil rope-like tendrils of the hair that emerged from between her horns around my wrists for safety, before she launched herself into the air. My stomach felt like it had stayed somewhere below, and my head spun. I held tighter.

I hated heights, but with No-Thing and his voidwalking powers busy elsewhere, a dragon was the quickest way to cross the continent. Archon was on the opposite side of the world, past Solheim and Darrub, and all the once-conquered human kingdoms. It was the edge of the world. I'd been there before—armed with nothing but rumors, books and travelers' tales—but this time I had even less idea what I'd be facing.

16   GHOSTS OF THE PAST

Olyvandra flew fast as the sun could fly across the sky, able to traverse a continent in a day, but we had barely crossed the wall that bordered the Three Kingdoms and Old Solheim before I told her to stop.

"What is it?"

"I feel something." It was like a fragment of a dream. A feeling. I struggled to recall the details or when I had dreamt them ... and then I remembered it was a memory of the future. What I had seen when I first drank Celon's blood. So many images had cascaded over me, but there was something important I didn't want to miss. A conversation barely remembered ... but which I still needed to have.

Olyve circled lower, and I pointed to an outcropping of rock. The plain was sprinkled with rusting swords and armor, and the decayed skeletons of the soldiers who had once worn them. This was where the war against Lili of Solheim had been fought. With the Dead God gone, no one had reaped their souls, and ghosts lingered everywhere. The Risen who had once roamed, dangerously devouring anything in their way, were now decayed. Only the newly dead who escaped cremation in the towns and cities wandered here, before they too slowly rotted, leaving only their bones and shades behind. While I was good at ignoring ghosts, I always felt their hunger—for life or the freedom of death, either would do. Their confusion, stuck between worlds, was heartbreaking, so I ignored them.

But there was one soul here I couldn't ignore.

Olyve landed, her keen eyes seeing what I had only felt. Her massive nostrils flared, detecting a scent she did not like. "Risen."

"Don't harm him. This one's mine."

I climbed down and made my way to the figure crouched on the outcropping. He had not moved, like a cairn of bone and rusting armor. He could have been a grave marker, but his flesh had not decayed as much as the corpses on the battlefield below him. His armor was so rusting and flaking it could not deflect any weapon, but it covered his nakedness. He still had shame and vanity, all the things that had made him human, although he was no longer what he had been. He was a ghost trapped inside a body like other walking corpses, but his flesh still held some life, his soul some sanity, because I had fused him into this form when I had been at the height of my power as the Dead God's bride. He was true Risen but not of a god's making. I had created him.

"Conrad,' I said when I stood next to him.

I reached out a hand. I didn't have the power I'd once wielded, but I was still a Solhan and a Thorne, and so I was able to feed him a bit of my lifeforce, which made him stir like a puppet come to life. My soul could speak to his directly, could control it if I chose, but I spoke to him like the old friend he was.

"It's good to see you," I said. I meant it. He was no longer alive, but he was also not dead.

"Eva. I was waiting. I knew you would come."

"I didn't. Not until I remembered. There's something you need to tell me."

"Yes. Fharen. He has been here."

"I know."

"You thought his body vanished with Thane, with the Dead God. I watched from afar. I felt through you everything that happened. So, I knew what it meant when you had gone, and the body came back. Fharen walked out of Solheim, and none of the Risen touched him, for they still smelled their god upon him. That was six years ago. He has been here all this time, building up alliances in Darrub, all the old human lands. Hiding his elvish nature and playing up his Solhan. I followed where I could. Watched and listened and learned. He wants to rebuild Solheim. He wants a new empire."

"I know all this, old friend."

"I had to tell you. Warn you. Ilsa was to be his queen, but the dragon took her." Conrad had been staring at my feet like some supplicant as he spilled all he had wanted to say, all the information he had collected for me. Only now did he look up, and I saw his hazy blue eyes. I'm not sure how well they saw, but they noted Olyve's form not far away. "The dragon took Ilsa away, and so Fharen spoke to his lieutenants of a new queen. Another Thorne by his side."

"Me."

"No. Dawn."

"That bastard." She was just a little girl, but a child bride was the kind of sick thing Fharen might just contemplate. I was gladder than ever that I'd sent Duane and Calka's remaining magic back to protect her.

"Fharen is willing to wait as long as it takes, to plot and grow his power. He is patient. And now he has gone to Archon."

"That I do know."

"Good." He sighed, as if worried I had missed that feint. That's why he was here in Solheim, afraid my sleuthing would have led me only here and not where I needed to be. "Know also that the Verang, the plant he unleashed on the Three Kingdoms, is not the only seed they found there."

"What?"

"There is another power dredged from the ancient swamps. Another old god."

"The plant is an old Solhan god? I always thought it was an alien, from another world. That's the sense I had when I first touched its soul years ago?"

"It came from here, as so many dark things do." It was fitting he looked at me with dead eyes when he spoke that condemnation. "According to the story I heard, the Verang wandered across worlds," he continued, "bending all to its will, until it was defeated in some far-off land by some forgotten being. It was forced back into its seed, back into the bogs of old Solheim to regenerate."

It wasn't an alien visitor, but an old terror returned home. And a god. Crap. Maybe fire wasn't enough to kill it then? We had blown it up with goo, though, just as Calka said to do, and the plant had released its hold on everyone. We must have sent it into retreat at least. I hoped.

And there was another?

"Are you talking about Celon?" I asked. "I know he's a god. I felt it when I connected with him, but he's been in Highcrowne, not Archon. And he's supposed to be here in Solheim now."

"He was, but he left to join Fharen. There is a pantheon they plan on reviving."

"Pantheon?"

"All the gods of old Solheim, before the Dead God rose to prominence. Enough of them could defend Fharen's empire against a Primal—against you, if the Dead God returns and obeys you as Fharen fears He will."

I tried to remember what I knew of Solhan gods, which was almost nothing. Most of the gods on Uncle's shrines aside from the Dead God had been there for show, to blend in among his human neighbors. Nanny had not let him pray to the Devourer, but Viktor had, and I had seen that shrine. I had not known about Celon, let alone other lesser deities. So much had been forgotten in the dreaming times when Solhans lost interest in all except Death. Olyve was there and might know.

But if Fharen had more allies—more potential gods to raise in Archon.... "I have to hurry. We have to stop him," I said. "I'm sorry, Conrad, but I must go. Thank you."

"I'll be here if you need me again. I'll be wherever you need me."

"I want to set you free." I had been working on a means of setting souls free, as the Dead God had once done, but I wasn't ready yet and certainly not ready to experiment on Conrad. I had already done this horrible thing to him, I needed to atone, not accidentally make it worse. "I'll be back when I can do that."

"I exist only to serve."

"That's because I made you this way. I'm sorry. I didn't mean to. You will be free one day. I promise." I squeezed his bony hand covered in leathery skin.

"Goodbye, Eva."

"Goodbye, Conrad."

I scurried up Olyve's leg like a squirrel and was glad when she took off at speed. I did not complain about holding on for my life. She had heard what Conrad had said. There was more than Celon to worry about.

"Do Kerrik and No-Thing know about this pantheon?" I asked, trusting her keen ears could hear me over the rushing wind.

"No." The reply rumbled through her massive form, felt more than heard.

We were in trouble.

The wind made it too difficult to speak further, so my worry only grew as the land sped away below us. It was near sunset when we reached the border of Archon. I itched to keep going, but it was wise of Olyve to land. We needed to collect ourselves and plan.

"I have sent a message through the void. No-Thing is coming with the others," Olyve said.

"How long?"

"Soon. As you are aware, many among our membership have no care for time, so it is difficult to convey urgency. It may already be too late."

"Can't you just chain Celon up again?"

"Perhaps, but there must be a reason Fharen brought him here, where the ancients slumber beneath the bogs of Archon. A Solhan god to wake more Solhan gods."

"Which gods? And why are they sleeping?"

"I forget you were never raised in Solheim, never learned at your mother's knee. She was my friend, she and Nanny, before your mother's ambitions grew too great for this world. I thought she would choose to become an Unmentionable, but Lili chose empire instead. Just as Fharen is choosing. The old Solhan gods were asleep even then, nearly forgotten. I knew of Celon because of the legends of the Thorne Empress, the first of the line of rulers, a story your mother read avidly her whole life. I think that is why she chose to marry your father—he was a Thorne—and she craved such power for herself and her line. A new empire.

"Until she learned she could bargain your powerful soul, Eva, for control of a Primal, of the Dead God Himself. That was power beyond her dreams. Worship of Death had superseded all other worship in Solheim for some ages, as your race looked beyond this world to others. But, in the old libraries of Solheim, in books I read as I waited for a chance to visit Nanny during the day, I learned of the old gods. Celon, Verang, Tarsel, Kilbrecht, Lilon, a pantheon who weakened as their worshipers lost interest in them. They faded and sunk into the bogs, statues and ruins, seeds. That is what happens when young gods die. Only Primals exist no matter if they are worshipped or not.

"Trickster learned this when he became a god with the help of the First Soul. My old friend thought it would be better than being an Unmentionable, but a lesser god's power needs to be fueled in the absence of something like the First Soul or the Dead God. Celon was sustained by Naren's devotion, by those who used the goo not knowing what it was, but marveling at what it could do for them. The plant, Verang, returned to life when it was given bodies to inhabit, souls to control. Trickster plays his games and is worshipped by some for it, but I sometimes think he hopes to fade now. Hopes he can go back to being one of us. There is no going back. There is only a need for more power. The awakened Celon, an awakened pantheon, will need power, devotion, prayers to live again."

Olyve usually never spoke so much. That in and of itself was scary.

"Where do you think Fharen is getting the power to feed newborn gods?" I asked.

"I do not know. But we need as many Unmentionables as possible here to stop him. Even Celon, weakened as he is, is still a god and exists on another plane. He can see through time, see what we might do, and prepare. At best, we can chain his body again, but not his full power."

"What about that trick we pulled with Leviathan, a Primal? We got him out of our way."

"You had the First Soul then. It is a Primal itself. Now, we have just our magic, woven from this world or borrowed from the Void. We have no prayers of the devoted, for Unmentionables are unknown and unseen."

"You make it sound hopeless."

"I fear ... No, you do not need to know my fears, child. We have you as a distraction, and at that you excel and more. We will stop Celon."

Now she was giving me a pep talk. A very bad sign.

"Hurry up, No-Thing!" I said aloud. I took advantage of the break to go to the bathroom, which euphemistically meant a bush, stretch my legs, and forage for some food. I'd survived Archon before. I was really hoping I survived it again.

As hours ticked by and I couldn't sleep, the night alive with the chirping of bugs, hooting of owls, plop of creatures slinking into the water. Hunters and prey. Skies bright with stars, fireflies, and the eerie glow of marsh gas ... it was worse than the city. At least in Highcrowne's frozen blanket of snow, there was silence, peace, which I missed desperately. I missed Dawn, even though I was sure she did not miss me. She would be having the time of her life questioning Calka to death and pestering Princess Glau with riddles and clever mind puzzles she liked to make up for 'fun'. I had a strange daughter.

I hoped Duane had found them—if anyone could it was him—and was watching over them with a Shadow King's arsenal. I hoped Sandy was watching Little Viktor, as I was sure she hadn't heeded No-Thing' summons to come here and fight. She liked to stay out of harm's way. Nanny, at least, would be watching out for Viktor. Morgan too, when he wasn't looking out for Ulric as he was bound to do.

My family.

How things had shifted since I lived in Uncle's house under his thumb, when he was a gangster rather than the priest he'd become, trying not to be poisoned by Nanny's cooking—although that hadn't changed. Nanny was the one constant. At least, there was no more Ilsa at my throat. My sister was imprisoned somewhere dank and deep that only Unmentionables knew about. Gypsum, my old friend who turned traitor, was in prison too, but she was set to be transferred to the stockade in Gernwold, where her family might visit her from time to time.

Karolyne was long gone, living on some beach somewhere, but I missed the old café so much I was thinking about buying it myself with some of the gold Hilja owed me. I'd name it "Burnt Traitor" in Karo's honor, as she'd been labelled a turncoat too during the war and the café burnt to a woody skeleton. Maybe that was too morbid, too Solhan? I should think on it. Maybe Jorg, my grall friend, would come be chef again, and all my other friends would work there too. Not that I could think of many. Bell and Kali were on the enemy list, really.

I had Katherine and Doctor Ghunnan, but they'd be busy in their laboratories and not wanting to hang out at the window attracting customers with me over a cup of whisky-spiked kaffe. Maybe Olyve and No-Thing? I laughed, imagining a mug being raised by invisible hands and spilled everywhere ... or guzzled by a pretty little blond girl with a dragon under her skin. I'm sure Hilja and Mister Gardens would stop by from time to time, hooded and clandestine, to check on Dawn and try to convince me yet again to let them raise her as an elvish heir.

It was all so sad.

Maybe it was better to let Archon's swamp swallow me like it had the old Solhan gods? Maybe it was better to fade and let the world go on without my melancholy and nostalgia? Was I getting old? Is this what it felt like? Solhans could live centuries, but I'd been hard used in my few decades. So much power had flowed through me, it was certain to have burnt me up a bit inside. I was like the charcoal skeleton of that café, timbers held together by ash, ready to collapse at any moment.

I should just go into the bog, follow one of the fey lights into murky depths. Better than facing Celon and Fharen, laughing Aguragas and Gallan's gloating nephew, all the unknowns that lay ahead. If I couldn't sleep with all this damn noise and light, I might as well die. Then I'd finally have some peace.

I found myself with a toe in the water before I snapped out of it. Olyve was snoring, her golden dragon scales rattling like coins as her chest rose and fell. Something had affected her too, for she slept too soundly. Then she stopped breathing.

Everything stopped.

The buzzing was gone, insects frozen in midair. Clouds of mist stood solid and unmoving, ripples in the water like waves of sand in a Darrubian desert garden.

"Trickster," I said.

"You caught me." A laugh filled the night, like a crystal chandelier all bright and sharp and musical.

Trickster slowly materialized before me, a shadow at first with glowing coals for eyes, and then clapping hands, until he was a full-fledged beast. His wings and tail were new, I thought. I couldn't recall if I'd met him fully formed that first time before I went to face the Unmentionables. I had not seen him since. A capricious younger god, I had hoped never to see him again. Until now.

"Are you here to help stop Celon?" I asked, excited.

"I had you contemplating suicide a moment ago, so how can you be so annoyingly chipper now?" he asked.

"I'm Solhan. Depressed is the default, but you being here means the Unmentionables are not alone. You will help. Won't you? Wait. You are a trickster, so I should be contrary.... Don't you dare help or get involved. We don't need your kind of interference!"

"Ooh, that almost worked. I felt a knee jerk reaction to help you against your wishes. Not enough though. Not planning on getting involved."

"Oh." I slumped. The swamp was looking appealing again. "Why are you here then?"

"To watch."

"To watch me and your Unmentionable friends die when we face off against Fharen and his new 'pantheon'?"

"I'm not like your old lover. Death is not what excites me. No, I've come to watch sleeping gods wake. I may need such a revival myself one day. Good to learn how it's done."

"We can't let old Solhan gods rise...." I began.

"Why not?"

"Well, they're Solhan, which automatically means not good. And Fharen wants them awake, which is once again, not good. And the world just barely survived 'my old lover' as you put it walking around. Gods are trouble."

"The good kind, like me," Trickster said, putting a hand to his chest. "We liven things up, and we are not all bad. We save babes from sacrifice. Case in point."

Trickster had saved me from being sacrificed by my mother, so that was a good argument. He had just been causing trouble though, no morality behind the choice.

"Why do you want other gods running around? Isn't that more competition for you and for worshippers? Do you have worshippers?"

"Some. *He he he.* You keep expecting me to give you a rational argument, girl. How odd."

True. I still hoped I could convince him to help, but Trickster was a spur of the moment kind of creature.

"Fine," I said. "Do what you will. But unfreeze Olyve and stop interfering with No-Thing and the others. I presume you're why they're not here yet?"

He smiled guiltily, eyes ablaze with joy at being so naughty.

"It will be so much more fun with them mucking up things," I argued, knowing just how to manipulate him.

"Oh, all right. See you soon, Eva." He vanished into shadow and the world came alive again. Olyve snorted awake, setting some marsh gas on fire with her breath.

Then a curtain of nothingness opened before me, spilling out a nightmarish ensemble of Unmentionables.

I instinctively backpedaled as the giant spider with its transparent limbs scurried toward me. He might have been wanting to say 'hi', but I didn't care. I hid under one of Olyve's wings. The spider paused, looking a bit disappointed that it didn't get to greet me with its feelers like last time. I shuddered, remembering.

There was the three-headed ghost woman—we'd never spoken, so I still hadn't gotten her name—but she helped during the war, as far as I could recall, so I classified her as an observer. Then there was Tikaban, the glacially slow horse fellow who was, surprisingly, not the last out of the portal. He was followed by the mummy—meaning desiccated corpse with spindly limbs, not my mother, although they bore a striking resemblance—and, finally, the bunny of death, a giant rabbit with crazy eyes and blood smeared claws.

Not as many as I would have liked. Quite a few had died in the war, or at my hand, like Harbinger and his cronies.

After the rift in the air sealed itself, I heard No-Thing right beside me say, "Eva. You shouldn't be here." It made me jump. He was invisible and hadn't bothered inhabiting any inanimate objects as he usually did.

"You almost recruited me to be an Unmentionable," I pointed out.

"That was when...." He stopped before saying 'you had real power'.

He was mistaken. I was not powerless. "I'm the distraction. Fharen and the others will focus on me. You take care of Celon. Now, let's go."

Nobody moved, which meant I wasn't in charge. Olyve was. She smiled her dragon smile and said, "You heard my goddaughter. Move!"

She took to the air, me on her back, with a plethora of creatures running, hopping or wisping through the bog below us. I thought there would be a planning session, but I supposed such fiercely independent beasties never worked together for long, and never in a coordinated way, so it was more important to point them where they needed to go.

We weren't far from the ruins Ilsa had shown me, where my family name was writ on the wall. I felt the magic of that place, but it had changed in the short time since I'd been here. The ruins had been cleared of plants, and there was now a temple made of new stone with a road leading up to it that had been carved out of the jungle. The road and the steps of the temple were crowded with thousands of pilgrims, adults and children in tattered clothes, people of every description, light to dark, short to tall, all chanting—all human.

"This is where Celon and the other Solhan gods plan to get their power," I said. "Worshippers." I didn't understand why all these humans had come here, braving the Archonian jungle and swamps. Had Fharen offered them gold or power or simply food? They looked starved, desperate, and I knew refugees would do any-thing for the promise of a meal.

As Unmentionables scurried across the ground toward them, and the dragon I rode cast a shadow from above, people screamed. I wanted to tell them we were the good guys, but it probably didn't look that way. Especially when Olyve spewed a stream of fire out of her muzzle that set trees and people ablaze.

"Stop!" I cried. "What are you doing?"

"Taking out their source of power."

LOREL CLAYTON

17 THE GREATER GOOD

I shouldn't have been surprised. Unmentionables who liked to deal with problems by eliminating whole dynasties or cities would, obviously, see killing thousands of human worshippers as a simple answer.

I had to inject some morality into the situation and fast.

"Olyvandra," I said in a fair approximation of Nanny's 'I am so disappointed' voice. "You will stop burning people right this instant and order the other Unmentionables to herd the humans away from here—without eating them. Are you in charge of this mob or not? If so, then prove it."

The flames stopped, and she twisted her long neck, so her huge, yellow eyes could glare back at me. "If you want to stop Celon from raising more of his kind, we must consider the greater good."

"Not if it means all these innocents dying. For all you know, the Solhan gods require sacrifice, so killing these people may be giving Celon exactly what he wants."

That argument worked. "Stop!" Olyve called to the others, diving and buffeting an overeager spider with her wings. Humans were knocked to the ground, but the delicate spider creature went flying. "Get the humans safely away from here. Their lives are not to be sacrificed. We must protect them at all costs."

I wasn't sure that theory was correct, but I wasn't about to protest. It had the desired effect, and soon people were fleeing away from the temple. It helped that Olyve and the others had already murdered a few dozen of them, leaving charred statues behind or husks drained of blood or life, so they had good reason to run away.

Old Eva would have been wracked with guilt and endlessly replaying what I could have done differently to save those people, but the pragmatic New Eva understood the past could not be undone.

Or could it? Something whispered in my mind.

Trickster. Maybe? I always distrusted whispers in my head. Meant I was either going crazy or being manipulated by a powerful being that could speak mind to mind—which was the same result. Letting someone else make my decisions. I was too stubborn for that.

"Alright," I told Olyve, who was a good dragon godmother and indulged me by letting me believe I was in charge. "Set us down. I'll run in there and distract everyone, stop whatever ceremony is happening, listen to the villains gloat, yadda yadda, while you and the others do some flanking maneuvers and fancy Unmentionable stuff to take out Fharen and Celon before they can enact their evil plan."

"Very well," Olyve said in that patient, godmotherly tone of hers.

"What's wrong with my plan?"

"Nothing, dear. You are the ever-so-important distraction after all, so act as you see best. We'll do our 'Unmentionable stuff'. Don't concern yourself with the details."

"Right." She set me down, and I suddenly doubted everything.

I'd interrupted enough ceremonies in dark temples and caves to know how this worked. Didn't I? There was always an altar. Someone tied up as a sacrifice. It wasn't me this time, so I'd probably be shocked to learn they had Karolyne or someone else important to me. If it was Ilsa, I'd laugh. If it was Dawn or Duane, I'd kill Fharen slowly. I knew how these things worked.

I had this. Didn't I?

"Okay. See you soon," I told Olyve. She just snorted and flew off. She obviously thought the frontal assault through the temple main door wasn't 'Unmentionable stuff'. I watched a bit to see what she was up to, whether she'd circle back to talk me out of my idiocy, but she didn't. She vanished into the trees, and everything went quiet. Too quiet.

"Stealth attack. Right." I could easily have been an Unmentionable if I had wanted. I didn't. I still didn't. Did I?

So much fun. The voice in my head said, and I knew it had to be Trickster. He was probably feeding me all this doubt for giggles. Nothing mattered more to him than his own entertainment.

I stood straighter, dusted off my clothes and strode through the huge archway like I owned the place. "Here I am," I called. "Come out and face me, Fharen."

It took me a moment for my eyes to adjust to the gloom. For a newly built temple, they could have included some modern amenities like gas lights or even Celon-powered glow lights—they had the god himself there. He could have opened a vein and powered the whole place.

There was a bit of a mechanical feel, a slight hum rattling the back of my teeth, and an iron metallic taste to the air. Acid, like batteries from the south. Human technology. How pedestrian.

A skylight cut in the stone was the only light source, and it illuminated an altar. Told you. I knew this stuff like the back of my hand. The stone was new and clean, so no blood sacrifices yet. Good. No one tied to it either. That probably meant they had been waiting for me.

"I warn you—I didn't come alone," I said to the gloom. Fharen and his cronies were nowhere to be seen. This place was too quiet too, aside from the hum. Were all of them using the ambush tactic? What happened when two rivals both waited around forever for a trap to spring? Get tired and take a nap? Well, it was my job to go in and muck everything up.

I avoided the altar—I'm not stupid—and took a stroll around the edge of the chamber. It was circular. The outside was square, so this was some sort of inner room, shaped for the ritual. There must be secret passages in the thick walls, or maybe that's where the batteries and iron was? Was this some sort of electrical trap? I should have brought Doctor Ghunnan. He was good at dealing with these things. They hadn't zapped me yet, so they were probably waiting for Olyve and the others. Or maybe they had meant to zap all the human worshippers at once and we'd already foiled their plan?

"Where did you get all those dupes?" I asked the empty space, hoping to lure a gloating villain into the light. "Thousands of refugees headed for a sacrificial altar? I stopped the plant alien, Verang or whatever, burnt it to a crisp, so they weren't its puppets. Did you use elvish glamour on them? Maybe good old-fashioned bribery and promises you never intended to keep? ... Fharen. Hello?"

"I am here."

Had him! I knew he couldn't resist a chance to tell me how clever and powerful he was.

"You want to know how I lured those humans?" Fharen said. "They are Darrubians, a few Archonians among them, scattered tribes with no real gods of their own, none powerful enough to have protected them from the Dead God anyway. They want Solhan power. Humans are mirrors of Solhans from another universe, so it is easy enough for them to adopt Solhan gods. They came to pray and ask for their protection. They never want to be victims again."

I still couldn't see him. His voice carried through the walls, amplified like one of the speaking horns on the great airships. I kept circling, looking for the source, and couldn't find it. There were carvings on the rounded stone surface, mixtures of dwarfish, elvish, and human designs. Ancient Solhan also. I came to a section with writing I had learned to read. I didn't spend all my days staring into a glass of whisky. I had read every tablet, scroll, and book in the Central Library on the old Solhan empire. There had been no gods mentioned but the Dead God, which is why I had been thrown by Celon. Maybe they had been deliberately erased from the records? Why?

"I don't like speaking to a wall," I said. "Come out and say hello, Fharen. Face to face. Don't you miss me?" I asked coquettishly.

"I do, Eva, I really do. I was disappointed when you figured out my ruse. Being Thane was so ... delicious. How did you discover me?"

"I didn't love you. It's not what's on the outside, Fharen. It's not even what you know, all the details, the mannerisms and turns of phrase. There's something in the soul—and that's what you lack. A soul."

He laughed. "Probably because I sold mine long ago. Not literally. But I don't care about these strange boundaries you and others cling to, these self-imposed limitations. The powerful can be and do anything. Why would you pull back when the world could be yours?"

"Because the world would suck even worse with me in charge. My room is a mess, my life is a mess. When you are powerful, you can do anything—but you are still always you. You can only remake the world in your own image, and if that image is flawed, so will it be. And you are very flawed, Fharen. That's why I've come to stop you. Your world would be a twisted fun house mirror of elvish privilege and human slavery, where the rich laugh at the misery of the poor. It would be a world of all the small, boring things you have always done, but on a larger scale. Yawn."

"Oh, but I am not remaking the world in my image," Fharen said. I could hear the smile in his voice. I had him right where I wanted him. He was about to spill all his dastardly plans. Now, where was Olyve and the others?

"Whose image then?" I prompted. I started pressing glyphs on the stone wall, hoping to find a hidden door and whatever chamber Fharen was gloating from.

Something clicked, and the hum of machinery grew louder. Oops. Was that my doing?

"Celon's and the other Solhan gods," Fharen said, as if I was simple. "I am restoring the old empire and the powers that led it to glory. I am not as vain as you believe me to be, Eva. I am open to the counsel and grace of Celon and the others. It is not my eternal, personal power I wish to secure, although a few millennia more of life will be good. No, I seek to establish a legacy. A dynasty. That is why I want our daughter. I want Dawn. What a terrible name. What is her secret name? More elvish or Solhan I hope?"

"I'll never tell you or anyone her secret name. I'm not stupid, but yes, it's more traditional, you might say. The main thing is: you can't have her. She's her own person. And if you think you can marry her—gag—and start some incestuous imperial line, I am going to find you and cut off your bols right now."

"That is so Darrubian. You really think so little of me? Have you even read your own history? Solhan history?"

"Not much, I have to admit. Magic necromancy stuff, yes, but when they start with names and dates and places I've never heard of, I start to fall asleep. When you're drooling all over rare texts in the Central Library people get angry and kick you out before you can finish reading everything, not that I really wanted to read more after the falling asleep bits." I was doing my best to stall, but where was everyone?

Sandy had a horrible sense of time. Tikaban was slow, but Olyve and the others had no excuse. Were they hunting down and eating humans after all? None of them could follow orders.

The mechanical sounds grew louder and the hum along with it. There was something familiar about that hum that made my hairs stand on end. Where had I heard it before?

Panicked, I started pressing on glyphs, hoping to turn the machine in the walls off, but the walls started moving. The sphere I was inside began to rotate, and my finger got pinched in a groove. I snatched it back before I lost it entirely. I sucked on it.

"Any blood by chance?" Fharen asked.

Could he see me?

"Where are you? And why do you want me to bleed?" I wasn't getting anywhere near that altar if that's where he was hoping I'd spill some blood.

"I'm assured it's not necessary, but I think it must be my vicious, primitive nature that desires a bit of blood for a sacrifice. They tell me all that is needed is your soul."

"Who is 'they'?"

"Your dear sister, Ilsa, for one. I cannot help her now, caged by the Unmentionables as she is, but before her piece was taken off the game board, she helped me discover the ritual and was ever so helpful in countless ways—probably because she thought she would be empress. That's why she killed Emily, to ensure your brother would have no female heirs to compete with her. She improvised and switched sides to Harbinger, and the immediate power he offered, but when you killed him, she came back to my side. By then, we had Dawn, and she was no longer necessary. So tragic for her."

I'd really gotten Fharen spilling not only his evil plans but my sister's too. Best to keep it going. "You don't seem that worked up about it."

"She should not have lost faith. Still, I used her. Ilsa worked with Aguragas and his insurrectionists to help eliminate my political rivals and destroy the protections around the Avian Sanctuary, so we could reach Celon. Naren and the Shadow King proved too powerful of a protection, still, so Mister Rose had to be taken off the board as well. Clever of me to arrange for him to be framed for Hilja's murder. I needed Hilja eliminated, of course. My daughter or not, she was not Solhan enough and not pliable. Ilsa tried to kill her before but never succeeded. She did, however, perform the most crucial task. Ilsa visited your friend in prison, Gypsum, who revealed the location of the device we recovered and transplanted here."

"Device?" What device would Gypsum know about that would be at all useful to Ilsa?

Oh.

I'd nearly forgotten. I hadn't known Gypsum believed me, but she'd been tasked by the Dead God to spy on me, and so she must have investigated herself after I came out of that trap. She must have used her influence as sister to a Matriarch to secure it before the authorities in Gernwold could. If any of them even understood the purpose of such an ancient, Solhan creation.

The walls of the room had confused me. Deliberately, I supposed. They'd been decorated in too many styles and languages. The real ritual markings were hidden within the noise.

I looked down at the floor. That part was the same. Oh, crap.

I was inside a time machine.

Worse. My soul was no longer protected in one of Ulric's soul jars. It had been reunited with my body at my coming of age ceremony. But I was not the weak girl I'd been. No one was extracting my soul to feed to a machine.

"I see several flaws in your plan," I said, taunting Fharen. I always loved to taunt the villains.

"Really?"

"First. You are not in this room, so only I will be sent back in time to when Solhan gods ruled or whatever. I won't help you bring them back. Second, if it requires the soul of a Solhan, my soul, which is probably why the last sycophant had tried to use me to operate this thing, then it also needs someone with enough necromantic power to extract the soul from my body. No one living is as powerful as me. Not Nanny, and I daresay not Ulric."

That was an outright lie, but maybe it would give him pause.

Fharen's laugh made me shiver even more than the growing hum of the machine. It felt like I was in the middle of a lightning storm, the charge building in the air, until even my straight hair was sticking out at all angles, and my skin was covered in gooseflesh.

"Quit. Laughing," I said through gritted teeth.

"I am so sorry." He hadn't stopped and even sounded like he needed to pause to wipe away tears of mirth. "It's just that you are so terribly wrong, my lover."

His glamour dropped away and suddenly he was there, sitting on the altar in the center of the room. Thane but not Thane. Fharen.

He was wracked with giggles, but managed to say, "I am the one who will be going back. And I don't need to extract your soul. I just need it to be here inside the machine—and you are here and your soul along with you. There is no stopping this."

"Your death should do it." I lunged for him, drawing my blade in the same instant, really hoping this wasn't another illusion, so I could finally skewer him.

He held up a hand. "Sleep."

An elvish sleep spell wasn't about to work on me. I was too powerful for that. Admittedly, Fharen was very good at glamour, but not other forms of magic. I knew because ... wait. There was a rune in his hand. Archonian. Powerful. The edges of my vision went dark,

my arm already limp, sword dragging on the floor.
Before I knew it, the room spun, and I was falling.

LOREL CLAYTON

18 LESSONS REPEAT

When I awoke, the hum was gone. The room no longer spun. I stumbled to the doorway, at least where I remembered the doorway had been, but it was still sealed off. I was trapped. Why did I fall into traps so easily?

Because I thought being the distraction was a good thing.

It had bitten me in the ass this time. They needed Solhan—likely Thorne—power to run this contraption, and I'd given it to them on a platter. Fharen obviously wasn't Solhan enough, despite all his claims to empire and hamming up his Solhan looks every chance he got.

Where was he? Glamoured again? I set my sword to swinging randomly in zig zag patterns everywhere I walked, while looking for another way out, hoping I'd get him, even if by accident.

No luck. Finding a door or drawing Fharen's blood.

I was so frustrated I shouted, a real visceral scream. It felt good. I wanted to smash the wall with my sword, but I refrained. It was my one useful inheritance, and I didn't want to dull or damage it. I used a fist instead, a mistake, and was quickly rubbing my knuckles and saying 'ouch' over and over. It did calm me down at least. Pain focused me on vengeance, which was more useful than blind anger.

I studied the writing on the walls, trying to tune out the distractions of other styles and languages, until I found the ancient Solhan script I was looking for. I had been learning to read what I could. There were some books hidden in the attic of my house that had helped, as well as fragments of knowledge from Solhan refugees in Highcrowne. I didn't drink whisky all the time. Only when my brain got full and needed a vacation from itself.

This wasn't like the writing Ilsa had first shown me in an old ruin here in Archon. I wondered if this temple was built over it or in front of it? I sensed it nearby, because it sung with Thorne magic. Simply touching it had revealed knowledge of the past. This writing was not as powerful, although someone had made an attempt—it was written in blood.

After a few hours of contemplation, study, and generally wracking my brain until I wished I could drown it in alcohol, I made out that the writing referred to a particular time in history, after the rise of the Solhan Empire but before it devoted itself to worship of the Dead God and the Devourer alone.

I wondered why Celon had not been in here, travelling with Fharen? I would have thought a fallen god like him would have loved to return to his heyday and redo things. The more I read the more I understood, though. Beings could not travel to a time where they already existed. The magic would not work. Fharen and I had not been born yet, so only we could come.

My stomach growled. Fharen wasn't planning on living in this time forever, was he? He wouldn't just leave me locked in here to starve. Would he?

Just as I started to get nervous, the doorway rumbled open. I readied my blade to finally get some vengeance on a particularly annoying Elf King.

What stepped through the doorway was not Fharen. It was hugely muscled, skin a blue so deep it was nearly black, with thick horns that formed a semicircle around its forehead. The beast grabbed the blade of my sword and snapped it in two.

What?

The scream of trapped souls, the fragments of all those I had killed, all those my mother and her mother before her had killed ... the power released was immense, and the blue beastie smiled and breathed deep, as if inhaling a delicious scent.

"Who are you?" I asked, pissed as hell that he had destroyed my heirloom, but trying not to show it, as this was one obviously powerful being.

"Grom."

Grom. That sounded so familiar.

I backpedaled as more giant creatures stalked into the chamber. There was a beautiful Solhan woman, pale as death with a gown to match. She was so tall she had to crouch so as not to catch her head on the massive, vaulted ceiling. Stars sparkled like decorations in her inky, black hair, and when I mean 'stars' I don't mean a simile for diamonds. They were real, miniature stars in every color, some orange like the sun and fiery. I knew who she was right away.

"Darkness, Night Mother," I whispered, beginning to tremble. She was a god. Grom was a god—god of rage and hunger. I hadn't realized they were Solhan gods. Many races knew of them, remembered them, even if my people had forsaken them.

The other gods, twelve in total, spread around the chamber, eying each other warily, like this experience was as strange for them as it was for me. There were many I had never heard of, lost to time, but obviously as powerful as Grom at least, for they showed no fear of him. They all bowed their heads ever so slightly to the Night Mother, however, the greatest of them. There was a willowy being, more tree or mushroom in shape, and a pair of sleek cats, one black and one white, entwining around one another and hissing from time to time. The most frightening of all was a black snake whose tail burned eternally with a red glow, like charcoal, and its matching red eyes never stopped looking into mine, as though it was trying to crawl inside my mind and burrow there.

When Fharen returned I felt the strangest relief. I ran forward, dodging giant feet. The chamber door was open, and I almost ran out, except this was not my time. Part of me was curious to see it, see what the old empire looked like, my ancestors, Archon before it was overgrown with jungle, but my curiosity was not enough to overshadow my fear.

"What are you doing?" I hissed to Fharen. "One god nearly destroyed the world, what do you think will happen when you bring all these back?"

"Gratitude. Power beyond anyone's comprehension. Now, be silent, for your usefulness is nearly at an end."

I went to strangle him, but he vanished in a glamour again, and then the room was spinning.

I stumbled, saying "sorry" when I touched Grom's leg to catch myself. I lunged for the altar in the center of the room, hugging it first for balance as reality tumbled around me, but then part of me wondered if it was the control mechanism, not the writing on the walls. I still had the bone handle of my Ashur, a broken blade no longer than a dagger remained attached, and I used it to slice my finger. Red droplets welled, and I began writing on the altar in ancient Solhan. A new destination.

I must have been onto something, because Fharen's invisible form grabbed my wrist, trying to force me to stop. I fought him off and finished the line of text.

The room shuddered, like a motor carriage on a bumpy road. We were off the beaten path. I heard Fharen make a surprise sound as he went flying. He hit his head and went unconscious, because he could no longer maintain his glamour. I saw him lying at the feet of the Night Mother, who picked him up and cradled him. None of the gods were disturbed by the turbulence or the change in destination. They were all looking at me curiously now, not just the snake, as I clutched the altar for dear life.

When the turbulence finally stopped, the temple door rumbled open of its own accord.

"Go," I told the Night Mother. "Before it closes again." I wasn't entirely sure how to control this thing. I was figuring it out but not well enough to open the door on command.

"You work with the elf?" Night Mother asked me.

"No. Never."

"He promised us a new world without the Dead God or the Devourer, a world where we would reign supreme among all gods."

"You'll have that here too," I said. "All you could ever want. Remember it was Eva Thorne who helped you, not Fharen. Now, go." I figured it couldn't hurt if she owed me one.

"Thank you," the Night Mother said, gracing me with a slight nod. She was the first to glide out, still cradling Fharen in her arms. The others followed suit and nodded to me as well before they each took their leave, the snake the last of them to go.

"Why are you staring at me?" I had to ask.

"You have no comprehension of who I am." The god's voice was smoother and less sibilant than I had expected—if I had expected a giant snake to speak.

"There's lots of important beings I tend to insult without meaning to," I said, "because I really don't give a damn who they are. No offense."

"You have been touched by tricks and chaos. I see it in you. I see what is in the dark, what lies beneath, the unseen world, and I know what others do not. Do you wish to taste of the knowledge I can give you?"

"Tempting ... but no. I'll figure it out on my own."

"Not even a nibble?"

I remembered some story about an apple and shook my head.

"Pity. For it is knowledge of self I would grant you, and there is no greater power. Remain in the dark if you so wish, but I warn you not to let the chaos touch those you hold dear, the young one especially. Keep the chaotic one away from her. Tell her I will see her one day and give her the knowledge she hungers for."

"You mean Dawn? Stay away from my daughter."

"I am her salvation. Know they enemy." With that the giant snake slithered away with the sinuous grace of a dark river spilling over the white stones. The door rumbled shut just as his glowing tail disappeared through the gap.

I took a deep breath. I had done it. No one had seen, but I had done it. The world was spared a pantheon of dangerous new gods. For now.

Time made my head hurt, and I really needed whisky. I wiped away the writing on the altar, nicked another finger, and spelt out a fresh destination in my blood. The rumbling became a groan, and I could tell the machine was running out of power.

"One more trip. Please," I begged.

The walls spun, my head along with it. No Archonian charm to blame this time. I think the adrenaline and unacknowledged fear was catching up with me. I needed to hold on.

The walls shuddered and stopped spinning, and the ground jerked beneath me. I fell hard on hands and knees. The door opened, and I crawled toward it, but I felt sluggish, like I was moving through mud. The door began to slide shut again, and I still wasn't anywhere near it.

"Keep going, Eva," I told myself through gritted teeth. Through sheer will, I climbed to my feet and threw myself forward, ready to roll beneath before it shut. I didn't need to, because a strong pair of hands gripped the lowering stone and forced it back up. Slowly, with more grinding, shuddering sounds of protest, a screech of protesting gears, and then it was freed. The door was open, and I climbed to my feet. I looked into a Solhan face, pale eyes and glowing white skin, and then the eyes too began to glow—green.

"Celon," I said.

"I know what you did, I saw, for I see through time," he said.

"But you didn't see it coming."

"You are chaos."

"The second god to tell me that today. Recently. Whatever. Time hurts my head."

"Unpredictability such as yours is dangerous for me. The Empress had it, your ancestor, else I would never have been captured, betrayed, and imprisoned for centuries. I can't risk that happening again. I am sorry, young one, but you must die before you kill me and all I dream for your people."

Those same strong hands that had just lifted a massive stone door reached for my throat. I tried to back away, but they came inexorably towards me. I forced myself to calm, to think, to summon power, all that I had. Celon was no living thing to be drained of life or putrefied by necromancy, however. He was like stone. I needed sheer force to shatter it.

I heard a snicker in the shadows. "He, he."

Trickster.

"Help me!" I demanded.

There was no response. The hands drew closer, now on my throat, squeezing.

Fear and anger fueled me, and I unleashed that stone-shattering power in all directions with a scream of rage: "Go away!"

It felt like all the frustration that had built up over the loss of my magic, at the chaos in the Kingdoms, at everyone who wanted to use Dawn for their own evil purposes and make my world a torment—all that sense of injustice tapped into the fire deep within me, like a volcano inside, and raw power poured out. My magic— pure, free, and ... chaotic.

Celon pulled back, but he was not stone and did not shatter. The walls did though. They fell away all around, blown outward. The entire temple crumbled into rubble. I saw open sky and Olyve's golden form circling. She descended along with a horde of Unmentionables, converging from all around now that the barriers were down.

The spider was the first to jump Celon, wrapping legs around his head and biting with mandibles, trying to inject poison that was strong enough to kill anything, I sensed, but not strong enough to kill even a weakened god. Celon threw the creature off.

More Unmentionables assaulted him with bolts of magic, fangs, or weapons, and Celon grew annoyed, like someone engulfed by a cloud of mosquitos. Even as Olyve's massive claw encircled him, Celon did not fear. She bit into his neck, ready to tear his head off, but even her sharp teeth could not penetrate his skin. One tooth broke and fell at my feet. Like my broken sword.

There was no chance when mortals fought gods. Even Unmentionables were still mortal.

"Trickster. Please," I begged again. "I'll owe you."

His shadowy form appeared before me and hefted Olyve's broken tooth appreciatively. He slung it over one shoulder. "You already owe me your life."

"No. I wasn't old enough to agree to that. That was a gift."

"Hmm. Fine. I'll help, but you will give me Dawn."

"No," I said automatically. I would never sacrifice Dawn, not for anything. I was curious as to why he wanted her, though. "Why her?"

"She will be fun," he lied. "You will not bargain with her, I see. That is what your mother did with you, sacrificed you to gain power and all she desired ... but you are not her."

"You have been paying attention."

"A more palatable agreement, then. Your life."

I almost said, 'no', again, but Celon had shattered one of Olyve's claws now too. The dragon shrieked with pain and dropped him again. The spider lay in a broken heap, feet in the air, dead possibly, and Tikaban was now reaching out a hoof, casting some spell that did nothing, fear on his usually kind face. No-Thing had created a travelling portal, but this was not like the one we'd cut into the void with the First Soul. It was too small and weak to draw Celon in. The others were trying to drive him toward it, but with a wave of his hand, the portal closed.

"Alright," I told Trickster. "You saved my life, and so now I give it back. Take it—as long as you stop Celon and save all of them. Save Dawn and Duane and Little Viktor, Nanny, Morgan, and everyone I care about. If I know they are safe, then I'm willing to die here and now."

"It will not be now. I will choose the best time."

"When it will create the most havoc, I suppose?"

"Of course."

"Just uphold the full bargain."

"I swear." Trickster gave the most mischievous smile as he held up his hand to swear, while also crossing his fingers.

"Hey—" My words were cut short because the world tilted again. It felt like I was swirling around in the time chamber again, but it was gone. This was a whirlwind of sheer force that picked me up, along with Olyve, and all the Unmentionables. A few bits of rocks and trees swirled around with us too, like we were in a tornado.

The world below flew by, jungles and bogs, until we were past the great river that bordered Archon and the smaller human kingdoms of Kell, Trist, and Selene.

We finally stopped on one of the rock formations of Metora that were the highest elevation in the region, nothing compared to the Avian mountains, but Highcrowne was half a world away.

Olyve and the others looked as stunned as I felt. No-Thing was invisible, but there was a sound of shock from him as a wall of green light arose from the distant Archonian river. It looked like the aurora in the polar skies, a glowing plasma of green, white, yellow, and blue.

"What is that?" Olyve wondered aloud. She had taken on her elf girl form, probably because it was smaller and less likely to be torn apart in the tornado we had just endured. Her finger was still broken, and she was missing a tooth. The damage Celon had done was not easy for her to repair.

No one knew the answer. There were mumbled theories among the wounded Unmentionables. I saw the spider's crumpled form, which had been carried on the wind too. I hesitantly touched a chitinous leg, pulling back as soon as I felt the rough dryness. It did not move. He, she, it, whatever—they had tried to protect me and died for it. They had saved my life. "Thank you," I whispered.

"You're welcome," Trickster said, appearing before me in all his shadowy, burning-coal-eyed glory.

"Not you. Why didn't you intervene sooner?"

"There was no entering the chamber once the door closed. Even I had to wait for you to return."

"Why not before I went in? Before they had to die? Before Fharen went back in time to retrieve those gods? You could have..."

"I could have," Trickster snickered again, "but I chose not to. It's more interesting this way. You'll see."

With that, he vanished.

"Trickster," Olyve muttered, her and the other Unmentionables looking as annoyed as I felt. "That green light must be his doing."

"What do you think it is?" I asked.

"Nothing good."

19   RETURN TO EMPIRE

Olyve was right—Trickster was trouble. The Unmentionables failed to penetrate the barrier he had created, and it surrounded Archon entirely, from river to mountains and all the jungle in between. There was no entry from the air or water, or even underground, as the deranged rabbit-looking Unmentionable tried burrowing. Even No-Thing could not find a portal through the Void that would reach to the other side.

"I presume this is Trickster fulfilling his bargain and stopping Celon," I told Olyve. Trapping the god was a solution. Not what I'd been hoping for, but something.

"Fortunate you convinced him to help at all—I suppose. We are alive, but knowing Trickster and his games, we may soon wish that were not the case."

I hoped she wasn't right, but she was far older and wiser and knew Trickster better than I did.

"What happened that you're not telling me?" Olyve asked. More of that pesky wisdom—she guessed there was more to the story.

"What do you mean?" I batted my eyelashes innocently.

"I know what that device was. It was hidden in the temple, but once it stopped functioning, and we were able to enter and fight Celon, I recognized it immediately: A dangerous artifact. We thought it destroyed until now."

"I encountered it once before, when I was at school in Gernwold. A dwarf had reconstructed it, a professor of magical archeology ... and a Solhan hater. She had needed me to operate it, so she could go back and destroy the Solhans before we had a chance to unleash the Dead God on the world."

"Impossible." When Olyve snorted in her dragon form, little flames plumed out of her nostrils, and I took a step back. "Solhans were never weak enough to be destroyed by anyone. Only they were able to destroy themselves. Foolish dwarf. Yet ... she was smart enough to realize the device required the soul of a Thorne to operate it."

"Lucky I didn't have my soul on me at the time. It was before my coming of age ceremony. Anyway, Gypsum was there, and she must have told the Dead God about it, which was how Thane must have learned about it, and that means Fharen knew about it. He used it to go back in time and bring back the Solhan gods. There was the Night Mother, and Grom, and—"

"—He what!?" Olyve interjected. The flames were rumbling in her throat now, flickering just behind her teeth. She was scary when she got upset.

"Don't worry," I soothed, gesturing for her to calm down before she set us all on fire. "I took care of it. Fharen told me the machine could only take us to a time where we didn't exist. That's how he and I, but not Celon, could go back to the Old Sohan Empire. The gods he collected are dead in this time, so they could come here, or ... they could go to any time in the future. I read all the writing on the walls, literally, and figured out that you could write with blood in Old Solhan to give the device directions. I used my blood to instruct the machine to take all those gods to the far future. After I'm dead. That's where I left them and Fharen. A great solution if I do say so myself."

Olyve grumbled, but the flames subsided. "I suppose it gives us time to prepare, at least. We can't defeat even the one god now, and at some indeterminable time, we will have....?

I counted on my fingers. "Five or six more ... maybe twelve," I admitted.

Another grumble. "How long do we have?"

"I don't know. I didn't want to know. I just specified a time when I wasn't there."

"Let's hope you live a long life," Olyve sad. "In fact. I will make sure of it."

Looked like my dragon godmother wasn't going to shirk her duties anymore. Good.

I wondered what Celon would be doing behind that magic wall in Archon? Something nefarious. Would it hold until the other gods showed and set him free? I hoped so, but … There were still worshippers in there, ready to restore him to full strength. More horrors and forgotten artifacts to be unearthed from the bogs. Lots of problems brewing. Problems for another day. Maybe even another Age.

"Give me a ride home?" I asked Olyve.

"Are you certain you wish to return to Highcrowne? You and Dawn could live with me in Illul Faellion. With the island abandoned, I decided to move in, along with No-Thing and a few other 'friends' to keep it deserted. Don't want any pesky mortals returning to disturb Sandy's pristine beaches."

"That's where she's been, not watching over Little Viktor? She's a terrible fairy godmother."

"She is what she is," Olyve said, shrugging. "As I have been a poor dragon godmother. Come stay with me, so I can change that. No more snow and freezing winters, just warmth and sun and ocean breezes. Bring Nanny, as I would love to have tea with my old friend more regularly. With me, you and Dawn would be safe from Queen Hilja and her politics, safe from Ulric and his schemes. No more squabbles between dwarves, elves, and humans. No more—"

"—Shadow King. I don't think Duane could leave all he's worked for behind. I don't think I could."

"What have you achieved? Highcrowne never changes—it is always dangerous, always at war with itself."

"Always alive. I've seen most of the world, and there is no place as frenetic and crazy—like me. No place I'd rather be. Take me home."

"As you wish."

The return was quick, me lost in thought, and I barely noticed the world fly by below us. Olyve settled on the Avian plateau. The clouds were low today, so we arrived unseen, shrouded in white mist. My clothes and hair were damp, and I shivered as I made my way into the sanctuary. Olyve followed in her diminutive, elf girl form. Naren was gone, and all the pools of Celon blood were dried up. I found the goblin doctor there on hands and knees using a scalpel to scrape traces from the stone.

"Finally made it into the Avian Sanctuary," I noted with a smile.

"It is more wonderous than I thought," he said, indicating the hieroglyphic-covered walls and shattered stone all around.

"You should have seen it before," I mumbled, but if the doctor was happy with these remnants, then good for him.

"Do you know where Naren is?" I asked. "And Duane."

"Still in the High Reaches—although most have dubbed them the Avian Reaches now—where Doctor Suttner and I deposited them."

"Almost home," I told Olyve, hitching another ride.

I thought I'd have to drag Dawn away from Calka and the Avian princess when I arrived. She'd talked about nothing else besides the princess for months.

Olyve had no issue finding the way, although she did need to pause outside the cave and ask permission to enter. Duane had returned Calka's bracelet and, along with it, the remnants of her power. I was glad to know they'd been locked away safe here when Fharen and Celon were on the loose.

"I can't stay in this dark hole living like a superstitious primitive for another second!" Dawn told me, storming up to us, grabbing Olyve by a spikey leg ridge and climbing her like a squirrel. In no time, she was mounted, arms crossed, foot tapping and impatient to leave. For only being partially elf, she managed a good approximation of Hilja's haughtiness when she wanted to. And she was only seven. Help me.

"I want to say goodbye to Calka before we go," I said. And check on Duane.

I knew better than to ask Dawn about her sudden souring towards all things Avian, as she was an acrobat at dodging questions and twisting things around for her own purposes. I let my soul sense lead me to Calka and the princess. Kerrik was there as well—he had not joined the other Unmentionables in the battle against Celon. Finally choosing his own people first? Or had Olyve assigned him here? I was glad they'd had the extra protection.

Princess Glau, who resembled a grey owl with an orange beak, was playing with her father, Roosal, on the floor. It looked like a game of marbles but there was some complex color and mathematical pattern to be achieved in little grooves in the stone. It hurt my head just looking at it.

No sign of Duane, but he was always watching from somewhere, in the shadows.

Their new home was even grander than the old one. I had no idea there were such elaborate structures inside the mountains. A palace of stone surrounded us, with carved pillars and arches. Was it here all along or newly built with their magic? A new throne for Calka looked resplendent on a raised dais, plated in gold and other precious materials. She had not yet had time to amass a nest of junk around its base like her old throne, so it looked more regal. I felt a sudden urge to tap into long-disused etiquette training.

"Queen Calka," I said, bowing formally. "Thank you for protecting my daughter. I am sorry I did not manage to stop Fharen from freeing Celon. The god has taken up residence in Archon, but I believe he is trapped there—for an indeterminate time."

"I know," Calka said. "I also know about the other Solhan gods. I have some remaining Celon, which showed me what is to come."

"Far in the future. Nothing to worry about right now." I waved dismissively.

"We may not pay the price of your choice, but our children will." Calka looked at her daughter with worry.

Dawn. She would have to face those gods when I was gone. Something else to prepare her for. I sighed.

'I'm sorry,' I said. "I didn't know what else to do."

"I understand. Thank you for trying and thank you for rescuing Naren. He is exiled but still one of us. I have sent him to recuperate in a secluded cave in one of the peaks north of here."

"Helping Naren was what Duane wanted. You're all his family."

"I hope we can count you among our brood as well?" Calka asked.

"I'd love that. Although, Dawn seems in an awful hurry to leave."

"She is clever, but young, and realizing her current limitations wounded her pride. It is a good lesson, to know there is always someone better than you at something. It should not keep you from trying."

"I suspect she will try even harder now. She probably wants to go lock herself in the Central City Library and not come out until she can beat the princess at that marble game. I assume that's what sent her over the edge?"

"No, Dawn is quite good at that. It was magic where she faltered. She has natural talents, even more than you, but believes she can think her way into harnessing them rather than feeling her way on instinct."

"Instinct is something I have in spades. And my instinct is telling me to get my daughter home before she makes me suffer. I will visit again some time."

"I do hope so. Bring your shadow back when you do." Calka indicated an alcove from which Duane emerged. He looked hesitant to ask, but I saw his gaze searching all of me, looking for any sign of what I had faced.

"A god broke my sword," I told him with a pout and showed him the bone handle that remained. "Otherwise, it wasn't that kind of battle. Just using my wits against Fharen and Trickster, giving some old Solhan deities a ride and the like. You know—a Tuesday."

He laughed.

He reached out to touch me then, and it was awkward, as we had an audience, his family really, so I took the lead and pulled him in for a kiss. There were coos of approval from Calka and Roosal, although

Kerrik
managed to squint disapprovingly.

The awkwardness returned, though, when Duane climbed up Olyve's leg and sat behind me, Dawn at my front. He was quiet the whole ride, holding me and thinking. I could feel him thinking.

When we got back to Highcrowne, I had Olyve drop us close to home for Dawn's sake, and the shouts and screams when she swooped in and cleared out the bazaar were hilarious.

Only a few people remained, Katherine among them, and Sir Markham and a few others who had been under the plant's control. I worried the fungus in their brains was back, but they didn't move in unison. They were just election supporters wanting a word.

"The election is tomorrow," Katherine pointed out. "These few here want to make their case—to both of you."

Dawn rolled her eyes and went into the house calling for Nanny. It seemed she thought as little of politics as I did. I knew there was no escaping Katherine when she was determined, so I stayed rather than running and hiding too.

Duane and I spent nearly an hour listening to our potential constituents.

"We know we're biased," Sir Markham said, clearly representing the others who all looked chagrined, hats in hands. "Our minds were not entirely our own before, but we experienced something when we were connected with the plant. We experienced—unity. Peace. A desire to work together for the common good. It's a feeling all of us here sorely miss. We may not yet be able to elect our Dwarf or Elf Crown, but the humans can elect one of you—and that is beautiful. Democracy is beautiful. It's the whole, the collective, coming together to rule— many voices becoming one. Whichever one of you becomes the voice of the people, I hope you will remember that we need that unity. Most have never felt it, but those touched by the plant have, and they will never forget. It's something worth striving for."

I quirked my brow. "You're not asking me to put new plants in everyone's heads and make them listen to me this time, are you?" Part of me was tempted by the thought.

"No," Duane said, "getting what they were aiming to say better than I did. "They just want to make sure you—or I—listen to everyone. Make them all feel important and heard."

"That's it exactly," Sir Markham said. "And think about what's best for the majority without sacrificing the minority."

"Of course," I said, agreeing but having no clue how to achieve such a thing. "I promise."

"As do I," Duane said. We both shook hands all around and then turned and faced each other to shake.

"Good luck with the election," Duane told me.

"You too. You'll need it." I smiled mischievously and signaled Katherine to follow me inside the house for a secret election strategy session. I wasn't sure I wanted to be a Crown, but I was looking forward to making Duane work for it. It was funnier that way.

After such intense campaign strategizing, Illul Faellion was very tempting. Olyve offered one more time before she flew off, promising to stop by and check in from time to time, more if she could. She wanted to be a better godmother. I resisted the temptation to vanish with her to the edge of the world. That was an early grave. I wanted to live.

I dove into the frenzied hubbub of campaigning, doing some door knocks and street corner handshakes late into the evening and first thing in the morning just outside the ballot boxes.

"Vote for Eva Thorne—that's me!" I said too cheerily over and over again as I shook hands and kissed babies. Most cried when a Solhan did it, either handshaking or baby kissing, but we all got through it.

It was a long twenty-four hours. Very long. Exhausted, I sat on a chair overlooking the bazaar from my balcony, whisky in hand, as I watched the town crier run around giving updates on the post-election ballot count. It was midnight before it was declared—only a few hours after polls closed—and it was unanimous.

"General Moore wins by write in!" the crier called. Goblins handed out newspapers with the headline: "Moore is back!"

The general found me a short while later in the dead of night. Duane arrived a moment after him. He must have been lurking nearby, probably watching my scowl from the balcony and not daring to get too close.

"Good," Moore said, "You're both here. I had no idea this would happen. It's not what I wanted. But it's democracy. I can't argue with the will of the people or shirk my duty. How am I to rebuild the Fortress of Mages, though? I have so many plans."

"I can help there," Duane said. "You can delegate to my workers."

Trust him to get another lucrative government construction contract.

"And it's important to bring order to all the human kingdoms, especially Darrub," I said, now that Archon and potentially a new Solhan Empire lurked on the horizon.

"Can I count on both of you to help?" Moore asked.

"Whatever we can do." I said, knowing I'd regret it. I should have made it clear there would be a fee involved.

"Good. There is no stopping me if I have the Shadow King and the greatest Solhan necromancer on my side."

"Greatest detective," I interjected.

He didn't disagree or agree. The consummate politician. He just smiled. "We will do great things, the three of us. Great things! Now rest up." He patted us on the backs, shook hands like a pro, and left us to the quiet of the night.

"I heard that, with Hilja's return, the elves have squashed any notion of their own election," Duane told me. "It's back to the same old same old. Status quo. Even the dwarves are less restless now that King Harley has set up a dwarven parliament to advise him. Elections for that are coming soon, which will be quite entertaining. There's a divide between the werewolf lineages who worked the mines traditionally, the Matriarchy supporters, and the common trades dwarves, which will be interesting to watch."

"You know what else is interesting to watch?" I said. "You."

He smiled rakishly. "I'm irresistible."

"No. I mean how you are talking about everything except us. If you are Shadow King again, and I'm that 'Solhan necromancer' once more, and Dawn is still Hilja's only heir.... Things are dangerous for her. The three of us have enemies, and we'll have even more when we start helping General Moore. Those enemies will grow faster than allies. It's not safe for us all to be together, one easy target."

"I was really looking forward to moving in and having Nanny cook for me every day," Duane said.

"And I was really hoping to move to that luxurious warehouse of yours with the Devourer shrine for Nanny to tremble at, and the huge bath for me to enjoy with you every night. But..."

"But. We can't be together. It's too dangerous."

"Always."

Thunder rumbled, and another rainstorm started like the one that had brought Duane to my door after he thought he'd killed Hilja. Like the night that had started all this. Lightning crashed, and rain fell like the tears I wanted to shed but couldn't.

"I know why you ran before," Duane said, pulling up his hood as drops splattered. "It was too painful after you lost Thane. But I promised myself then, and I promise you now—it doesn't matter how long I need to wait. I will wait forever for you, Eva. Until the time is right." He turned away.

More lightning lit up the sky in blue, and the air felt electric, the rain really coming down, and me shivering and wanting to get inside. So, I had to shout.

"You might be able to wait—but I can't!" I pulled Duane back to me and kissed him.

He pushed me up against the wall and looked hungrily into my eyes. "You mean it?"

"Yes. I want you now—and forever."

THE END

Did you enjoy this book? Please take a moment to leave a
review. What you say will determine whether someone else
takes the plunge into Eva's world, so please ask them to
dive headfirst. Thank you!

Join our mailing list at **lorelclayton.com**
to get a free Eva Thorne novella, short stories—and learn
about our other books!

ABOUT THE AUTHORS

Lorel and Clayton were teen sweethearts, brought together by a fierce love of books (and hormones) and have been married for 35 years. As writing partners, they meld logic, creativity, and genres. Fantasy, science-fiction, mystery, horror, steampunk, thrillers, the classics ... they read them all, and if they can mix them, they will!

Still reading? Want to know more?

Lorel has a PhD in molecular biology and Once Upon a Time did cancer research before turning to the dark side (aka marketing), but she uses her powers for good, helping to raise funds for charity. She loves books, movies and animals, and would gladly spend all day with a cat on her lap and the wind in her hair (Conan reference there), while tapping out a story on her keyboard. Or maybe a movie script. With coffee of course. And lots of chocolate!

Clayton is a classically trained artist who learned digital painting, mostly because there's a hyperactive fourteen-year-old boy running around the house (their gorgeous son, in case you were wondering if that's normal). Clayton is severely dyslexic but loves books and storytelling. He adds vast imagination and a discerning ear for effective prose to their creative collaboration, not to mention the book cover art.

Born and raised in the western United States, they traveled to Sydney, Australia in 1997 and never left, finding the sunshine and beaches of "Oz" too irresistible. Look them up if ever you're Down Under.

Connect with Lorel Clayton

Website: www.lorelclayton.com
BookBub: bookbub.com/authors/lorel-clayton
Instagram: www.instagram.com/lorelclayton
Facebook: www.facebook.com/AuthorLorelClayton
Goodreads: www.goodreads.com/lorel_clayton